DESTINY'S PRIZE

Andrey Kretsch

Publisher:
ASPG (Australian Self Publishing Group)
P.O. Box 159, Calwell, ACT Australia 2905
Email: publishaspg@gmail.com
http://www.inspiringpublishers.com

Author: Andrey Kretsch

Title: **DESTINY'S PRIZE**/*Andrey Kretsch*.

ISBN: 978-0-6450559-7-9 (Print)
      978-0-6450559-8-6 (eBook)
      978-0-6450559-9-3 (Hard Cover)

PART 1.
NEW YORK.
1957.

TO

My beloved parents (dec) my mother Mara' (Maria), my father Ferenc (Francis) Kretsch. Who selflessly, decided to leave Hungary, for Australia, in 1947. In order to provide me with a better life and greatly enhanced life and career opportunity. I'm eternally indebted.

To my family. Although, somewhat sceptical about my literary ambitions, they did provide a stable, loving environment, so I could concentrate and pursue my dream.

Acknowledgements

A host of people have been extraordinarily generous with their valuable time and insights. Those whom I would specifically like to acknowledge are (in alphabetical order);

Mike Brady; a hugely talented musician and a great bloke. He made my original dream possible (Destiny's Prize the Stage Musical).

Patrick Edgeworth; talented and accomplished writer for TV (Cash and Co-), Stage (Boswell-West End. Georgy Girl – Melbourne and Film (BMX Bandits). He has patiently guided me through the writing process and sustained my enthusiasm with his wise, professional advice.

Malcolm Robertson (dec); accomplished, writer, director and actor. His bubbling enthusiasm and wise counselling, were invaluable. He is sorely missed.

Prologue

iklos (Mike) Goldstein, left Hungary, via France and came to America in 1930, at the age of 30, one of millions of immigrants. He moved to Queens, in New York, lived there for some years, then moved to Brooklyn and stayed there, until his death in 1957. To his few, old friends, or his Chabad congregation members, if they ever thought of him, his name evoked no great sense of loss, or sadness. His passing, barely caused a ripple, in the relentlessly moving stream of life. But to his only son, Dov, his death, felt like he had been dumped, by a massive tidal wave. For him, this stoic, taciturn man, had been a revered, reserved hero and his passing, was a constant reminder of the fate that awaits us all.

In his later years. Dov Goldstein, a Hasidic (ultra-religious), Jew. Would occasionally reflect back and review his life. He'd ponder whether, his life would have turned out to be significantly different, without that pivotal moment? Probably yes. But of course, he'd never know for sure. Then he would move on to the, next logical question. But was he happy and content with his current life? This was a question, he could readily answer and it was with an unequivocal – yes.

For Dov Goldstein, his initial pivotal moment occurred, when he was just fifteen. At the time. He struggled with his shock and the emotional trauma, so he was not aware and certainly not interested in obscure, philosophical reflections. Instead. He tried to console himself with the old chestnut. 'That whatever doesn't kill you, will make you stronger.' Combined with a quote, he found from Christopher Markus. 'Hardship often prepares an ordinary person for an extraordinary destiny.' However, neither sentiment helped or offered any solace.

It was only much later, as he reflected on his life and reviewed it through the prism of time, he realised that these events had shaped his destiny and his future. Without these incidents, there was no way, he would have found his true love and meanwhile, discover his vocation and destiny.

Despite a tendency for introspection. Dov was an optimist. For him, the glass was always half full. As a consequence of those reflections and his conclusion. Dov felt blessed and his belief in the Almighty was reinforced.

Some memories, remain vivid, etched technicolour, in our brain. This one in particular, since it marked the beginning of his new life direction. It had started as yet another, mundane, pleasant sunny day in 1957, suburban New York. The family, as usual, were running late. They hurriedly dressed, in their high-holiday finery and bundled into their, battered, old Chevy. His father (Mike), behind the wheel, his mother (Elizabeth) beside him, while he lounged on the back seat. He watched with an equal measure of amusement and apprehension, as his father ground through the gears, in their manual vehicle. He loved his ultra-religious father, but with a teenagers' facility for critical review, judged him to be a terrible driver. Hence, the state of their car. He also bemoaned his father's lack of overt affection and communication, so starkly different to his tactile, voluble, emotional mother.

As an only child, his mother doted on him. She had a guilty passion for daytime situation comedies on TV and would endlessly watch, while her husband was at the nearby synagogue. Her favourite programme was, 'The Adventures of Ozzie and Harriet.'

One day, in the mid-afternoon, when Dov was nearly 15 and at a time his father was praying at the adjacent Chabad synagogue. She bounded, into the kitchen where he was studying. Beaming, she conspiritually, guided him to the TV room and indicated the screen. The bewildered Dov followed her finger and silently stared at the young Ricky Nelson, in an episode of, 'The Adventures of Ozzie and Harriet.' Frustrated by his silence, she muttered. "Nu, can't you see the resemblance?" Dov stared, but for the life of him, couldn't see what she was on about. Talk about a mother's love being blind, he thought to himself, but was too sensitive to say it. Instead, he mumbled. "You've got to be kidding me, Mum," she was undeterred, hugged him, and nudged him closer to the TV screen, again indicated, as she exclaimed. "Check his eyes, cheeks, lips, and his smile. You could be brothers," Dov obligingly, looked, but couldn't see the resemblance.

Certainly, Ozzie and Harriet bore no resemblance to his parents. But he didn't think it would be appropriate to tell his mother. Years later, he still smiled and felt a warm glow and profound love, when he recalled the incident.

It was only a pleasant 30-minute drive, from their home in the Jewish ghetto of Williamsburg, Brooklyn, next to a small Chabad synagogue, to the Reception centre in Brooklyn.

Chapter 1

Chapter 1
The Start of Dov's Odyssey

The Goldstein's arrived late at Deity, situated near the banks of the Hudson. It was a popular venue, for larger Jewish weddings in Brooklyn, an affluent near city suburb, of New York.

The large, multi-level, underground car park was near-full and Dov's father had extreme difficulty, in finding a spot, without damaging adjacent vehicles.

Eventually, after several close calls, each one initiating a heated argument with his wife and generating considerable stress, he parked. Relieved, they clambered out and hurried to the Reception.

At the entrance, they were greeted by the parents of the bride and groom. They were dressed in their finest garments and offered a warm welcome to the parade of arriving guests. Mindful, that they were late and of the long impatient, queue behind them. The Goldstein's offered a brief mazeltov (congratulations), to their hosts, before moving past and placing their wedding gift on an adjacent table. The table was already covered, by an assortment of gifts. Dov could clearly hear the sounds of; laughter, talking and loud upbeat music. It drew him and he hurriedly strode through the foyer, trailed by his family, into the main reception area.

The huge, high ceilinged area had a wall of glass that overlooked a lush green garden. Several dozen big round tables, draped with bright, white linen, lined the roomy, polished pine dance- floor. Each table, had a prominent centrepiece, filled with an assortment of, brightly coloured flowers. The band was playing an upbeat number and the dance floor was packed with dancing couples. When the band switched to a well-known Jewish melody. Suddenly, the bride and groom were now lifted high above the heads of the guests. Sitting in armchairs, they nervously smiled, as they anxiously clutched the armrests, while their chairs were violently thrust up and pulled down, like a yo-yo, during their spirited journey round and round the dance- floor.

Not long after. The Jewish band began, an energetic rendition of Hava Nagila. A well-known and beloved Jewish song. Caught up in the music, the guests and in particular, his father responded, like generations of their Jewish forebears. They began to vigorously dance to the music. Arms clasped around adjacent guests, they whirled around and around. A sea of bobbing, 10 inch high prominent, circular fur hats. Each Hasidic guest, was wearing their, expensive, treasured Shtreimel Hat.

As Dov watched, he noted, that his father was red-faced, sweated profusely and laughed uninhibitedly, as he enthusiastically, whirled round and round. Dov was surprised and thrilled to see his normally restrained, stoic, perpetually worried father was enjoying himself, so uninhibitedly.

Suddenly, he stopped, clasped his chest and crashed to the dance floor. Dov watched puzzled and terrified, as several doctor guests, rushed over and hastily commenced CPR. When after a brief flurry, they stopped and solemnly approached his mother. He grasped, it was all over. He thought his heart and stomach, had literally plummeted down, leaving a gaping, black abyss. He felt, as if he had suddenly, stumbled from a skyscraper and was hurtling remorselessly, to the ground. Crushed: lightheaded, unsteady, drenched in a cold sweat, he stumbled over and hugged her. They embraced and this released mutual, dammed emotions. They began to sob uncontrollably and clung to each other. The embarrassed guests, uncomfortable by the display of such overt grief, backed away, from the confronting island of palpable misery.

A year later, his mother was diagnosed with breast cancer. For the next twelve months. Dov was constantly at her side, while she valiantly fought it. Eventually, she died when he turned seventeen. Technically, Dov was now an orphan. He was unable to comprehend, what had suddenly happened to his happy, sheltered, organised, stable, contented world, in the past few years. All his security, support and expectations had been turned upside down, obliterated. He felt lonely, lost and vulnerable. His protectors and advisors were both gone. His uncle and his family were kind and caring, but were not and could never be a replacement.

Years later, Dov was still plagued, by vivid flashbacks. He intensely recalled: his grief and all the details of these tragic events and the subsequent, unexpected journey that had irrevocably changed his life. A journey that unexpectedly, led him to his love and gave his life consequence and an unexpected, new direction.

His mother's recent death, had immobilised him with a sense of crippling grief, paradoxically combined, with a dose of guilty relief. He'd been unable to cope with her constant suffering and the inability, of anyone to do something about it. Dov had prayed for her to be pain-free. When she eventually died, amidst all the grief, there was also a sense of shameful relief. She was finally pain- free and at peace. This was when the bizarre nature of his father's death, finally sank in and he began questioning his faith and his belief in the Almighty. What sort of G-d, would rip such a G-d-fearing, good father and beloved husband from his family in such a cruel and undignified fashion? To Dov, it seemed an act of divine maliciousness. To kill this stoic, sombre man, at one of his brief, rare moments, of unbridled, happiness and joy.

By this time, he realised how much he had loved his father and despite his father's stoic, reserved, understated nature, how much his father Mike (Miklos), loved him. Dov just wished, he had been more like his mother and had been able to openly show it.

When Dov recalled, Miklos' account of his family history, it was abundantly clear, how selfless his grandparents (Feri and Maria), had been to advise their only beloved son, Miklos, to pack up and leave Hungary in 1920, (when Miklos was in his teens), to get out of the virulently anti-Semitic Hungary and travel, initially to France and then, some years later, Miklos, at his own initiative, travelled to far-flung America. He was desperate, for information regarding his parents, in Hungary. He thought his uncle Reuben, in America, may know something?

For his grandparent's; life in Hungary was relatively comfortable. But they realised that the future for Miklos would be bleak, with poor prospects and limited opportunity, for work or a good education and this would be doubly valid, for any future grandchildren.

The catalyst for his grandparent's decision was, the institution of a new anti-Semitic movement called 'Awakening Hungarians', after the First World War ended. The National Army units, often encouraged people to chase Jews, out of their communities and in 1920 the Government reduced the number of Jews, in higher education of learning to 5%. Special camps were established. Camps that became in Hungary, as notorious as have become the name of Auschwitz.

Miklos was reluctant to go, he wanted to stay, be with his family and help in any way that he could. To leave seemed an act of betrayal, to the family unit. He thought, his parents were exaggerating the situation, until an incident occurred that changed his mind.

A long time best friend, whom he'd known, since pre-school, school and Yeshiva. Had somehow managed to enrol at the University. He told Miklos, how he had been made to sit, in the last bench of the classroom, called, 'benches of shame.' One day, Miklos was called to the hospital and found his friend in the ICU. He was barely recognisable, broken nose, swollen, near closed black eyes. An arm and a leg in plaster. Semiconscious, he was attached to a battery of monitors. Barely, clinging to life. He was kept alive. By a series of 20th-century medical equipment and through the skill of the attending doctors and the professional nursing staff.

He was obviously, severely beaten and in a critical condition. Miklos spoke repeatedly, to University officials, the police and the Army, but no one was interested in investigating the incident or punishing the perpetrators. This was a wakeup call for him and the situation had now become personal. Reluctantly, he decided to leave, but made his parents promise if the situation got worse, they should join him.

Dov wondered, would he have had the love and strength to do what Miklos' parents had done?

Dov's resentment against G-d and religion boiled over as he brooded over his circumstance. His questioning and resentment had increased as he witnessed his mothers' prolonged, pointless suffering. He consoled himself that questioning and searching was integral to anyone with faith.

The funeral and the seven-day sitting Shiva (mourning), for his mother, at his uncle's (Rueben), was a blur of sad-faced, downcast, dark clothed mourners, offering doleful condolences.

He struggled to finish his current school year. What was the point? Depressed and discouraged, he wondered, what he'd do the following, his final year? He was paralysed by his loss and drifting, directionless and apathetic regarding his whole life. The future by definition, is daunting. Currently, for Dov, it was now, a complete mystery and totally intimidating.

After what had happened, any thought of religion, or becoming a Cantor and follow a fourth generation family tradition, had been quickly discarded. His only comfort these days, was his music. It offered an escape and a release. Could this be his vocation? He was uncertain, he waited for a sign. In the interim, he moved forward mini-step, by mini-step.

Some weeks later. Out of the blue, Marge Cornhuckster, his mother's, schoolgirl, best friend, phoned and brightly announced. "I've enrolled you at our local High School. Be sure to be here by, "named a date, then hung up.

Dov had spent the first 17, now approaching 18 years of his young life in the sheltered, Jewish-friendly environments', of Queens and more recently Brooklyn, with intermittent times secluded, in the Yeshiva (a place where devout Jews, intensively studied their religion). He had never travelled beyond these boundaries. He felt secure in this familiar environment and was accepted as part of the street-scape.

The prospect of traveling to Denton, Kansas and staying with an unfamiliar, non-Jewish family, while he completed his final year of High school, loomed as an uninviting and daunting prospect. His mother had certainly talked glowingly, about meeting Marge, when they both attended Denton High school. She had rhapsodised, how welcoming the town -people were, particularly Marge, and how pleasant the lifestyle. But it was not something, Dov would choose to experience. Dov was still uncertain, when a week before he was due to leave, he received another call from Marge. "Don't forget. I expect you next week. I promised your Mum. She told me, you had promised her as well," Dov felt trapped. Marge didn't play fair and relentlessly added. "So ring me the day before you're coming. We'll meet you at the station," not waiting for his reply, she had hung up. Dov had no option, he had promised his mother. He needed to make arrangements.

The next few days were frantic. He dropped the keys of his parents' house, around to his uncle (Rueben), since he was the Executor of his parents' will. They co-signed several documents, his parent's lawyer had previously provided. Next came the formal goodbyes. Sad farewells to his remaining family (Rueben and his family: Ruth, Adam, and Renée), as well as some Brooklyn and Queens friends. Dov packed a few belongings, including his trusty guitar. Booked a ticket and rang Marge with the details.

Wanting to make a good impression, Dov put on his best black suit, despite the mandatory torn left lapel, forced on him by Jewish tradition. When a parent died. Rending was a controlled, religiously sanctioned act of destruction. Anger was a component of all mourning. A purpose of the grieving process was to help diffuse this anger. Also, tearing the apparel, signified a torn heart.

Dov travelled to New York Penn Station, nervous about what lay ahead. When he arrived, the platform was already crowded. He noted that his appearance was met with a barrage of strange, startled looks and whispered derogatory comments, from the assembled people. He wondered, if his appearance caused such a profound reaction in sophisticated, cosmopolitan New York, how would they react in an isolated country town? He was about to enter uncharted waters. But decided not to fixate on that, at this moment. He would address and worry about it, on his arrival. Although, he did regret his promise. He consoled himself, it was the least he could do. Since, it seemed to provide so much comfort, to his dying mother.

He was thankful, he had the carriage to himself. Already it was hot and he regretted the need for his Hasidic clothes. But he was a Hasidic Jew.

Finally, the train started. Dov gloomily gazed at the passing landscape of tenement apartments. Dilapidated, brick buildings, with gaping slate roofs, broken windows, and cluttered, junk filled, overgrown back gardens. A depressing view from the passing train.

The journey was going to be long (over a day), and tedious. To define, the next chapter of his young life; possibly, as a singer-songwriter? Dov decided to spend some of the time drafting lyrics, for a song he dedicated to his Mother.

DOV. (NOW YOU ARE GONE).

Your loving shadow has passed on.
As has the sunlight, the laughter, and the song.
A dark, deep pit is now my home.
Since you are gone.

As Dov drafted the lyrics, his emotions welled up and he had to stop. After some time, he regained composure and continued. As he reviewed the lyrics; he bleakly noted, the passing landscape was now: sporadic farmhouses, clusters of tall, hardy oak and maple trees, with random herds of idly grazing cows.

A debt repaid, to promise made,
Brings me to this place, light years from home.
An outsider in a foreign land.
Isolated, so alone.

Dov looked up from his writing pad and realised, a substantial part of the trip had now passed.

You were my compass My homing beacon
Now I feel rudderless and lost
Oh, how can I carry on?

Dov took his acoustic guitar, from the luggage rack. Eased out chords, as he softly strummed and sang the lyrics.

You were my rock the
The bosom I could cry on
My sheltering shield
And now you are gone

Choked with emotion, he had to stop again. He was tired, mentally exhausted and there was still a long journey ahead of him. He decided he should try to get some sleep, he got his jacket from the overhead rack and using it as a pillow, lay along the seat, of the empty carriage. He woke some hours later, disorientated and wondering where he was? He felt stiff, but otherwise better. His dismal musing was disrupted- when the carriage door was flung open. A forty-something, stout, uniformed figure strode in. The man was briefly, taken back by the appearance of the passenger, but regrouped. "Ticket please," he demanded and watched amused; as the black-suited Hasidic teenager, scrambled to check all his pockets. The flustered Dov, finally located the item and offered the ticket. The Conductor checked it, looked up and smiled. "You're going to have an interesting time. Not too many Jews in Denton. Good luck buddy."

As the train approached Denton, Dov reviewed the passing landscape, with moody indifference. The flat brown, burnt, arid landscape was now punctuated by occasional lush, green vineyards and colourful, geometrically laid out - wheat fields. A far cry from the bustling city, he'd been used to. Finally, they neared his destination. The prospect of alighting was daunting. Nervous, he delayed the inevitable, he was reluctant to face this strange new town and to meet his unfamiliar hosts. His Hasidic outfit was absolutely not ideal. By now, he was sweating profusely. Then, the train eventually arrived.

When Dov was about to get off the train, he caught a reflection of himself in the dusty carriage window. A figure dressed in all black: with a long black coat, extensive beard, prominent bushy moustache, and long dangling payus (side-locks), all this, was topped, like a cherry on a cake, by his traditional, 10 inch high, circular Shtreimel, fur hat. Even in his smart (torn) black suit, by any definition, he was a bizarre sight. And certainly wouldn't be mistaken for Ricky Nelson. But he had no choice. He was a Hasidic Jew. He treasured the hat, it represented tradition and had been a generous gift from his parents for his Barmitzvah. He cherished it. It was a priceless reminder of his parents. However, he now had to face his host family and Denton. He suspected, his look would be deemed freaky. He feared his arrival would be, as if an Alien had landed in town.

He was not reassured, when he observed the crowd on the platform. They were all dressed in multi-coloured casual. Clean shaved men, in light blue jeans and bright dyed short-sleeved shirts. While the made up, coiffured women were wearing short, vivid patterned, floral dresses, with matching shoes and handbags. The crowd looked like the off-Broadway cast, for Oklahoma, a film he had seen the previous year. An even more dramatic contrast, to his appearance.

His equivocation, was cut short, by the -sudden jerk of the train. It was about to depart and erupted, successive clouds of light grey steam. Dov realised, he had better hurry. Clutching his gear, he jumped off and was enveloped in a Cumulus cloud of grey steam. He made his way through it and nervously, trudged along the platform. He noticed by now, the platform was near- deserted. Suddenly, he heard a hesitant, female voice shout. "Dov?! Dov?" He looked around, it was Marge. He dropped his suitcase and faced her.

As he approached with his guitar case, Dov could see the look of shock and utter horror on the faces of her two companions. Marge observed the negative reaction of her family and regretted, she hadn't, prepared them for this meeting. From her letters. She knew, her schoolgirl best friend, had converted and then married a religious Jew. However, she hadn't thought, it was a big deal. But, seeing Dov in the flesh, she was forced to admit, he was a weird sight, particularly in Denton.

As Dov came closer. He offered a big warm smile and waived his guitar case, as he addressed her companions. "Who did you expect, Pat Boone?"

Dov was introduced to her husband. Clem Cornhuckster, looked like an overworked, fifty-something -bank manager and seemed to be always sucking on a lemon. Then to the most beautiful girl, Dov had ever seen, their teenage daughter. Jane Cornhuckster, possessed a luminosity. To Dov's eyes, it seemed, as if Jane had swallowed a light bulb. She had long flowing Topaz yellow hair and a figure that stirred his imagination. Reed slim, with a narrow waist and the suggestion of bouncy, perky breasts. When she smiled. His heart flipped - as her red lips parted and revealed gleaming white teeth. Dov stared and felt as if he was drowning in her malachite green eyes. The family bustled the stunned Dov to their car. In awkward silence, they drove to the Cornhuckster home.

During the short ride, Dov mulled over his current circumstance. Even though, he felt a complete outsider. The prospect of spending time with this gorgeous, young woman, was exhilarating. He concluded that the fates (or in his case, the Almighty), had been extremely benevolent.

Meanwhile, Jane was also reviewing her situation and had come to a contrary conclusion. When her mother pleaded and she had agreed to babysit, their guest. She never imagined, he would be such a freak, so weird looking. She had felt sorry for his tragic history, but now, dreaded her assigned role. She was apprehensive, how the town and in particular, her schoolmates would respond to him. She resented, the imposition, it would place on her own life. But somehow, she would just have to make the best of it. Her mother had committed to the situation. She had promised, Dov's dying mother, her schoolgirl best friend. However, Jane sensed, her father was less than thrilled.

Chapter 2

Clem, considered himself a devout Catholic and a good Christian, in the full non-religious sense of that word. So, he was surprised and troubled, by his instinctive apathy, for the teenage, ultra-religious Jew, especially given his recent tragic events. He reflected on this. However, it continued to puzzle and disturb him. Subsequently, a few days after Dov's arrival. He attended his local Church, in the outskirts of town.

It was a sandstone and wood building, with a spire, topped by a large metal cross. He sought out the local Priest. A man he respected both, as a priest and also as a Church and Catholic scholar. The fifty something, grey-haired Priest, greeted him warmly. Clem, arranged to see him for Confession. The Priest was somewhat surprised, by this request. It had been many years, since this devout Catholic, had felt the need, for confession. The priest wondered, what had happened?

After hearing Clem's confession, the Priest, was somewhat reassured. He spoke earnestly, to Clem, then he began to glibly outline, some relevant history. ""Look. Anti-Semitism, has been present, since Roman times. Emperor

Tiberius (the second Roman emperor, from 14 to 27 A D), expelled the Jews from Rome in 19 AD. As did Claudius again in 49 A D," paused for breath and asked. "Clem, tell me, if this is too dry and boring?"

"No, it's fascinating," Clem quickly, responded. Without missing a beat, the Priest continued. "Regarding the Catholic Church. The fourth Council of the Lateran, was convoked by Pope Innocent III, in 1213. The Council gathered at Rome's Lateran Palace in 1215, the delay caused by the need for all the Bishops to attend. This Council, was the first to proclaim the requirement of Jews to wear something, that distinguished them as Jews (and Muslims the same). In addition, on many occasions, Jews were accused of 'blood libel', the supposed drinking of blood of Christian children in mockery of the Christian Eucharist", again the Priest paused and asked. "Should I continue?"

"Yes, please," Clem promptly replied. Given the green light, the Priest resumed. "Anti-Semitism in European Christian culture escalated beginning in the 13th century. The Church often added to the fire, by the myth of 'blood libel', that the Jews would kill a child before Easter and use their blood to make matzo. Anti-Semitic imagery, also recurred in Christian art and architecture," the Priest paused, then apologetically added. "Clem, I'm sorry to be going on and on. Last chance, should I stop?"

"No way. This is all interesting and relevant," Clem, enthusiastically replied. Once again, the Priest happily recommenced. " In 1555, Pope Paul IV, issued a papal bull, which revoked all the rights of the Jewish community and placed religious and economic restriction on Jews in the Papal States. The bull established the Roman Ghetto and required Jews in Rome, which had existed as a community since before Christian times and which numbered about 2000 at the time, to live in it. The Ghetto was a walled quarter with three gates that were locked at night, Jews were restricted to one synagogue, per city. Subsequently, Paul IV's, successor, Pope Pius IV, enforced the creation of other ghettos in most Italian towns".

The Priest sensed, Clem had been, intently listening. He took a deep breath, and sincerely offered. "I wanted you to understand, the history of anti-Semitism. So, as you can see my friend, anti-Semitism dates back to ancient times and has involved the highest level in the Catholic Church. It is not your doing. It is not your fault. Maybe, you have been influenced by history, but you can disregard it,"

"Thank you Father," the grateful, relieved Clem responded. He felt much better. The Priest was probably right, he was just responding to years of past, Church actions and teachings. Plus; probably his own devout fathers', bias and behaviour.

He resolved, to try and correct this inappropriate and UN -Christian tendency. Despite, the years of constant brainwashing.

Chapter 3

Then, the drive was over. They had stopped, outside an imposing two-storey, red brick Terrace. They showed Dov, his upstairs room, it was adjacent to the Cornhucksters' bedroom and across the corridor from Jane's room.

Dov's room was bright, it had two windows that looked onto a quiet, tree-lined street and were framed by floral curtains. There was a single bed, covered with the same floral material, a bedside table, on it- a small white vase, with a single rose stem. The room also had a large wooden wardrobe and a small armchair, also covered with the same floral material.

Later that evening, Dov came downstairs, into the dining room. He was uncertain and apprehensive about the situation and how he would handle it. He immediately, noticed that the dining room table groaned under the weight of food. The centre-piece was a large silver tray, with a huge silver domed cover. Along one wall there was a massive, mahogany sideboard, almost hidden by a collection of bright Ralph Kovel pottery. He deduced, Marge clearly had an obsession. Jane was engrossed, reading. "Jane. Manners!" Mr. Cornhuckster rebuked. Jane slammed the book down onto the table. A passionate reader, Dov checked the book. Surprised, when he read the title, 'Catcher in the Rye.' He turned to Jane and exclaimed. "Didn't expect to find this here," for a long moment, their eyes locked and he felt like an art collector, who had just found a Rembrandt. He was brought back to earth, when she retorted. "It's probably too way out for you," gathering his wits, Dov managed. "It's about a teenager, who's estranged and alienated. What's not to like?"

"So you've read more than the title," she replied, somewhat taken back. "I am Holden Caulfield," he emphatically added.

During dinner. Marge, as usual, was most considerate. She struggled to break the awkward silence that hung over the room. She tried to engage Dov and cheerily offered. "It's a pleasure to have you with us. Isn't it Clem?" After some prompting, Clem muttered. "I can't say how much," Marge jumped in and filled the awkward silence. Again she hopefully, addressed Dov. "You'll have to tell us all about New York."

"You mean criminal city," he replied, tongue in cheek.

"Is it really full of crime?" the gullible Marge asked.

"It's okay, but you do have to be wary," Dov responded.

Marge was undeterred. "What about the shows? Have you seen, Annie get your gun?"

"No," Dov confessed.

Marge persisted. "Oklahoma?"

Dov looked down at his plate and admitted. "Only the Film."

Marge was running out of ideas. "You must have seen something?"

"Not many Broadway shows get to the Brooklyn yeshiva," he explained.

Marge was puzzled. "Yeshiva?"

Dov explained. "It's where devout Jews, study our religion. So I-"

Clem, tired of being silent, aggressively cut in. "First the Russian spies, now that bloody Commie satellite, that Spudnik's perched over our head,"

Jane interjected. "It's Sputnik dad!"

Marge tried to change the subject. "Jane's dying to hear all about the latest fashions." Jane reviewed Dov's outfit, then sarcastically offered. "I'm not into funerals." Dov's eyes remained on Jane, as he adjusted his black jacket and gave it his best shot.

"Black is all the fashion, this year."

Clem was determined to have the last say, he snapped. "Not in Denton!"

Jane took Dov's breath away and he had trouble not staring. He sensed she was less than eager about his arrival, but still tried to make conversation with her, he tentatively asked. "What's the school like?"

Offhanded, she replied. "Okay, I guess. You will see for yourself, tomorrow."

Dov felt rebuffed and decided to remain silent for a while.

Clem was quietly stewing. Later at the table, he offered comments like, "Those Russian spies, the Rosenbergs, weren't they Jews?" Even as he said it, Clem felt, huge remorse. He noticed Marge's disappointed stare and that made his him feel worse. He had lapsed, despite all his good intentions. He vowed, to try harder in the future. This teenager, was like a red cape to a bull and he couldn't seem to help himself. He wondered, if he should go to confession again and review the situation, with his Priest? However, he decided, to try harder and see how it went. In addition, he was somewhat ashamed of his lapse and convinced himself, he deserves another chance, before Confessing to the Priest.

Soon after. Clem made a great show of saying Grace before the meal. Dov still stewing, decided the situation should become more even-handed. So, shortly after, he stared at Clem and said a brief Jewish prayer for the bread. The Cornhuicksters were somewhat taken back. But when Dov finished, they half-heartedly joined in with. "Amen."

Clem was disgruntled by the turn of events. He scanned the food on the table and grumpily said. "I'm starving. Marge, as usual, has done us proud," he stood, rubbed his hand in anticipation. Lifted the domed cover- with a flourish and revealed a baby roast Pig, in a bed of assorted vegetables. Stared at Dov as he said. "The specialty of the house, roast pork, A La Marge," still looking at Dov, lifted the carving knife. "Wait till you taste it, you'll think you've gone to heaven," Dov had not eaten on the train and was hungry after the long train ride. He admitted. "Smells good."

Jane brusquely, cut in and sarcastically offered. "Thought Jews can't eat pork?" Embarrassed by her gaffe, Marge asked. "They don't?!" Dov was disinclined to make it a big issue. "Don't worry Mrs. Cornhuckster. I'm finished with religion." Jane doubtfully, reviewed his appearance. "So I see." For a short time, this killed any further conversation until Marge, anxious to break the silence, turned to Jane. "How come, we haven't seen Bob around?"

Clem perked up. This was a topic he was pleased to discuss, he exclaimed. "He's quite a nice lad" and -stared meaningfully, at Dov as he added. "He comes from a good churchgoing family," Jane was unhappy with the subject, but finally responded. "He's history. Haven't heard from him, the whole Christmas break," she stood, faced Dov and offered a curt. "Good night," then left.

Dov was tired from his trip and exhausted from meeting his hosts. So he stood, faced the Cornhucksters, offered. "Good night, "and also left.

A few minutes later, in his room. Dov desolately, unpacked his meagre belongings. He paused and gazed sad-faced, at his mother's photo. As he looked, he was flooded with emotion and experienced, a kaleidoscope of fond, tender memories. The way she hugged and comforted him if he was ever unsure or distressed. The limitless concern for his happiness and well-being. He got choked up just thinking about it. He comforted himself with the thought, she'd be happy that he had travelled to Denton. Whatever lay ahead, he wanted to make her proud of him.

Dov had kept his promise, to his dying mother. He had come here to complete his final year and graduate. But his Dad's long-held wish and to a less extent his mother's that, he should become a Cantor and continue the four generation, family tradition, was beyond him. After what happened to his father and the way his mother had suffered- Dov had lost faith in G-d and religion. Fourth generation or not, how could he devote his life to religion and lead the singing in the synagogue?

But his parent's philosophy and their example did have a profound effect on the young Dov. He had often joined them, as they volunteered for the Jewish Home Care Program. Two or three times a week they would, visit sick or disturbed people and help them with their medications and their medical visits.

Each Sabbath, (Friday nights, Saturdays) they would visit any Jewish patients, in the nearby hospitals. They would wish them, a good Shabbat and all the best with their health. In addition. They gave each, a small parcel containing; a small challah (a special bread), a small bottle of kosher wine and some kosher sweets. Dov loved to see their gratitude and appreciation that someone actually cared.

He would also accompany his parents, as they regularly visited the aged, and the disabled, loaded with all sorts of baked food and groceries. His parents had schooled Dov to do 'good'. Whatever he decided with his life, he should aim to make the world a better place, even if he was not a Cantor.

All these thoughts scrambled through his head and triggered ideas for a song. His parents' great wish, regarding his future, had turned out to be unacceptable. He was forced to disregard it and somehow find a direction, he was comfortable with and that suited him. Dov grabbed his guitar and teased out some chords, as he searched for the lyrics and began to sing.

DOV. (DESTINY'S PRIZE).

Too long I've been burdened ...
By others...Aspirations....
There alien hopes and. ... False ... Expectations...
Worn ill-fitting dreams...Their fears and... Reservations...
But no more. . . I've shed this load... It's time for me...
To find ... My destiny.

Satisfied, with the sentiment and the lyrics: Dov fell back on the bed and held the guitar above his head. The ceiling light, struck the gleaming surface and bounced off. It seemed as if he was holding a shiny trophy. Dov took this, as a sign. The song seemed right, like a bespoke suit. It felt true. He sensed this confirmed it. He should follow his dream, as a singer-songwriter.

But he would do it in the context of his parent's philosophy. No matter how long it took, no matter how hard, it became.

Chapter 4

Next morning, it was the start of a new school year. Although it was just 7 am, it was already quite warm. Jane had grudgingly offered, to show him the way to school. Dov was thrilled, they would spend some uninterrupted time together. It would give him a chance to get to know her and vice versa. However, she rapidly set off and silently marched with fixed intent, to the local High School. Dov strode behind her, sweating in his black Hasidic outfit, as he valiantly, tried to keep up. He marvelled at the clear, fresh air, the bright blue sky and the loud chirping, twittering birds, the absence of cars and the near-deserted streets, plus the delightful scent of pine, with a touch of honey, from the abundant, red – brown barked Maple trees, with bright green foliage, that lined the roads. Everything felt novel, clean and full of promise. Like a fresh, bright beginning, for this next chapter of his new life. It lifted his spirit and added an extra bounce to his step.

Eyes straight ahead, Jane tried to ignore him. But following her, did offer fringe benefits. With guilty pleasure, Dov studied her well-toned calves and swaying hips. Unbidden, sensual thoughts flooded his mind and refused to disappear. Pare back all his religion. Dov was still a normal, hormone awash teenager. The mode of dress and wigs for females, in the Hasidic community and the need to be segregated, removed temptation. But undeniably, out in the general community, he had sometimes ogled, attractive young women.

In his extensive reading, Dov had often come across, the concept of, "love at first sight." Naïvely, he had ridiculed such a notion. He had put it down as an invention, of the author's imagination. A literary device. Not anymore. From the first moment he saw Jane on the station platform and reinforced when they locked eyes at the dinner table, he was downright besotted and love-struck. He was head over heels in what he assumed was love with this wonderful girl. In love with her beauty and her essential essence. Being a total novice. He assumed this feeling of joy and well-being, whenever he saw her, particularly when they talked, was love? Otherwise, he had some, new and undefined, mysterious malady.

Clearly, he was attracted to her, but felt guilty about the sensual thoughts that repeatedly intruded, instinctively, he felt his love should be better-purer than that. But in his subconscious, he rationalised, he was a man. This was normal, wasn't it? He had no frame of reference, no advice to guide him. He struggled in a choppy, treacherous sea, of newfound, sensual emotions and at a loss, how to handle it.

Near the school. He hurried, to catch up and offered, an apologetic. "I hope I'm not going to be too much of a drag."

"Drag doesn't cover it," she curtly replied, as she hurried on.

Soon they arrived at the school gates. A prominent high metal arch, with an arcing large sign, 'Denton High.' Jane walked through and casually, said over her shoulder. "Stop here until you hear the School bell," without waiting for an answer, she continued along the gravel road towards, the majestic two-story red brick building, with a tall, notable tower, topped by a large flagpole with a huge Stars and Stripes, which fluttered in the gentle breeze.

On the left of the driveway, there was a parched brown, gridiron field, with a tilted, weary, wooden Scoreboard showing, 'Denton zero. Visitors zero'.

On the right of the driveway, there was a large rect-angular, asphalt Schoolyard. The whole School area was enclosed by a chest high, wire mesh fence. In his mind Dov, asked himself, was this to keep the animals in, or to keep them out?

As Dov waited, he wondered, what this new School and his fresh schoolmates would be like. His reflections were interrupted, by the sound of the loud school Bell. Dov tried to suppress his anxiety. He took a deep breath, squared his shoulders and strode into the Schoolyard.

As he entered, Dov was aware, all the bustle, laughter and noise - just stopped. As though someone, had turned the volume off. In the eerie silence. Dov tried to suppress his apprehension. He took several deep breaths, then a few tentative steps, but halted when he heard a loud chorus. "Whooo eeee! Is it a bird?" It was shouted by a group of students, all wearing brightly dyed football jump-ers, the 'Jocks', members of the school football team. Then, another question was shouted in a loud voice. "Is it a plane?" It was shouted by a student with slicked- back, black hair and wearing a tight, yellow T-shirt, Rip, the vice-captain of the football team. This question was answered by a tall good-looking student with piled high, greasy style duck-tail and wearing the garish, school blazer, he mock-ingly shouted. "It's a scarecrow!" Bob, the captain of the school football team and Jane's boyfriend.

Dov stopped, confused and intimidated, by his welcome. He had never experienced anything even remotely similar. He had spent his life, in Jewish friendly neighbourhoods, like Queens and Brooklyn. He had been accepted and was part of the usual streetscape. Similarly, in his Jewish schools. So, this hostility and intolerance, was completely foreign to him and unsettling. He wondered whether it was outright Anti-Semitisms? Whatever, this experience was, was it unique to Denton?

He watched surprised and gratified as Jane, stepped for-ward, confronted her schoolmates and announced. "This is Dov Goldstein. He's from New York," his beautiful host, had been brave and dampened the hostilities. Dov's already high estimation of her was, further elevated. Her interven-tion had momentarily silenced her schoolmates. He stared at her besotted. He was forced to hurriedly reappraise her. Sure, she was a beautiful young woman, but obviously she was much more. She was compassionate and brave, to stand up for him, against her schoolmates.

His lovelorn musings were rudely disrupted when - his Hasidic hat was sent flying. He spun around and was confronted by the smirking Bob.

Meanwhile, his Hat had been scooped up by Rip. When Dov attempted to retrieve it from Rip. It was thrown to Bob. As Dov began to dart, to and fro between the taunting pair, like a ball in a tennis match. He heard a loud sarcastic chorus. "Whooo eeee! It's forty-love," it was shouted by the 'Jocks'. They had formed a Circle around the trio and had begun a loud, rhythmic clap.

Though Dov was embarrassed, by his futile, to and fro dashes. He was determined to regain, his precious Hat. Having Jane present, was an added incentive. After a few minutes, a short figure, burst through the circle and grabbed the hat from the surprised Rip. The short student, had an incredible Bill Haley cowlick hairstyle. An irresistible force, he strode over to Dov and offered the hat. Then, he enthusiastically introduced himself and pumped Dov's hand. "Hi, Alberto Baca," he looked Dov over, as he exclaimed. "Groovy outfit. Love the hat, great beard and moustache. You remind me of someone", after a moment's thought, he had a lightbulb moment and brightly announced. " I know,' Rebel without a Cause'. Saw it six times. Now, what's his name?" After he was prompted, he remembered and bellowed. "Sal Mineo!" Alberto pointed to Dov and declared. "You're taller, but if you got rid of the beard, moustache, the sideburns and dumped the outfit, you could be twins," Jane forcefully cut in. "Dov's a religious Jew, you idiot," to date, apart from Jane. Alberto had been the only friendly person at this school. Dov was struck by his courage and his warm, outgoing personality. He seemed to be another outsider.

In the past. Dov had a secure, supportive environment with his parents, his uncle's family, and the neighbourhood. Plus, he had always been, a bit of a loner. As a result, he had never felt the need for any close friends. But in this new alien environment, without all that support, the prospect of a friend appealed.

Bob strutted over, he brushed past Dov and Alberto, tried to engage Jane, and offered a cheery. "Hi honey, let's go to Jose's after-school," Jane indicated Dov and retorted. "Can't. Dov's our house guest." Bob glared at Dov, gave him a slow once over-look, and sarcastically proposed. "Your friend's a real snappy dresser." In mock shock, he turned to Jane. "He's staying with you?!"Jane nodded and said. "It was Mum's idea." Bob shrugged and again confronted Dov. "Hey, Duv, what's with the classy threads?" Dov mimicked Bob's action, he reviewed his gaudy blazer and slowly looked him up and down, then retorted. "Thought it was fancy dress. Just trying to fit in," Bob was not impressed, he snapped. "Hey check this wet rag. Been in town, five seconds and he's already putting down our colours."

The 'Jocks' and Rip joined in and belligerently, loudly, shouted. "Yeah!" They surged closer and invaded Dov's personal space. They bumped and pushed him. Then, began to shove Dov around, from member to member, like a pinball. Until Dov pulled free and escaped from the circle.

He quickly joined Jane and Alberto and the trio strolled into the School building. Dov's first morning, had not been dull. He wondered, if it would be like this for the whole year?

At lunchtime. Jane insisted Dov, should sit with her in the noisy Cafeteria. The large sparse rectangular area had a wall of glass looking onto the Schoolyard. Along another wall, there was a long laminated counter with trays, utensils, crockery, glasses, and containers of, water and different fruit juices. A fifty-something, bored looking, brown-haired woman, was behind the counter and supervised.

Three parallel rows of laminated tables, matched with plastic chairs, ran the length of the room. The tables were crammed with eating, talking, laughing Students. The confined area reverberated with the loud noise. The tables seemed to be occupied on a hierarchal basis. Bob, Rip and the 'Jocks' were at the table nearest to the counter. At the next table, there were a group of teenage girls, dressed in colourful casual and wearing the school football socks, the 'Jocketts,' the cheer squad for the Football team. The rest of the student body filled the remaining tables. Dov and Jane found a space that, was the furthest from the counter. Literally, they were at the bottom of the food chain.

The two ignored the whispers and the strange looks from the other students. They shared a sandwich and Dov sipped a glass of fruit juice, while Jane ate an apple. When she finished. She sat back and thoughtfully appraised him. "You're a bit of a surprise packet," unsure how to answer,

Dov remained silent. He was gratified, for any time he spent, close to this beautiful young woman.

The silence was broken when Jane's best friend, Betty-Lou interrupted. She was an outspoken: curvy, dark-haired, teenage, dark flashing-eyed, small bundle of energy. She was accompanied by Alberto. She offered a bright smile as she regarded the silent pair and brightly announced. "Check out, Denton's beauty and the beast," Alberto cut in. "I think he's cool. Love his outfit, it's a one-off," reluctant, to disabuse his new-found friend. Dov merely said. "Sorry to disappoint you. But there are loads of similar cool guys in Brooklyn."

Alberto, ignored the comment. Bursting with excitement, he faced the two girls and exclaimed. "You should have been at Bartle Hall, Kansas City, last night. Bill Haley was awesome." He whipped out a pair of drumsticks from his back pocket and played a flashy drum roll on his thigh. It was something, Alberto was prone to do whenever he got excited. Betty Lou pointed to his cowlick hairstyle and retorted. "I wondered if this accounted for that!" Then she turned to Jane and sarcastically said. "Plays drums at assembly and thinks he's a muso," Alberto was stewing, he snapped. "That's great from a wannabe Southerner. I've known a Betty and a Lou," in a pronounced Deep South accent, he said. "What's this Betty- Lou nonsense?" Betty Lou was not one, to take a backward step and promptly responded. "Wake up Mr. Mindless. Your people came from Cuba and mine from the Deep South. You dummy!" Dov felt envious, as he observed their good-natured banter. At some stage, he hoped to have the same casual, exchange with Jane.

During the conversation. Bob, Rip, and the 'Jocks' had menacingly gathered around the group. Jane had something she wanted to share with Dov. But the arrival of her schoolmates was a catalyst, to bring it forward. She decided it would be prudent to remove Dov and avoid any further argument, or confrontation. She turned to Dov and softly said. "I want to show you something, concerning your mother." Dov was surprised and buoyed by the unexpected proposal, and exclaimed. "Great, lead away."

The assembled students were startled, as Jane jumped up and led Dov from the Cafeteria. They walked along, a long corridor, with classrooms on either side: and then, walked up a flight of scuffed wooden stairs, along another corridor, lined with framed photos of past Graduation classes. Jane stopped at one and pointed. "Look, there they are," underneath the photo, there was a brass plate, with the inscription, 'Graduation class 1923,' she added. "Check the front row, third from the left, that's mum and next to her is your mother," Dov eagerly checked the photo. Sure enough, he could identify the attractive features of the teenage Elisabeth Cummings and next to her the teenage Marge Sullivan. As he studied the smiling young women, full of life and hope. Dov felt a sense of incredible sadness. Holding back tears, he struggled to speak. "Thank you. This... This was the best gift ever," choked up, Dov stared at her and grasped her hand. She seemed embarrassed and turned her eyes away, but let him still hold her hand.

Eventually, discomfited by his overt emotions. Jane pulled her hand free and seized his arm and announced. "Look. There's something else, I want you to see."

Dov allowed her to lead him along the corridor and into one of the large, empty classrooms. She hurriedly looked around. "I'm sure this is the room, Mum showed me," she muttered, as she went up and down the aisle and checked the wooden desktops. Dov was intrigued and trailed along, until Jane triumphantly indicated a desktop, and exclaimed. "Look, here it is," Dov hurried up and stared at the desktop. Inscribed in the aged wooden surface, in uneven letters -standing out amidst the backdrop of indiscriminative scratches, choked with emotion, he haltingly read. "Elizabeth Cummings and Marge Sullivan, friends, -"Dov had to stop before he could finish. "Forever," they locked eyes. Dov's whole world was reduced to her green eyes. The cicadas,' chirping outside the window, irritating, buzzing blowflies and the distant sound of voices and laughter from the Cafeteria, all irrelevant. The only thing that mattered, were those deep green eyes, with the multiple islands of tiny, gold specks.

Chapter 5

The next day, before school. In the school playground. Rip, with creamed- back hair, bursting, tight shirt, sidled up close to Betty- Lou. The small bundle of bubbling energy, blatantly, turned her back on him and started chatting with her friend Kate.

Preppy looking teenagers, suddenly flooded in. The 'Jocks' and 'Jocketts,' greeted each other boisterously. Meanwhile, Rip hailed Betty Lou, like the,' Fonz.' "Heyyy!" Still ignored. Rip, was in danger of losing face. Hand over his heart, he played to the crowd and began to sing;

RIP (TEASE QUEEN).

Come on baby
Don't be a tease.
Come on baby
Don't be such a tease
Love me baby
I'm here to please

The 'Jocks', gathered together and offered Rip, their support.

JOCKS

Wow, wow, wow, wow, wow,

Rip smirked as Betty- Lou swayed up and stroked his face. Startled, when she ran fingers through his slicked- back hair and then disgustedly, wiped her hand on his jumper. Kate and the Jocketts, gathered around Betty Lou, in support.

JOCKETTS

Wow, wow, wow, wow, wow,

Rip was undaunted and continued to sing.

RIP

Oh baby,
You drive me crazy.
What can I do,
I'm so crazy for you

The' Jocks' reassembled and joined in.

JOCKS

You, you, you, you, you,

Rip, reenergised, recommenced to sing.

RIP

Drive me crazy
Sweet, sweet lips

You drive me crazy,
Luscious hips.
Make me crazy.
For your charms,
I want to hold you.
In my arms.

Betty Lou was not intimidated. She confronted Rip and began to sarcastically sing.

BETTY LOU.

Cool it greasy
You're such a sleaze
Cool it greasy,
you're such a sleaze
Shoot through greasy
Hit the breeze.

Sensing they had Rip, on the ropes, Betty Lou and the 'Jocketts', combined forces and sarcastically sang;

BETTY LOU and 'JOCKETTS'

Oh greasy
You make us queasy,
Lost all your glue
We're so over you
You, you, you, you, you.

Rip, gathered the 'Jocks' and confronted all the females.

RIP and JOCKS.

Drive me crazy
Sweet, sweet lips
Drive me crazy
Luscious hips
Make me crazy
For your charms,
I want to hold you,
In my arms.
Oh come on baby
Don't be a tease
Come on baby,
Don't be such a tease
Come on baby,
You're such a tease
Tease, Tease, Tease, Tease,
Tease Queen.

Betty Lou, had enough. She confronted Rip and snarled. "Arsehole!" Then flounced off, trailed by all the females, animatedly, they chatted amongst themselves. Rip and the' Jocks', testosterone's surging, slapped each other on the back and they also left.

On the same day, after school. Dov took the opportunity to explore the town. The residents, went about their usual business, until Dov passed by, then they all stopped and gaped. As Dov wandered down Main Street, he passed a Bar. Although it was early afternoon, he could see there was a crowd already drinking inside. Lounging, on the wooden bench outside, were several sixty-something, men, with beer guts, wearing cowboy hats, contented, as they puffed away, on their pungent, rolled up cigarettes. Several mongrel dogs, lay on the pavement near their feet, tongues lolled in the heat. In his Hasidic gear, Dov wished he could do the same.

As Dov stood outside the Bar: a horse and cart laboured past on the road, then, a dusty green 1957, Chevy, with windows down while the radio blasted out, Bill Haley and the Comets, 'Rock Around the Clock.' It passed in a pungent cloud of black smoke. It was trailed by a battered, 1950s red Crosley station wagon, with a bale of straw and a barking dog in the back.

As he continued along the sidewalk, Dov passed the: Post Office, Bank, a Cafe named Jose's, then a Movie house, the Palace. It was advertising its current attraction, 'Rebel without a Cause.' On an adjacent wall, there were several large, bright, posters, listing the coming attractions.

Soon after, he arrived at a Record shop. As he checked the window display, his attention was caught by a glossy poster for Angeline Dubois' new album, 'Tease Queen.' The singer/ film star was in her mid-30s, she was dark haired and drop-dead gorgeous. Inside, he saw that Jane was interested in the same poster. Dov studied the shop. The tiny store was stacked with Vinyl records. The walls were plastered with photos of, fifties Pop-stars and on prominent display, several Angeline posters.

When Dov entered the shop, the young male Attendant had an upbeat song, on the turntable. He turned and did a double take, at the sight of Dov.

MALE (TEASE QUEEN)

You broke my heart
Little Tease Queen.
You said we'd never part.
Now alone, after our tiff.
Alone with my teen dream.
Oh baby, baby, baby, look at this stiff.

Jane, exuberantly swayed to the music. Spying Dov she shouted. "Come right in, this is super," teasing, she came up close, then swayed away. Dov was both confused and stimulated. Enthused, he turned to Jane and exclaimed. "It's great."
"Angeline Dubois's new single. Welcome to the fan club," she enthusiastically responded.
"But it doesn't rock like Elvis," he added.
"You've just been blacklisted," she said, as she started to dance.

ANGELINE

Shoop, Shoo-ah, ship, ship, Shoo-ah
Shoop, Shoo-ah, ship, ship, Shoo-ah

This was a far cry from any dancing Dov was used to. Trying to make a good impression, he attempted to mimic her moves but failed miserably

MALE

Come on baby
Don't be a tease
Come on baby
You're such a tease
Love me, baby
I'm here to please
Wow, wow, wow, wow, wow

After a moment, he gave it up as a bad job. Jane had also stopped, but continued to sway to the music. Smiling, she gently rested her hands on his shoulders. "You need someone to help you polish up your moves," Dov eagerly responded. "That would be great," he wondered if she was volunteering? Jane resumed dancing. Hoping to please her. Dov also restarted dancing, as best he could.

ANGELINE

Come on greasy
Don't be a sleaze
Come on greasy
Don't be such a sleaze
Love you greasy

Sarcastic) like hell will freeze.

FEMALE ENSEMBLE

Wow, wow, wow, wow, wow

Embarrassed, by near tripping over himself. Dov ground to a halt. He felt a total klutz.

MALE

Oh, baby,
You drive me crazy
What can I do
So crazy for you.

Jane crossed to the stationery Dov, sympathetically patted him on the shoulder and kindly announced. "You've got to get a girlfriend." Dov couldn't believe it, was she offering herself, for the role?

MALE ENSEMBLE

You, you, you, you, you.

When the chorus kicked in, she started to dance with abandon. This left Dov stumped.
He stared, mesmerised and stimulated, as Jane continued to dance uninhibitedly.

MALE

Drive me, crazy
Sweet, sweet lips
You drive me crazy

Luscious hips
Make me crazy
For your charms
I wa-na hold you in my arms.

Dov was brought back to earth and out of his contemplation, when she stopped.

She took her time, checked his appearance and caringly offered. "I know one girl who wouldn't worry about your look and all that gear," Dov hoped, she meant herself?

"But, it might upset her guide dog," Jane added and Dov's face and spirits fell.

She laughed at his discomfort, and hurriedly added. "Your face! Sorry! I was joking."

ANGELINE

Cool it greasy You're such a sleaze Cool it greasy
You're such a sleaze
Shoot through greasy
Hit the breeze
Wow, wow, wow, wow, wow.

Later as they're walked home, Jane was carrying the Angeline album. When they passed the Palace, she held it up and announced. "I'm dying to hear it." Dov noticed the poster for an upcoming attraction. Angeline Dubois's new film, 'Tease Queen. When good girls go bad,' he indicated. "Would you like to see this?"
"Would I ever," she enthused.

"Great! When? "Dov was ecstatic. Would this be his first date?

"I'll find out when Betty Lou can make it."

"Oh!" Dov was again, disheartened.

Seeing his expression, she offered. "You can come with us if you like." Again his mood was squashed. This was not what he hoped for. But, better than nothing. Dov was silent and miserable, as they walked back to her house.

That night after dinner. Still discouraged and brooding about Jane not returning his interest. Dov got his guitar, sat on his bed and teased out chords, while he searched for lyrics. Dov wanted this song to express how he felt about Jane.

Having zero experience, with girls and relationships. Dov wondered, if he was being ridiculous. He questioned, what could she see in him? She was way out of his league. She had beauty, brains and also a compassionate heart. All Dov knew was, he had strong feelings for her. Feelings and emotions, he never had before and at this stage, there was no way, he could tell her. But that didn't stop him from dreaming and imagining, what could be. When he was dreaming, anything was possible. Nothing was beyond him. Even Jane.

The next morning as they walked to school, she was content to walk beside him. It gave Dov a huge lift. The day seemed brighter and the world a better place. He soon noticed, she had taken a different route, he asked. "Are we going a different way?"

"Yes. We're meeting up with Betty Lou," she replied. Dov was somewhat disheartened. He wouldn't have Jane, all to himself.

Sure enough, at the next corner, Betty Lou bounded up and cheerily offered. "Hi."

The girls hugged and started to walk side-by-side as they chatted.

Once again Dov was relegated, to one step behind Jane. He was excluded from their conversation. Although, sometimes they would laugh and dart a glance back at him.

Chapter 6

The next day at school. Dov attended the mandatory Bible Studies class. The windows of this small, first-floor classroom, overlooked the playground. From his seat in the front row, Dov could see the red – brown trunk and branches of the adjacent large Maple tree. Dov sat isolated. Though Jane was also in the front row, she was away from the window. The remainder of the wooden desk were all occupied.

The late 20s something, moustached male Teacher sat at his desk and waited for the chatter to subside. Behind him written on the blackboard, in large capital letters, 'Bible studies, the 10 lost tribes of Israel, fact or fiction?' Satisfied, he had their attention. The teacher addressed the class. "Following, the conquest of the northern kingdom of Israel, by the Assyrians, the 10 tribes over time, disappeared from history. But the belief persists that one day, the 10 lost tribes would be found."

Bob and Rip whispered and loudly giggled in the back row. Bob suddenly thrust his hand up. The teacher nodded. Bob couldn't maintain a straight face, as he remarked. "Looks like one of 'em, ended up here, sir."

"That's enough Brown," the teacher snapped.

The silence was suddenly shattered by - the sound of a shrill, blasting Siren. When it stopped. A voice screamed over the PA system. "This is a nuclear alert drill. I repeat this is a drill."

The teacher faced the class and shouted. "Everyone under their desks. Now!" The students scrambled under their desks. The confused Dov, hastily followed suit. Meanwhile, Jane in the front row looked pale and rested her head on the desk. The Teacher observed and asked. "Are you all right?"

"I'll be okay," she casually replied.

"Any problem, see the nurse", the teacher added.

After class when Dov asked her, she brushed it off with. "It's nothing. I just seemed to have lost my zing," then, she turned and quickly walked away.

Chapter 7

Some days later, after several more episodes. Jane decided she couldn't just keep ignoring her symptoms. Reluctantly, she made an appointment to see the local doctor. Doctor West's, surgery was located in a small: single storey, modest, wooden cottage, on Main Street. It was some 50 meters past the Record shop. She tentatively entered the cream-colored wooden cottage and approached the 50-something, stocky, uniformed Receptionist and announced. "Jane Cornhuckster, I have an appointment at 1 pm with Doctor West," the Receptionist checked the appointment book, nodded and asked "Are you a new patient?" Jane replied. "Yes," then hurriedly added. "No, I was delivered by Doctor West and saw him again, when I was probably three for my measles," the Receptionist checked the file. "Yes. But all that was years ago. I'll need you to fill out a form," she handed Jane a clipboard with a form and an attached Biro. Jane took them and sat down on a wooden chair in the small reception room. The only other person waiting, was the lady from the Cafeteria, Mrs. Harris. She was engrossed reading an old National Geographic magazine and studiously avoided making any eye contact. Jane quickly finished the form and returned it to the Receptionist. She checked it and said. "Good. While he finishes with his patient, Nurse will do some basic measurements. Please go to Room one," she indicated a nearby door. Jane entered and was greeted by a 40- something, sturdy, cheery woman, wearing a blue Nurses uniform, she politely ordered. "Please, lie down. I'll take your blood pressure," Jane laid on the examination couch. The nurse wrapped the blood pressure cuff around her upper arm and began to pump it up. Jane felt increasing compression on her upper arms, to the point of discomfort, as the Nurse kept pumping. Satisfied, the Nurse began to release the pressure, while she placed a stethoscope on the inside of Jane's elbow. "Not bad," she finally said. "You're probably a bit anxious. I'll wait a few minutes and do it again," she bustled around while she engaged Jane, in idle chatter, about the weather and the town. Jane replied in monosyllables and soon the Nurse gave it up as a bad job. She reapplied the cuff and again pumped it up and listened with her stethoscope, then offered. "That's much better,she quickly scanned the form Jane had filled in and asked.

"Now, tell me about these dizzy spells?"

"It's nothing," Jane re-joined.

"Does it happen often?"

"Several times. In the past week, but after a few hours, I'm over it," Jane brushed it off.

"Just as well you're seeing Doctor West," the nurse rebuked.

"You sound, just like my mother," Jane wryly responded.

<h1 style="text-align:center">Chapter 8</h1>

Jane attempted to make herself comfortable on the hard examination couch. The nurse had draped a sheet over, her exposed abdomen, before she left with, a curt. "Doctor West will be here shortly."

While she waited. Jane idly studied the stark examination room. Facing the couch was a mahogany desk with a black leather swivel chair. Adjacent to the desk were several shelves of medical textbooks and medical journals. Near her couch, there was a shiny metal, two-door medical trolley. On the top, there was an assortment of intimidating medical equipment. On the wall behind the desk, there were several framed degrees that verified that Doctor James Edward West was a graduate of, Kansas City University. The graduating class of 1935.

Finally, Doctor West bustled in. The 50- something: stocky, jovial man, had receding grey hair and wire- rimmed glasses. He kindly reviewed Jane. "So how long have you had these recurrent episodes?"

"Oh. About three- or four months."

"What made you come now?"

"I thought they would go away. But they haven't," she sheepishly replied.

"Let's have a look at you," he said, as he gently removed the sheet. "I'm just going to feel your tummy," he declared and began to gently palpate her abdomen on the left side, just below the ribs, began to tap the back of his hand and kindly explained.

"I'm just checking your spleen," paused, then offered. "Seems a little enlarged," he saw Jane was confused and alarmed, he quickly added. "Not to worry, let me also check your Liver," he repeated the procedure on the other side, just below the ribs, and announced. "Much the same," he paused and reflected, then added. "We'll need to do some tests," he wrote something on a form and gave it to Jane, then he replaced the sheet and instructed. "Give it to the receptionist, she will make an appointment for the test." Jane looked worried as she hopped off the couch. Dr West noticed and attempted to reassure her. "it's probably nothing. I am just being cautious and running these tests," Jane wasn't completely reassured, but she left, without any further question.

Chapter 9

A week later. Dov was at last, satisfied with his effort on Jane's song. He had rewritten the lyrics, several times. He named the song, 'Bring on the Night.' It had been an eventful week.

That night. Unable to sleep. Dov got out of bed, pulled the floral curtains wide apart and moonlight flooded into the room. He opened the window, leaned out in his pyjamas and breathed the warm Maple scented night air. The street was deserted. The moonlight and the occasional street lamp cast bizarre (Rorschach), tree shadows on the roadway. He thought he could pick out a man's face? No, it was a girl. He moved the small armchair near to the window. Sat in it and softly sang Jane's song.

DOV (BRING ON THE NIGHT.)

How can she not see?
My heart's on my sleeve
How can she not
Notice my yearning

He thought, he heard footsteps outside his door. They stopped and he heard a loud cough. He softly sped through the first verse, closed the window and the floral curtains. The footsteps started again, but moved away, then there was just silence.

He returned to bed. But his mind was still racing and he couldn't sleep. After, considerable more tossing and turning, sleep still eluded him.

It was still quite early. So, he decided to take a walk. He got dressed and carrying his shoes, crept downstairs and out of the dark, silent house. Outside, he put his shoes on and decided to head to Main Street.

It was deserted. But the tranquil, full moon night and the walk had been therapeutic. He felt calmer and less depressed. As Dov walked, he was enveloped by the warm summer night. In the distance, he could hear a dog's forlorn howling. It was in sync with his mood. As he continued with Jane's song. Dov had a flashback, to the moment, when they had first locked eyes, at the dinner table.

DOV (BRING ON THE NIGHT.)

How can she not hear?
Hear my heart
How can she not notice?
It's breaking
To her, I'm a nonentity
A shadowy stranger that she cannot see.

Dov remembered, the night he joined Betty- Lou, and Jane at the Palace Cinema and watched, a black-and-white screening of, 'Tease Queen,' starring Angeline DuBois. Regrettably, he had to sit in the middle of the near-empty cinema, by himself, three rows behind the girls.

So bring on the night
For my dreaming

Dov recalled, Jane, flirting with Bob, on the phone. Oblivious to his persistent, longing gaze.

Bring on the night
Fantasies scheming
Bring on the night
Now she is seeing

Dov remembered, playing chess with Jane, distracted and unable to focus on the game.

Bring on the night
Love all revealing
Made bold by the mystery of the night

In the darkness, above the nearby Café, a flashing neon sign: 'Jose's,' suddenly, lit up the darkness. Dov was drawn to it, like a moth to a flame. He opened the door and nervously entered.

Wide-eyed, he checked out this strange new world. A big red Jukebox, blasted out, 'Blue Suede Shoes.' The cosy milk bar on Main Street had large plain, plate glass windows, on either side of a central, technicolour stained glass doorway. The Plate glass, gave unimpeded views of Main Street and the streetscape.

Inside, the scattered laminated tables were covered with red- check tablecloths. The tables were packed with rowdy students from his High school. They boisterously sang along with the tune on the Jukebox. Several teenage waitresses, in candy pink costumes -bustled around. A lengthy serving counter, with a grey, granite top, ran the length of the room. It had a long row of large glass jars, each crammed with an assortment of brightly coloured tempting sweets. At each end of the counter, there were two shiny silver milkshake mixers. Below the counter, a broad glass cabinet displayed an assortment of cakes and open sandwiches.

Behind the counter. There was a massive bright Mural of the Johnsonville Fossil Coal Power Plant, 1951. Operated by the Tennessee Valley Authority (TVA). The Mural, filled the entire back wall. The remainder of the walls displayed a collection of classic film posters such as, Casablanca, Mr Smith goes to Washington and The Marx Bros in Casablanca.

Scattered between these posters, were coloured posters of pop stars such as, Elvis, Little Richard, Desi Arnez and Buddy Holly.

A fit looking, man in his 50s, with distinctive Che Guevara facial hair, struggled to hang - a large photo. It was a photo of Che. Alberto smiled at, Jose's, clumsy efforts. The

Cuban-born owner/operator of the Café was Alberto's father. They swung around, when Dov entered.

Jose offered a big welcoming smile. While Bob, Rip, and the 'Jocks', at a front table, gave Dov a loud Bronx cheer. Jose glared at them and growled. "Any more of that and you're out," then Jose smiled at Dov and pleasantly offered. "Been a lon time since I last saw a Yeshiva guy. I wasn't that old. About your age –" Alberto abruptly cut in. "Dad! Not that old story."

Irritated, Jose continued. "They were very good to me. So, I'll never stop telling it!" Trying to settle things down. Dov asked Jose. "What's a guy from Cuba doing here?" Happy to launch into his story, Jose began. "It's a lon story," darted a guarded glance at Alberto as he continued. "Let me just say, that life here with great guys, muy better, than with that bastard Batista. So – "Alberto unable to help himself, again cut in. "Dad!"

Jose indicated Alberto and bemoaned. "He nags me more than my poor Rosa," quickly, crossed himself. Stepped back and admired the Che photo. Then turned to Dov. "Now how about a milkshake on the house?" Dov gratefully nodded. Jose shuffled behind the counter, with a pronounced limp and began to make Dov a milkshake. Finished, he spoke to a waitress and gave it to her. Dov turned to Alberto and asked. "What's with your dad's limp?"

Alberto smiled and offered, "It was our lottery ticket." "What?!" Dov remained baffled.

"He was working for the T VA and had a bad accident, "Alberto explained.

"Yeah. And?" Dov waited for more details.

Alberto crossed himself and announced. "Thank God he was okay, apart from the limp. And he got a big compensation payout."

"And-?" Dov was mystified and intrigued. Alberto indicated the Cafe. "It paid for all this. So we stayed here, ever since," behind the counter, Jose had overheard, he smiled and began to clean up.

Alberto and Dov looked up, as Jane and Betty-Lou sauntered in. It was obvious, Alberto quite fancied, the feisty, small dynamo with the big smile and the curvy figure. They all sat down and started chatting. Betty Lou's eyes had been swivelling between Jose, behind the counter and the blown up Photo of Che. She appeared puzzled, then after a time, quizzed Alberto. "How come your dad's got identical whiskers?" She pointed to the photo and demanded. "Who is this guy?!" Alberto was a little taken back, he announced. "Che Guevara; of course."

"Guevara. Thought that was a fruit juice?" Betty- Lou replied.

"Maybe in the Deep South where you come from," Alberto snapped back, then stood to attention and proudly added. "In Cuba, he and Castro are leading a revolution." "Ah-ha, a fruitcake!" She mocked, then gently straightened Alberto's cowlick. "So this imitation thing's genetic. What about poor Desi?" She derisively asked. Now it was Dov's turn to be mystified. He threw a questioning look at Betty-Lou. She explained. "Alberto's named after one of Cuba's most famous exports." Dov turned to Alberto and tongue in cheek quipped. "Hi, sugar," Alberto didn't reply. Instead, he drew himself up to full height, clicked his heels, bowed and announced. "Desiderio Alberto Arnez, the Mambo King. Left Cuba and look at him now. A big muchacho. Bill Haley is great, but Desi is my man. Our destinies are linked."

Betty-Lou, couldn't resist, she scornfully snapped. "Sure. You're dateless and desperate. While he loves Lucy," Jose finished behind the counter and left.

Not long after. Bob and Rip approached their table. Alberto nudged Dov and whispered. "The Cojone cousins, small and smaller," Bob and Rip ignored Dov and Alberto. But tried to chat up Jane and Betty – Lou.

Betty- Lou ignored Rip and Jane was still annoyed with Bob.

Dov was surprised when Jane started to be blatantly, attentive to him. He suspected, it was, all for Bob's benefit, but never-less, welcomed the attention. Bob, wasn't impressed and strutted up to Jane and exclaimed. "Doll you're the ginchiest. Missed you, baby," Dov was pleased and surprised when she said. "Get used to it. I told you, I've got a house guest," now, Bob was annoyed. He made it clear he couldn't understand what Jane saw in him. To be honest, Dov was uncertain as well. He was prepared to keep quiet until Bob glared at him, then sneered, as he said to Jane. "Why are you hanging out with this reffo dipstick?!" Then he decided he had enough. He glowered back at Bob and snapped. "Maybe she's tired of someone who thinks Holden Caulfield, is the latest model car." Alberto appreciated and laughed at this comment. This catapulted Rip into the game. He confronted Alberto. Grabbed him by the jumper, dragged him to his feet, pushed him over and stood over him, in a threatening manner. Dov leaped to Alberto's defence and shoved Rip away. Now, it all escalated when Bob joined in. He swung Dov, around and jammed him hard against a wall.

In no uncertain terms, Bob and Rip made it clear, Dov was not wanted, he didn't belong. All the 'Jocks' joined in. Dov had never faced such overt, mindless, intolerance and hostility.

As he looked at the distorted, jeering, antagonistic faces. He was reminded of images from the Movie-Tone film clips, he'd seen during the afternoon matinees at the Queens Movie theatre. Films of Nazi Germany with the crazed, aggressive people, as they screamed, over and over: Juden Rous (Jews out), Juden Rous (Jews out), at the terrified, silent, cowed German -Jewish residents. And the stories of the Holocaust survivors, who would drop by on winter Sundays and have coffee, cake and chat with his parents. Dov had difficulty, not staring at, the faded blue numbers on their fore-arms. He listened mesmerised by, their stories, told in low measured voices and was fascinated by their, lined faces and tired eyes which, hinted at a terrible past, best not remembered. He wondered how they could bear to retell their nightmare, in such an apparently calm and measured manner.

He was puzzled, astounded and in awe, of their philosophy and uniform, message; 'do not hate, be grateful, smile and feel joy every day', it was inspiring.

Dov was particularly, in awe and stunned, how these survivors, had invariably retained their faith and maintained their Jewish religion. By comparison, after his recent tragedy, he had doubted and abandoned his faith and his religion. Although, his recent tragedies were life shattering, they couldn't be equated with, what these people had experienced, or the unimaginable, horrors, they witnessed on a day- to- day basis. He was in awe of their resilience and also felt a sense of shame for his reaction. He pondered, 'why does G-d let bad things happen'? And in particular, 'how could G-d let the Holocaust (Shoah) happen?' These two questions, continued to plague and haunt him.

Chapter 10

Eventually. After considering these questions and the associated, emotional issues for several days. He decided to seek advice from his wise Yeshiva Rabbi, who was also a respected scholar. A few days later he was in the Rabbi's office at the Yeshiva. He sat in a chair, across the desk, he faced the, sixty something, lean, Rabbi with horn rimmed glasses and a typical bushy beard, moustache and payus. Dov haltingly explained his dilemma. The Rabbi, respectfully listened, occasionally offering a slight nod of his head. When Dov finished. The Rabbi spent some minutes considering the question and his proposed reply. Meanwhile, Dov fidgeted impatiently.

Finally, the Rabbi slowly stood, came round the desk and faced Dov. He gave a weary sigh and solemnly commenced, in a thick European accent. "My young Yeshiva student. You ask a good question, but it's very difficult to satisfactorily answer," he briefly paused and instinctively began to slowly sway side- to- side as he gravely, slowly intoned. "Many, many Rabbis, scholars and mystics, have extensively considered this issue, over the ages. They finally, came up with a multifaceted response, unfortunately, with no clear right or wrong answer," he paused, while Dov waited in anticipation. Finally, after another weary sigh, still swaying, he slowly resumed. "They can be classified, under seven broadly based categories". He saw that Dov was, all ears. He paused briefly, then resumed swaying and resumed, to gravely intone.

"First. 'G-d is dead.' This is understood to mean, either he does not exist, or he has changed in some way. For some it means that G-d has abandoned them, while for others, it means, G-d never did exist," between each item, he would invariably briefly pause, regather and heave a deep sigh before he recommenced, swaying and continued to intone.

"Second. 'The Eclipse of G-d'. There are times when God is inexplicably absent from history", paused then added. "Martin Buber made this phrase famous, suggesting that the 20th century was passing through a period when G-d, for reasons unknown to us, refused to reveal himself," a brief pause, then he recommenced, swaying and intoned.

"Third. 'A Distant G-d'. The experience of the Holocaust (Shoah), calls for Jews to reinterpret their belief in G-d. For reasons unknowable to us, refused to reveal himself," another weary sigh, while he darts a glance at Dov, then he recommenced, swaying and intoned.

"Fourth. 'Free Will and G-d'. Terrible events, such as the Holocaust are the price we have to pay to having free will. G-d will not and cannot interfere with history, otherwise our free will would effectively cease to exist. This was the view of Elizabeth Berkovits," yet another brief pause, before he recommenced, swaying and intoned.

"Fifth. 'Jewish Survival'. The event issues a call for Jewish affirmation for survival. The rise of the nation of Israel is one way of reading this revelation. Emil Fackenheim, states that Jews are commanded to survive as Jews, lest the Jewish people perish; to remember the victims of Auschwitz, lest their memory perish", paused, then, recommenced, swaying and intoned.

"Sixth. 'Incomprehensible Silence'. The Shoah, exceeds human comprehension. It is so horrific as to strip away any attempts at explanation. Andre Neher believes that there can only be silence after the Holocaust – G-d's silence and our own," paused, then, recommenced, swaying and intoned.

"Seventh. Providential History. Some have suggested the Shoah had the providential outcome, of overturning old mediaeval Jewish structures and replacing them with modern Jewish life, and that this is what needed to happen," paused, then, recommenced, swaying and intoned.

Finally, the Rabbi finished, his long dissertation. Then, the relieved, weary Rabbi straightened, gazed fondly at Dov and announced. "As I said at the beginning. Unfortunately, there is no right or wrong answer. However, I've given you all the information. Which one you favour, is up to you," he paused, while Dov sat trying to digest, what he had heard. The Rabbi studied him, then kindly offered. "If you need clarification in any area, let me know," Dov acknowledged his comment with a grateful nod. Satisfied, the Rabbi cheerily added "Well then. Good luck!" He shook hands with Dov and left. Dov clearly remembered this memory and all the information. It influenced his thoughts and his behaviour, for the rest of his life.

Chapter 11

Amidst, his current, aggressive confrontation, in Denton. He again recalled the meeting with the Yeshiva Rabbi and the Holocaust survivors stories. How their stories made him feel sick and sometimes have nightmares. He had the same sickening feeling now. He couldn't help himself. It was in his DNA.

Those poor, persecuted people couldn't stand up for themselves, or fight back. But he could. He was determined not to accept, this, overt, intolerance, and prejudice. Holding himself ramrod straight, he glared, with animal hostility, at each of the Singers.

BOB (YOU DON'T BELONG.)

A new boy in town, a real wise guy
Fancy words all bullshit lie

Dov confronted each Singer, he came up to their face, near touching close. Unblinking, he just glared at them. It was chilling. They continued singing, but some actually stepped back a pace. Dov continued to follow. He felt each step back, was a small victory. They couldn't ignore him. He was a person, a somebody. A mensch. Eventually, Dov was right in Bob's face. Both boiling mad, steaming. Jane's frantic, efforts to separate them was futile.

RIP

Tryin to muscle in, scheme an pry
Buzzing round, like a dirty fly

Jane, Betty- Lou, and Alberto watched riveted, by the sight of the lone teenager defying the derision, intolerance and hostility of his schoolmates. Alberto flitted about frustrated. His repeated attempts to intervene, was aggressively blocked by the 'Jocks.'

JOCKS

Pack your bags, hit the track,
Just keep movin.
Shove off, rack off, piss off,
The air, you're ruinin.
Clear out, get out, so long.
You don't belong.
You don't belong.

At the end. Bob angrily confronted Dov and snarled. "Come on, you chicken shit wanker. Let's see what you're made off." Jane tired of it all, wearily interjected. "Come on Bob! Grow up," it was obvious Jane was not comfortable with all the testosterone. She stalked out, pursued by Bob.

Dov was not unhappy with what had happened. He was proud. He had stood up for himself and by proxy, for the countless, past hapless Jews, who were not able to. During the proceedings, he had noticed, Jane had been surprised and he hoped, impressed by his stand-up attitude. Jane had indeed and it fascinated and confused her. She realised, underneath, the weird clothes and the outlandish hair, there was a sensitive, young man, with a lot of character and courage. Her mothers', repeated comment. "Don't judge a book, by its cover," had never been so apt.

Chapter 12

The next day, as they walked home from school. When they neared her home, she turned, walked alongside and timidly offered. "It was nice of you to stand up for Alberto. It could have got heavy," keeping a straight face, Dov replied. "I wouldn't have hurt Bob too much." Dov noticed that Jane smiled, despite herself. Encouraged, he shadow boxed around her and announced. "They call me the Yeshiva Kid," she was plainly disbelieving. "Sure."

"Would you believe the Yeshiva Yid?" He teased. Jane shook her head.

"What about Sackcloth Sammy?" He finally offered.

She laughed and responded. "That I believe. I mean, what do I really know about you?"

"What's to know? I'm Jewish and I'm an orphan."

"Forget the sunny boy routine. There is much, more to you than that," she emotionally replied. Then they were home.

Regretful, Dov followed Jane inside, but in his heart, he was jubilant. At last, she was seeing him as a somebody.

He skipped to his room and reviewed, the last verse of his song-

DOV. (BRING ON THE NIGHT);

In the black and velvet gloom
I can see her love glowing
It lifts me up
Transforming me
A dream's now a reality
No longer I'm a nonentity
Now I'm a face that she can finally see
A person, a being, a somebody
A somebody
Aaaahhh!

Dov remembered, the splendid Rose bushes, in the Cornhuckster's front yard, how he and Jane, admired them. Then, how their faces accidentally touched, as they bent and smelled them and he had marvelled, at the velvet softness, of her cheek.

So bring on the night
For my dreaming

That evening. It was warm and Dov took the opportunity to sit on the Cornhuckster's front porch; near the row of magnificent rose bushes. He checked, no one was around, then he selected one of the best, picked it and placed it under the fret of his guitar.

Dov desperately wanted Jane to admire him. He racked his brain, how he could impress her. His limited and perhaps only obvious talents, were his singing and his guitar playing. He decided to go for it and hoped she would hear him. Dov started to strum his guitar and began to sing a traditional Blues Number. He glimpsed Jane at the window. She appeared to listen and he was buoyed. Halfway through, he stopped singing but kept playing his guitar. After a while, he noticed, Jane had come onto the porch. He was delighted; then blown away when she began to clap along, on the offbeat. When Dov stopped playing, she said. "I can see why they wanted you to be a Cantor".

"Some hope," he snapped.

"Why is that?"

"No way. Not after how mum died. What sort of G-d puts someone through that kind of pain?" He growled.

Jane was guarded when she replied. "I ... I'm sure there's a reason."

"It's all crap!" He barked.

Somewhat taken back, by his vehemence. Jane took a moment to study his hair and outfit. "So why are you still decked out, like this?"

"I'm in mourning".

"How long before it's over?"

"Eight months to go, then all this is history," he indicated his Hasidic attire.

Jane flicked the Star of David over the neck of his T-shirt and asked. "And what about this?"

"That stays!" He emphatically exclaimed.

Jane seemed unwilling to drop the issue. "Why?"

"Because"

"Why don't you want to say?"

"Because. I don't want to say."

"Was it a present from some girl who broke your heart?" Jane teased with a smile. Dov was tired of it all and casually offered. "My mother gave it to me. Just before she died," this stopped Jane in her tracks. In the silence, Dov took it off and showed her the inscription on the back of the thick chain. Jane was curious. Choked with emotion, she began to read it out loud. "Just... Just because I'm not there... Doesn't mean... Doesn't mean... I'm not... I'm not with you," they stared at each other, without speaking. Dov drowned in her eyes and wondered if they glistened with moisture? As he watched, a tear welled, over her eyelash and started to trickle down her cheek. After a moment. Without speaking, Jane grasped his hand. It was only then, she managed, to hesitantly ask. "So if you're not going to be a Cantor. What are you going to do?"

Dov knew what he was desperate to do, but had never shared it with anyone: scared of their reaction, apprehensive, their response would shatter his fragile dream. But Jane wouldn't let go. She persisted and after a while when she promised not to laugh. Dov relented and confessed, "I want to get my music and my thoughts out to the world and try to make a difference like, Leonard Cohen, Woody Guthrie!" Then, picked up his guitar, played a loud chord and said. "I want to be the best, like Elvis!" Give Jane her due, she didn't burst out laughing. But she reviewed his weird appearance and with loaded sarcasm said. "Yeah! I can see that." Dov was unwilling to accept the verdict. He performed a loud, showy three-chord blues Bass Rip. Then he took the Rose from the guitar and gave it to Jane.

She remained unimpressed. "Thanks. But Dad's going to be miffed, if you pick anymore. And you'll need more than three chords," then she swayed inside the house. Dov was besotted, smitten. Still staring at her, he could see she remained, at the window watching. Undaunted and determined to make an impression. Dov began to play "his" song.

DOV (DESTINY'S PRIZE.)

Dreams delicate thread's easily broken
Unravel the web of promises spoken
Have I the will, the courage, the fire?
This is for me.
This is my destiny.

He was startled, when - Alberto erupted from the darkness. The excited Alberto - played a flashy drum roll on the front porch rail and announced. "Hey! That was great. You and me amigo, we could go places. Fame. Fortune. Fast women. It's destiny. The Jew boy and the Mambo King Manager!" Dov was sceptical. But, Alberto pleaded, for a chance to prove himself,

ALBERTO (BET ON ME.)

Forget the odds and stuff convention
Can't give you no warranty
No indemnity protection
My best shot I guarantee

Dov was well aware, Alberto was desperate to escape the rustic life in Denton, experience life in a big, bustling city and try to make it in Show business. But never figured Alberto as a manager. On the other hand; though Alberto knew Dov wanted to be a singer-songwriter. He had never heard him sing, until now. Alberto was excited, he had struck gold. He continued to plead his case.

On the level no deception
Go check out my pedigree
Won't accept no rejection
Take a chance n' bet on me

Since childhood, Alberto had obsessively followed the career of his idol-Cuban born Desi Arnez. He recognised he didn't have the musical talent himself. But was confident, he had the drive and the ambition. If he found the right talent, he could make someone else successful. Alberto felt blessed, fate had brought Dov to his doorstep. He figured Dov would be a good friend and an excellent first client. He regarded him as an original, major talent.

Chapter 13

Over the next few months. They did a lot of thinking and put in, a hell of a lot of hard work. Dov got down to some serious studying, interspersed with daydreaming about Jane. He followed her around like a moonstruck puppy. Sometimes, she'd snap. "Stop following me, check the traffic, anything," during this period, Alberto came up with ideas, regarding Dov's proposed career. Step one, he insisted Dov must change his name. He claimed, Dov Goldstein was not marketable. He suggested anglicising it, to Davey Gold. Dov had already abandoned his religion. He figured a new start, why not a new name? Dov had no problem with the name change and agreed. He considered his name, was just a label. It had no impact on the love and respect he had for his parents or grandparents. That was fixed and permanent. Alberto also decided, Dov needed to change his appearance. Knowing, Dov was a huge Elvis fan. He showed him a blown-up photo, of Elvis, with his long sideburns. Alberto insisted the beard, moustache, payus, and all that Hasidic gear had to go. After much argument, they reached a compromise. For Dov's first public appearance, he would lose the Hasidic clothes, the beard and the moustache, leaving only long sideburns. In the interim; Dov practiced secretly, each evening, in the Storeroom, at Jose's.

After Jose's closed, he rehearsed his songs, in the rear Store-room. While Alberto offered comments. He also, practiced, late at night, in his room at the Cornhucksters. Sometimes, Clem would shout. "Heaven's sake! Stop that row!"

One night. After he had practised in his room. Dov was ready to go to sleep. He was in bed, in his pyjamas and about to turn the bedside light out, when there was a soft tap at the door. He turned and saw Jane peering in, wearing a dressing gown. She closed the door, with care. It was obvious, she didn't want her parents to hear. She whispered. "Hi." Dov couldn't believe it. Jane in his bedroom. Wow! He answered. "Hi," realised it was too loud, quickly lowered his voice. "Hi," she's shyly whispered. "I thought you should know, somebody in this house likes what you're doing."

Dov was ecstatic, he hoped it was her. "Thanks!"

"My mum," she whispered and Dov's face and spirits fell. She hurriedly added. "I'm kidding. No, I really love it. It's great."

Somehow, Dov found the courage to say what he felt. "So ... So are you. Great!"

"Me? I don't know why you'd say that."

"Because you are," he replied, with enthusiasm.

"But I've been nothing but rotten to you. I wonder sometimes, how you put up with me?" She asked. "Anybody who loves, Catcher in the Rye, can't be all bad," he promptly responded.

"I dunno. I came to tell you how much I enjoyed what you're doing and even then, I had to make a joke of it. I'm so sorry."

"Don't worry about it," Dov replied, offhanded. Then he steeled himself and decided to protest his love. "Look, there's something I want you to know," he went to get out of bed. But Jane quickly, put her hand up -to stay where he was and hurriedly said. "Must go. If I'm caught in here, it won't be the Russians who start World War Three, "and with a wry smile, she was out the door and gone. Dov couldn't believe, what had just happened.

Alberto, urged Dov to keep writing songs and in particular a special song for his first public gig. But In the interim, he should keep practicing. Alberto also claimed, if they were going to market Dov, they needed a demo tape. Dov agreed, but the practicalities loomed as a major issue. Until Alberto learned, that the operator of the Record shop had some recording equipment. Recently, he had purchased a Mullin's magnetic tape recorder, from 3M, USA. It was a cumbersome and complicated machine, but it fitted into a 'Carry On 'and the sound reproduction was great. It would have to do. They met with the young man and he agreed to make a Demo tape of some of Dov's songs. Dov and Alberto decided to split, the modest fee.

Sometime later, they spent one humid Sunday, with the young man recording, what Alberto considered Dov's, 10 best songs. Afterward, Dov and Alberto listened to the tape. The machine may have been cumbersome and complicated, but to their ears, the sound reproduction was amazing, mind-blowing. If it was good enough for Bing Crosby to use one, on his NBC Radio show, via transcription discs for the 1946 – 47 season. That was good enough for them. After some haggling, they settled for a purchase price of 300 dollars. They were now the proud owners of a Mullins' magnetic tape recorder.

They hugged each other. They were excited and ready to move forward, to the next stage, of their adventure.

During this period; Dov still had nightmares, regarding his inept and awkward dance moves with Jane. They discussed it and Alberto bought an audio Jiving, tape. Each night after song rehearsal, they listened to the tape and practiced dancing. Though, dancing with each other, was somewhat awkward. They diligently practised. One night, José unexpectedly, came into the storeroom and gaped at the dancing duo. Alberto hurriedly explained the situation. José accepted the explanation with a degree of scepticism. Notwithstanding, they continued their practice and began to improve. They now jived like a couple of professionals

Nearing, the Graduation dance, Alberto approached the organiser (the young Bible Studies teacher) and after he heard Dov, in the Storeroom at Jose's, persuaded him, to give Dov a guest spot on the night. Some weeks, before the Dance, the final year results come out. Thankfully, all three had passed. This ticked off, another one of his mother's promises.

The night before the Dance. Dov was in the Storeroom at Jose's. The cramped warm room was crammed with, an extensive range of groceries and spices, which gave the room a pleasant, distinctive, exotic aroma.

Dov sat in an upright chair, draped with a sheet and was being lathered by Alberto. José bounded in, with a gleaming, cutthroat razor. When he approached, Dov tried to get out of the chair, but Alberto and José restrained him. They attempted to reassure him. But Dov only had eyes, for the shining, razor. Observing his fright, José implored. "Relax. You're in the hands of a maestro. In the old days I-". Alberto abruptly, cut in. "Dad! We haven't time." José shrugged and defiantly continued. "As I was saying. Without any false modesty, I was known as the best barber in Havana." Dov remained sceptical, but stopped struggling and sat back resigned, as José began his work.

Alberto watched with interest, while José expertly wielded the razor. When he had finished, Alberto nodded in approval and announced. "Good job dad." then faced Dov, and asked. "You want to check it?" Dov sure did, but was apprehensive, about what he would see. He nervously nodded. Alberto obliged and held a mirror up. Dov studied this stranger and had to admit, the makeover was dramatic. Looking back was: a clean-shaven, and not a bad looking teenager, with long hair and long sideburns, that was similar to Elvis'. A face that would look good, on a record album. To maximise the impact, on the night. Alberto suggested, Dov should keep out of sight, until the Graduation Dance. Dov regarded his friend, with new respect, maybe he would make a great manager?

Chapter 14

Graduation Dance.
Late 1957

Prior to his Stage appearance. In order to keep out of sight. Dov and Alberto hid on Stage, behind the Upstage Scrim. It was hot, cramped and dark, in the confined, dusty space. Dov was nervous as hell and sensed, Alberto, was as well, but he tried to hide it. Dov checked the Arena, through a chink in the Scrim. The High School Basketball Arena was festooned with coloured balloons and fancy, florid bunting. Above the stage and along the back wall, there were Banners with, "Graduation Dance – 1957".

In matched dark suits, white shirts, and thin dark ties: clean shaven, with slicked back, black hair, the smooth looking Band, played strict tempo ballroom music – 1950s Roger Webb sound. Bored looking couples, whirled round and round. Dov noticed Bob and Jane were doing a slow dance. Rip was dancing with Betty Lou. He whirled her between couples, all the while, his busy hands wandered.

Bored teachers sat around and monitored the proceedings, as they supervised the hormone-laden teenagers.

The Band finished the bracket, to scattered applause. It was their cue. Alberto and Dov scurried to the Wing. Alberto checked Dov. He was wearing a tight-fitted black outfit and clean shaven, apart from long sideburns. He looked amazing- like a Rock star. Satisfied, he patted Dov on the back and urged. "Go, get them, tiger." On the dance floor, Dov saw, Betty Lou had finally, snapped. She slapped Rip and pulled free.

Meanwhile, on stage. The Bandleader stepped forward and loudly announced. "Dust off your dancing shoes. Let's give a big hand for our special guest artist- Davey Gold!" Dov was so nervous, he thought he'd throw up. His heart was racing and his throat felt like the Sahara. He stood frozen. Alberto thrusts him on stage and disappeared. Standing in the Spotlight, Dov felt transformed- a Rock star.

He clutched his guitar, strode to the microphone and struck a loud confident chord. He was greeted by stunned silence. Dov spied Jane and Betty Lou near the Stage, They stared gobsmacked. Self-assured, Dov launched into the song, he had written for the occasion.

DOV (LOOK OUT WORLD)

Hey Janey hey Betty Lou

Near the stage. Both girls yelped with delight, when they heard their name. Dov was elated, when the band section played along. He saw Alberto, had joined the girls, near the stage.

School is out
So pack your bags
There's plenty more things to do
Hey, teachers!
Time to close your books
It's over now, your time is past
So keep your dirty looks

Jane gasped. "Oh my God!" Betty Lou exclaimed. "He's totally prime." Alberto, was smug, as he noted, the girls' reaction to Dov. He turned to them and boasted. "Guess who his manager is?" Dov was rapt when the Audience began to clap along. The attending teachers, were somewhat uncertain about the sentiments in the song, but they also started to clap along.

We're out of reach
So grind your teeth
It's time to be free
Buckle up with me
Now hang on tight
Roller coaster ride
You're trapped and we're free
We have earned our liberty
Couples surged onto the dance floor.
Look out world

The cage is bare
The animals are free
Parents, teachers, all you keepers
Look out now we're free

Alberto noted how Dov, owned the song and the Stage. How he belted out the lyrics. The couples began to dance with new found enthusiasm. They danced a showy, energetic Rock 'n' roll.

So step aside
Watch us as we stride
It's ours you see
It's our turn to be free
Ancients, oldies all you old fogies
We're the future, you're the past
Our star is up and rising fast

The dance floor was now, a sea of pulsating, heaving, humanity. Dov was lifted by the audience reaction. Buoyant, he switched into a higher gear, as he punched out the lyrics. The Band caught up in the mood, also went up a notch and hammered out the rhythm. A wall of sound that lifted Dov- even higher.

Look out world we're standing up
We've got lots to prove
Look out world the time has come
We're all on the move

Look out
Aaaaaaahhhhhhhh
Look out world

Dov took a bow to a thunderous ovation. As he looked around, he noted, that Alberto' had bowed to the two excited girls. When Alberto had finished, Betty Lou, enthusiastically hugged him.

Dov strode off stage and onto the dance floor. He felt awkward as he waited until Jane rushed over. She stared at him, as though for the first time and exclaimed. "You were like... Wow!" Jane was astonished, by the sudden feelings, she felt for Dov, as she watched him perform. She was already impressed by his intelligence, his character, sensitivity and bravery. Now, it seemed the, 'Book cover,' had been dramatically transformed and she was really impressed by this, 'New cover.' She could now honestly add, good-looking, to her checklist. No, she corrected herself, hot, really hot.

Lost for words. She came closer and gestured to his face. "Can't believe you did that." Dov tried to be nonchalant. "I've graduated. So that's all over," he stroked his now clean-shaved face and said with bravado. "No big deal," Alberto itched to get involved, said with disbelief. "Sure!" Then turned to Jane. "He screamed like a virgin when dad did the old shearing routine," Betty Lou, not one to be left out, turned to Alberto and mocked. "Yeah!- You'd know Romeo," Jane wanted to get back to the main game. Still staring at Dov, she declared. "Anyway, you look fabulous-Davey," Dov was speechless. This was beyond his dreams. Maybe, he did have a chance with her? During all this, the Band had started playing again and couples drifted back, onto the dance floor.

Dov and Jane's moment, was shattered when Bob and Rip strode over and butted in. Bob got in Dov's face and barked. "Piss off, you Elvis wannabe," then turned to Jane and ingratiatingly offered. "Honey, ditch these goofballs, let's dance," Rip piped in. "Yeah, what a pair of clowns."

Dov was surprised and encouraged when Jane forcefully, cut in. "He was great!" Betty- Lou also decided to join in. She turned to Rip and vehemently snapped, "So stifle it," Dov was over the moon. Both girls were rooting for him.

Betty- Lou now turned her attention to Alberto. "Move your size nines gorgeous! Let's shake booty," Alberto was delighted and eagerly responded. "I'm your man, baby," she led the eager Alberto towards the dance floor. They started to dance.

Dov was taken back and delighted when Jane turned to him. "Come on Do-, "she quickly corrected herself. "-Davey," they walked arm in arm onto the dance floor and started dancing, in a formal fashion. The lush music swelled. The stage darkened. The Spotlight found Dov and Jane, as they whirled about, cheek to cheek. Holding her firm yet soft body. Dov closed his eyes as they spun around and round. She smelt fantastic. It felt as if he was clasping fragrant sunshine. He was overjoyed, when he felt her soft hand on the back of his neck. Jane was still coming to terms with this 'transformed,' stranger. Up close he was even better looking and she was, unreservedly, enjoying yourself.

When the band switched to an upbeat Glen Miller number. Jane started to Jive. Just when Jane thought, things had become stable. Dov produced yet another surprise.

He responded and complimented her moves. For a brief time, she was thrown. Who was this smooth looking, polished dancing stranger? He seemed to be the complete package. Smiling, Dov maneuverer her, through a complex routine and she enthusiastically joined in. High-spirited and laughing, they executed a series of complex jive moves, totally coordinated. They were in perfect sync. Their enjoyment and exuberance were infectious. The captivated couples, moved back to give them room and started a deafening, rhythmic clap. Dov felt absolute joy. He focused on his body moving to the music and of Jane moving to the same rhythm.

Betty Lou and Alberto joined the clapping circle: that included the 'Jocks', the 'Jocketts' and the Teachers. Everyone, excited and smiling, as they watched the jiving couple -except for the sour-faced, Bob and Rip. Betty Lou turned to Alberto and shouted. "Wow! Look at him!" Alberto responded. "He's a triple threat. The looks, the voice, and the moves. But it took us a lot of practice," Betty Lou was openly sceptical. "Us?!" Alberto was nonchalant. "The voice was there. But the rest was a struggle," Betty Lou snapped. "Rubbish!"

"Come on, we practiced the Wurlitzer," Alberto explained and grabbed the startled Betty Lou by both hands and executed the Wurlitzer. Beaming, he continued. "And the Basic Zipper," again he grabbed the docile Betty Lou by both hands and did the Basic Zipper. She was impressed. "Cool!"

As Jane and Dov danced by. Alberto gave Dov an enthusiastic thumbs up. Dov smiled broadly, before they passed. When the Band finished. Jane and Dov remained on the dance floor, holding hands. Jane turned to Dov. "That was super. Let's go somewhere." Dov was over the moon, but bereft of ideas, he finally responded. "Great. Where do you want to go?" Jane hesitated, she could hardly believe, what she was about to suggest, but she couldn't help herself. She replied. "What about Lovers lookout?" Dov couldn't believe it. Lover's lookout with Jane. Far out! He knew from Alberto, this was a well-known romantic location, for the local teenagers. "Yeah. Great!" He finally managed. They remained silent, while they stared at each other. After a moment, Jane grabbed his hand and said. "Come on, let's go."

Chapter 15

Shortly after the Graduation Dance. Jane and Dov arrived at Lover's Lookout. They stood there, holding hands, on the high, lush grassy, hill that overlooked the scattered, twinkling lights of Denton. It was a warm, still night. They were overwhelmed, mesmerised, by the full moon and the bright, glittering stars. Suddenly a vivid light, cleaved the darkness, arcing across the sky.

Jane indicated and exclaimed. "It's a shooting star, quick make a wish,"

Dov replied. "It's the Sputnik."

Jane was taken back. "Sputnik? Wow! Make a wish anyway."

"Hear what Little Richard did when he saw the Sputnik?" Dov asked.

Jane had no idea. "What?"

"Freaked out. Thought it was the end of the world. Threw all his jewellery off the Sydney Harbor Bridge," Dov revealed.

Jane faced Dov and mimicked Little Richard. "Good Golly."

Dov smiled and replied in kind. "Miss Molly," then made out like an old time preacher.

"Hallelujah! He found the Lord and rejected that devil Rock and Roll."

Jane asked. "And so?"

Dov was elated. They had just traded easy banter, for the first time. It felt great. Jane was surprised and was enjoying their easy banter. She had never experienced that, with any of the young men in Denton, even Bob. This was something different, and special.

For a long moment. They just stared at the sky. Then, Dov faced Jane.

"I tell you this. After what happened to my parents. I am through with G-d and religion. But look out Rock and Roll. Tonight made anything possible," he paused, then stared intently, at Jane and emphatically repeated. "Anything!"

Dov had spent weeks on a song inspired by Jane. It was a declaration of his love. There was no way, he had the courage to tell her- how he felt. But singing it was a different matter. He thought he could do that. But had been waiting for the right opportunity. After what happened tonight, and in this location. He would never get a better chance. Dov sensed, he had to go for it. He had to be brave and express his feelings. He hesitantly began to sing.

DOV (OUR LOVE)

From that first glance
You overwhelmed my heart
You ignited something, that's burning deep inside.
Much sweeter than a thousand guitars.

Dov stopped and scrutinised Jane for her reaction. Jane felt 'mushy' inside. The setting, the ambience, the song, it felt like a scene from an MGM musical. This was what she had eventually, hoped to experience with someone. However, had been repeatedly disappointed. She concluded, she was being way too romantic and naive. However, this was really happening and she enthusiastically embraced, the experience.

When she smiled. Dov started breathing again. Emboldened, he continued, more confidently.

DOV

Never felt this way, but you stole my heart.
Sweeter than a Shakespearean sonnet.
More uplifting than Gandhi's marchers.
Stronger than all of the Eiffel's arches.
That's our love.
Aaahhh!
That's our love.

When he finished. Jane faced him with mock outrage, "Pretty presumptuous, to assume you know my feelings. How can you know?" Chastened, unable to meet her stern gaze, Dov looked down, shuffled his feet, and kept silent. Jane felt mortified. She prayed, she had not destroyed their magic moment and determined, to try to retrieve it. She decided she had to be bold and act decisively.

Dov looked up surprised, when feather light, she kissed him on the cheek. He was blown away, when she whispered, "Tonight topped off everything. The lyrics are pretty full on, but somehow you have captured my feelings." Dov hugged her and began the chorus, with fervour,

DOV

Our love's brighter than Haley's comet.
Sweeter than a Shakespearean sonnet.
More uplifting than Gandhi's marchers.
Stronger than all of the Eiffel's arches.
That's our love
Aaahhh!
That's our love

At the end of the song. They embraced and kissed. It was the first time Dov had ever kissed a girl on the mouth. He was in heaven. He lingered on her soft moist lips, inhaled her perfume and wished the moment, could last forever. The kiss for Jane, was yet another surprise. She had kissed a number of times and thought it was, no big deal. However, this kiss with Dov, set her back on her heels and emotionally rattled her.

For Dov, their first kiss seemed to be a promise of all the boundless, wonderful things to come. As they returned to her house. Dov felt as though he was floating.

After that evening, their relationship changed. In the past, he would walk behind her while she made a point of ignoring him and strode to school. But now they would always, walk side-by-side, laughing and chatting.

Chapter 16

Sunday, some days later. In the Cornhuckster home. Marge bustled around the kitchen/eating area, setting the table for the family's traditional Sunday lunch. Clem, still dressed in his Sunday best, impatiently checked his watch, between reading the paper. Finally, he irritably growled. "Church is a family affair. She should come home with us. Not with him!

Marge snapped. "His name is Dov," Clem muttered. "Damn," to himself. Seeing Marge's displeasure made him feel worse. It was much harder, than he expected, to be polite to this unwonted guest.

He had lapsed again. It was proving, much harder, than he expected, to their unwonted guest. He wondered, whether he should attend confession again?

"You sure? Since some shearers got to him, who knows? Clem retorted.

"You should be more reasonable," Marge accused

Clem was affronted, he retorted. "Reasonable? I'm not even charging him rent," Clem exclaimed. He considered himself a good Catholic and a reasonable man. However, this ultra- religious teenager, was aggravating and taxed

his patience. He faced Marge and decided to plead his case.
He began to sing;

CLEM (A REASONABLE MAN)

I'm a reasonable man,
Oh yes I am, oh yes I am.
I tolerate all types and creeds
Even fringe minor, breeds.
Though some consider Anglo-Saxon best.
I'll dine and sup, with all the rest.

I'm a reasonable man,
Yes I am, yes I am.
I tolerate all religious creeds.
The Jews, the blacks, and even Swedes.
Though some consider Anglo-Saxon Saxon best.
I'll dine and sup, but why wed, the rest?
Christian, Muslim, all shades of Islam.
Hindu, Vishnu, Mandarin and Manchu.
Black, yellow or brindle,
Watch me mix and freely mingle.

I'm a reasonable man,
Yes I am, yes I am.
I tolerate all foreign seeds.
The same treatment guaranteed.
Though some consider Anglo-Saxon best.
I'll dine and sup, but why wed the rest?

Christian, Muslim or shades of Islam.
Hindu, Vishnu, Mandarin and Manchu.
Black, yellow or brindle,
Watch me mix and freely mingle.
Catholic, Nordic, Baltic, Arabic.
Buddhist, Talmudist, Shinto, Schamanist.
Chinese, Lebanese, Maltese, Portuguese.
Greek, Sikh, Mozambique, Martinique- Aaaah

I'm a reasonable man,
Yes I am, yes I am.
Treat them equal, treat them well.
Ask anyone, they will tell,
I'm a reasonable man.

Just then. Jane and Dov bounded in. Jane held a rose under Marge's nose and announced. "From Granny Jones". Marge sniffed appreciatively and exclaimed. "Gorgeous," Clem still irritated, curtly, cut in. "Well, I've been sniffing our roast," looked meaningfully at Dov, as he continued. "Chicken and I'm starving." Dov attempted to defuse the situation and apologised. "Sorry. Wanted to show Jane the roses, while they were in full bloom," Clem wasn't placated and sarcastically responded. "Bonza! Never seen them before. Only every year, since she was three," Jane jumped to Dov's defence and exclaimed. "Not with Dov." Clem remained irritated. He stared at Dov, shook his head and announced. "Can't get used to you without the hair. And without that.... That?... Dov helped him out and offered. "Yarmulke." Clem, mulled the situation over and launched another attack. "How could anyone give up their faith?" Then turned slyl to Jane. "Would you give up your faith?" Jane was put on the spot and reluctantly responded. ".. No. But Dov had reasons, very good reasons," Clem, now pointedly looked at Dov and announced. "Faith doesn't have reasons, that's why it's called Faith, not Maths." Not to be intimidated, Dov stared at Clem and announced. "Marx was right. It's the opiate of the masses," Clem's irritation, now reached a higher level. Glowering, he snapped. "So we're a bunch of drugged out fools?" Jane attempted to settle things down, she offered. "Dov did not mean that," unfortunately, Dov couldn't leave it alone and he announced. "I don't have time for blind faith," this made Clem ballistic, he barked. "Now we're drugged and blind," he stood and glared intently at Dov, as he snapped. "For some people, Sundays' are for quiet contemplation," stomped towards the door, as the others watched startled. Over his shoulder, Clem added. "I'm off to the American Legion," Marge was startled and horrified, she shouted "Clem?!" Agitated, she grabbed her hat and rushed out after him. Jane was surprised and upset by the turn of events. She turned angrily to Dov and snapped. "You're as bad as Bob. You of all people, should respect other people's beliefs," Dov attempted to placate her and tried to take her hand, but she snatched it away. He lamented. "This is a small town, with small town attitudes," Jane wasn't buying it, she responded. "Have you ever thought it may be you?!" Dov retorted. "I could be here forever and nothing will change."

"You need to make the effort," Jane retorted. Dov gave a bitter laugh and exclaimed "effort!" Gestured to his face and added. "What's this?!"

"That's on the surface," Jane responded. Dov decided, he needed to eat humble pie and softly mumbled. "I'm trying. I really am. I don't want to fight..... I love you," he waited in trepidation, for her response. Jane with a Mona Lisa smile, sniffed the rose. Gently she kissed it. Teasingly slow handed the stem to Dov. He accepted it and heaved a sigh of relief, then jauntily exclaimed. "Then, nothing else matters."

Chapter 17

After Dov's successful debut. Alberto and Dov decided to review their future strategy. Most days, they met after school, at Jose's and discussed it.

It also allowed them to get to know each other better. Dov elaborated on his dream about becoming a singer-songwriter. How he wanted to make a difference, through his music like Woody Guthrie, Peter Seger, Leonard Cohen. But he was still a big Elvis fan. Alberto teased him. "Forget about making a difference. "Be a success and make money, like Elvis and Desi."

In turn. Alberto explained about his dream of emulating, his hero Desi Arnez. His family had to flee Cuba, just like José and Alberto. He had become successful in another country. Alberto figured he could do the same. He enthusiastically pointed out, that his and Dov's proposed journey, was a win- win situation. Working together, they could both achieve their dream.

Alberto had been thinking about what they should do and hesitantly, outlined his plan. "If we want to hit the big time, we need to get away from here," Alberto took a breath and continued his pitch. "Look at Pat Boone. He was born in Florida, raised in Tennessee and attended the University of North Texas", looked meaningfully at Dov, as he added. "In Denton, Texas," Dov was startled, by the coincidence and wondered, was it more than that? Was it karma? Alberto saw that he was listening intently and confidently continued. "He began his career by performing in Nashville's Centennial Park. He began recording with Republic Records and then with Dot Records, doing covers," Dov's hearts sank, he was disinclined to rely on doing covers. He wanted to sing his own songs.

Alberto saw that Dov was hooked, he began to reel him in. "He had his first number one single in 1956, 'I Almost Lost My Mind'. But his career really took off following his regular appearances on ABC TV's Ozark Jubilee, produced in Missouri," satisfied, he had laid the bait, he again looked significantly at Dov and added. "You need to move around, find and follow the action and the opportunities. For us, it is New York!" Dov's heart sank, as he thought of Jane. In his mind, he cursed Pat Boone. Using his name, when he arrived, turned out to be bad karma. Alberto observed his glum friend for a moment and smiled. "That's okay. I've got some dough from dad. I can lend you the money if you're broke," Dov was touched by his friend's spontaneous generosity.

"Thanks, but money's not the issue. Reuben recently, sent me a modest bank cheque, for the sale of my parents' house."

Now Alberto understood and faced Dov. "Sorry, amigo. You'll have to tell her."

Dov subconsciously, knew Alberto was right. Denton was certainly: no Detroit, New York, or Los Angeles. If Dov was serious, about making it in Show business, he had to leave. But how could he, when he had just found his first love? He couldn't risk losing her. Dov pondered on this dilemma. He'd need the Wisdom of Solomon to solve it.

A day later, he came up with a possible solution and knew he had to discuss it with Jane.

The next evening, Jane and Dov were sitting on the front porch. Dov was hesitant, as he explained his dilemma. "Look...I... I need to leave".

She looked shaken and promptly said. "Oh God. I'll miss you."

"No you won't," he answered obliquely.

"Of course, I will," she emphatically cried.

"You don't need to," Dov replied, mysteriously. Jane was puzzled and remained silent.

The next morning, a nervous, tentative Dov explained. It would be super, if she could come with them, on their adventure. This way Dov could follow his dream and they could still be together. Jane was startled by the proposal. Dov admitted, his suggestion, was self-centred and selfish. He knew it would be a huge sacrifice for Jane: to leave her home, her family and to forego her dream of becoming a teacher. He had agonised whether, to even ask her. Could being with him and sharing his journey, ever compensate for all she had to forfeit? He offered a heartfelt apology, for even asking.

Jane was touched by his concern and thoughtfulness. She seemed uncertain and made no response. Dov hoped, her silence meant a maybe? He was desperate to think of any way that, would be more even-handed. He pleaded for another 24 hours so he could come up with a proposal. Jane was conflicted, but agreed.

After considerable soul-searching. Dov came up with an idea and anxiously, outlined it to her, the following day. He suggested that maybe Jane could attend Teachers College in New York, or Kansas City? This way, they could both follow their dreams. Jane appeared, delighted at the suggested solution and volunteered to explore the practicalities.

Several weeks later. Jane bounced in, with a piece of paper and confronted Dov at breakfast. "A reciprocal course starts in Kansas City, in a few months. I've enrolled. I'll come with you initially, then go on to Kansas City, but it will have to be our secret, for the moment," she breathlessly announced. Dov hugged her and whirled her around and around. He was ecstatic, this confirmed how much Jane loved him. He was humbled, by the extent of her sacrifice. This was beyond his wildest dream. For days, he was in a state of euphoria. He had never felt so I live. Life couldn't get any better. Dov was on the far side of delighted. The three of them met regularly at Jose's and excitedly planned their big adventure.

Some weeks later. With their departure imminent. Dov felt that he should say goodbye and thank the Cornhucksters for their hospitality. The evening before their proposed departure, an uneasy Dov, faced them in the family room and announced. "I'll be gone by the time you get up in the morning," he stopped and checked their reaction. Marge was unsure. Jane looked uneasy. Clem was far from unhappy with the news. Dov continued. "So I'd like to thank you both for taking me in."

"It was no trouble. Was it Clem?" Marge volunteered enthusiastically and nudged the silent Clem.

"Oh, no - No!" Clem said, after the prompting.

Marge continued. "It won't be the same without you."

Clem offered a heartfelt. "No, it won't."

Jane remained silent, as she attempted to hide her excitement.

Chapter 18

The same evening. In the front part of Jose's. Alberto nervously, finally, revealed his plans to his father. As he expected, they had a heated argument. Seeking to end it, Alberto desperately implored. "I need to go. I want to be somebody." José remained adamant and snapped. "It's a crazy thing. Dov I understand, but you have all this," gestured encompassing the Café, shook his head and growled. "Loco."

"This is you and it is great, but I want more," Alberto, desperately responded.

"Si. Women and a good time," José retorted.

"You came here and worked for the TVA. You took a chance. I want mine," Alberto pleaded. Jose remained firmly unconvinced. "This is your home. It's muy dangerous out there. Bums, pimps, putas, banditos and-"

"-You left your home," Alberto snapped.

"Batista murdered the Lipsteins. I could have been next," José responded emotionally. Alberto reflected, then counter punched. "I can't let Dov down. He has no one," stared at José and added. "You know what, that's like," reeling on the ropes, José declared. "I promise your mother to protect you," seeing an opening, Alberto went for a KO and offered. "She used to say, I could be anything. She believed in me," tacitly admitting defeat, José lamented. "You no fight fair," he sighed with resignation and embraced Alberto, then stepped back and snapped. "You still here?! Go! Vamoose! Pack!" The relieved Alberto, hurriedly left, with his suitcase and a gaudy Carry On.

A few minutes later, he was knocking on Betty Lou's front door. While he waited, he put the suitcases down. Shortly. The door opened, they exchanged greetings and Betty Lou invited him in. He left the cases on the front porch and followed her inside. In the living room, he revealed his plans, to go to New York, then announced. "I'm off," she was stunned and hesitantly asked. "You'll write?"

"Of course. Every week," Alberto insisted.

"Rubbish. You'll meet someone, you'll forget," bashful, she added. "I'll miss you,"

"Really... I'll miss you to," Alberto confessed.

"I don't think." Betty Lou was openly sceptical.

Then Alberto decided to go for broke. He adopted a mock Cuban accent and announced. "JU will always be a flower in my heart," then parodying José continued. "It's muy dangerous out there," snapped to attention and saluted. "My outfit leaves at dawn. Cara mio, let us share a last tender moment," Betty Lou hid a smile, pecked Alberto on the cheek and offered a cheerful. "Good luck," Alberto was disappointed, he asked. "What is this, a Doris Day movie?" Betty Lou was puzzled, she asked. "What's wrong?"

Alberto tentatively explained. "How about the Playboy version,"

"What do you mean?" She asked.

"You know!" Alberto insisted. Betty Lou was becoming irritated and snapped! "No. I don't."

"You know. Some of what you gave Rip," Alberto revealed. Smack! Betty Lou unleashed a resounding slap to Alberto's face and shouted. "Another arse-hole," she turned and moved away, Alberto nursing his cheek, sheepishly watched her leave and apologetically shouted. "Only jokin," then ruefully muttered to himself. "Only hopin,"

<h1 style="text-align:center">Chapter 19</h1>

Early next morning, while the family was still sound asleep. Cornhucksters' crowing rooster, announced a new day. The kitchen door slowly opened and Jane furtively entered, the empty kitchen. She was wearing a coat and carrying a suitcase. She carefully propped a folded letter against a teapot and moved to the outside door. Realised, she had forgotten something, put the suitcase down and hurriedly, left the way she had come in.

Shortly after. Clem bustled in, from another direction, wearing a dressing gown. Puzzled, he picked the letter up and read it with growing dismay. As Marge, entered. She was also in a dressing gown. The distressed Clem, thrust the letter to Marge. As she reviewed it, she exclaimed. "Oh my G-d!" Then both turned and stared at the suitcase. Just then, Jane entered, clutching a Teddy bear. Startled, she pulled up short. "You're not going anywhere, with anyone," Clem barked. "You can't stop me. I'm not a child," Jane retorted. Clem indicated the Teddy Bear and sarcastically said. "I can see that," paused and snapped. "I said go and-"

"I knew you'd be like this. Knew you wouldn't listen," Jane lamented. Marge attempted to intercede. She turned to Jane and pleaded. "Please do as your father-" Jane, tearfully, faced her mother, and declared. "Mum. I love him," turned to Clem and beseeched. "I know he's different," ignored Clem's sarcastic laugh and pitifully, continued. "And I know sometimes, he can be difficult." Marge glared at Clem, aborting another laugh. Jane desperately continued. "But his life's been hard. If you got to know him, you'd see he's sensitive, gentle, talented and-"Clem harshly, cut in. "You're not going. Especially, to that crime infested New York," paused, then gently added. "What if something happens? You'd be so far away," Jane was adamant. "Sorry, dad. But I'm going. Dov has this dream. He wants to be a singer, a songwriter." Clem sarcastically, quipped. "Doesn't he like to eat?" Marge attempted to mediate. "Please Clem," but Clem continued to glare. Jane realised it was hopeless and bemoaned. "What's the point," she moved towards the suitcase. Clem speared a glance at Marge before he mounted another argument, he faced Jane and implored. "Jane, you have a lifetime ahead of you. Why rush things? Finish your studies. Get your degree, then you'll have our full blessing. Now isn't that reasonable? Right, Marge?" The distressed Marge faced Jane and pleaded. "True love, is worth waiting for." Clem jumped in and added. "And we'll help Dov in any way we can," but Jane stuck to her guns. "I'm. . . I'm so sorry," picked up the suitcase and began to move towards the door. She was abruptly stopped, by the loud knocking, on the front door.

Chapter 20

Marge and Clem exchanged a puzzled look. Irritably, Clem opened the door and Doctor West, slowly entered. Clem was surprised. "Doctor West! Bit early for a house call," Dr. West struggled, to find the right words. "I ... I ... Just wanted to catch you altogether.

Jane's blood results came through last night," but the look on his face implied, it was not good news. Marge and Clem instinctively edged closer to Jane. In the stifling silence. Doctor West gently enfolded Jane's hand in his, as he sympathetically said. "We need to do more tests," Jane was startled, she pleaded. "But I'm going away."

"You'd better cancel whatever it is," Doctor West bleakly replied.

"I... I... I can't," she implored.

"You have to," Doctor West was adamant.

"This is the rest of my life we're talking about," she beseeched.

"So is this," Doctor West declared. Tearful, Jane reached for her suitcase, but she was, gently restrained by Marge and Clem. "My dear. If he loves you, he'll stay," Marge tearfully, offered. Resigned, Jane hopefully, turned to

Doctor West and desperately asked. "How... How long will it take?"

"I wouldn't plan on going anywhere, for some time," was his dismal reply.

Fearfully, Marge pleaded. "But you can treat it?"

Again, Doctor West could offer little comfort. "We'll... We'll do our best," in the fearful silence. He added. "That's why we need to do more tests." Blindly, Clem reached out and grasped Marge's hand. Arms around each other they stared in stunned silence at Doctor West. Jane clutched her Teddy bear and stood rigid. On Jane's face, a series of fleeting emotions were plainly displayed: love, loss, and pitiful resolve.

Doctor West slowly left the frozen tableau. Clem edged closer to Jane and offered her a long, loving stare. He clearly remembered, as if yesterday. The day Jane was born. How ecstatic, he and Marge were. The countless plans they had for her future. How much they looked forward to the prospect of having grandchildren. But the Doctor's news, had threatened all their dreams. Clem faced Jane and mournfully began to sing;

CLEM (TURN BACK THE CLOCK)

Everything looks familiar, but nothing now seems real.
Your childhood a kept memory, like a never broken seal.

Clem patted his heart, as he sang. He cherished and guarded his memories of her childhood and his hopes and dreams for her future, in his mind and heart. Concerned, that if he exposed them, they may be damaged or lost.

Kept safe within. Kept safe within.

Marge sympathetically edged closer to Jane and speared her with a long, loving stare. Forlorn, she could also remember each milestone: Jane's first words, her first step, starting to speak.

MARGE

Each treasured memory, each remembered part.
Striking chords we know so well, still gently touch my heart.
Turn back the clock.
Turn back the clock.

Jane hunched her shoulders, head down, began to silently weep. Pause. Then, she slowly slipped out.

CLEM

Forgive the young, they are so young.

Clem was confronted, by his own mortality. He realised, all their plans for Jane's future and their future life together, were now all in jeopardy and maybe, in ashes.

They think in endless time, see no problems, all is well,
An endless summertime.

Marge also lamented, the threat to all her dreams and hopes for Jane and their life together. If Only they could turn the clock back, to yesterday. When the future and their cherished dreams, were still stable and remained bright and rosy.

MARGE

Turn back the clock.
Turn back the clock.
To those innocent and carefree times.
Bring back our summertime.

Forced to confront their Demons, their worst fears. Tearfully, they tightly clasped each other as they mournfully, sang;

MARGE and CLEM

Turn back the clock.
Turn back the clock.
Turn back the clock.
Turn back the clock.

Clem tenderly grasped Marge's hand. Tears flowing they continued to sing with resigned despair.

MARGE and CLEM (CONT'D)

Was it only yesterday, we planned her journey
to the heights.
Yesterday has gone away, today's put out the lights.
Put out the lights.
Put out the lights

Both understood the implication, of the Dr's message and were heartbroken. They realised. Time was not their friend. They desperately wished for the return of: innocent, bright, optimistic and care-free times.

MARGE

Please stop the unforgiving hands of time.

MARGE and CLEM

Where are the years?
Those precious years
those innocent and carefree times.
Turn back the clock.
Turn back the clock.
Turn back the clock.
Turn back the clock,

Arms around each other, they bewailed, all that was now threatened. However, they both held her cherished memory safely locked in their heart and mind.

Everything looks familiar.
But nothing now seems real.
Her childhood a kept memory, like a never broken seal.
Turn back the clock.
Turn back the clock.
Turn back the clock.
Turn back the clock.

Heads down, crying, arms around each other, they slowly shuffled out.

Chapter 21

1957

Early next morning, Dov waited on the deserted platform, at the Denton Railway Station. When he arrived, he had said a brief hello, to the bored Stationmaster. But was too excited and had little inclination to continue the conversation, the Stationmaster tried to maintain. As Dov paced up and down. He repeatedly checked his watch. His guitar and suitcase were behind him. Jane and Alberto were late.

Finally, Alberto arrived. He struggled with a large suitcase, and a gaudy small "Carry On", that contained, the Mullins' magnetic tape recorder. Sighting Dov, he jubilantly cried out. "Man is this exciting, or-"stopped when he didn't see Jane. Dov tried to defuse, the situation, he offered. "We thought it best, not to leave the house together."

A little later, they both turned, as Jane hesitantly, appeared on the platform. She had no coat and no suitcase. Dov's stomach lurched. The signs were ominous. Alberto sensed the situation and tactfully left them to it.

Dov was mortified. Jane was clearly distressed. She sobbed. "I'm sorry. . . I'm so sorry." Stunned by the situation. Dov demanded. "What's going on?!"

"I can't do it," she tearfully revealed.

"Why not?" He challenged, confused and bitterly disappointed.

Unable to explain, Jane offered only, a blunt. "I just can't." She was distraught, fragile and conflicted. She realised, if she told him the real reason, he'd probably want to stay. She couldn't let that happen, it would jeopardise his long-held dream. She couldn't bear to be the cause of this. She cared too much. She had to hide the real reason, irrespective of consequences and despite, any pressure.

Confused and devastated, Dov lamented. "I thought we'd decided."

"I should have agreed," she mournfully, replied. Without an acceptable explanation. Dov's paranoia kicked in. He wondered. Had he duped himself all this time, about her feelings? How did he get it so wrong? He decided to cut to the core issue and challenged. "Don't you love me?"

"Of course, I love you," she responded without hesitation. Dov decided not to pull any punches. "If you love me you'd come. "

"Don't say that. There's nothing, I'd rather do then, get on that train."

"So do it." He bluntly insisted.

Sobbing, she said. "I can't."

"Then, I'm not going." He desperately offered, as a last-ditch gambit.

Still crying, she said. "Please don't do that. You'd never forgive me"

"I'd never forgive myself, if I lost you," Dov insisted.

"You've got to go. If you don't, the rest of your life you'd be thinking, what if? What if?"

Dov sensed that all was lost and bemoaned. "What's success without you?"

Heartbroken they stared at each other. After a moment, from behind her back, Jane brought out a Rose. She shakily offered it, to Dov. Her voice was breaking, as she said. "Just because I'm not there. . Doesn't... Doesn't mean, I'm not with you," shaken to the core. Dov slowly accepted the Rose and carefully placed it between the pages of a pocket diary.

They hugged... Jane fought for control, then broke free and moved away.

They were isolated by an impassable gulf, as each battled their own dark demons.

DOV (THIS IS THE BEGINNING)

(In his own world. Dov wondered ;)

Can our love survive this savage blow?

Has fear replaced love in her soul?

Was this just all fantasy?

Can it resist cruel reality?

Is this the beginning of the end?

Or is this just the beginning?

Finally, Jane made partial eye contact with Dov.

DOV

(Dov experienced a twinge of hope. He now pondered)
This is so much harder than it seems.
Torn between love and chasing my dreams.
Do I go on or do I compromise?
Shelve my hopes and live a life of lies?
Dov and Jane now, looked intently at each other

DOV

(Dov's hope, had now become a certainty.
He was convinced :)
I'll struggle to the bitter end.
It's the beginning, not the end.
This is the beginning, not the end
This is just the beginning
This is just the beginning.

Distraught, Jane ran away. Dov was left heartbroken, he clutched the pocket Diary. He felt as if his heart was on the point of breaking, as he watched her disappear. In the distance, he heard the faint sound as a train approached. The sound seemed to skewer his very soul. It heralded his imminent departure and would cement, their separation, possibly forever. He couldn't bear the prospect. It was way too painful. His mind screamed. "No! No! He wouldn't, he couldn't accept this outcome.

Chapter -22

New York 1958.
The Arrival

Some weeks later. Dov and Alberto were in New York and stood gob-smacked, in Times Square. Neither one, could believe it. Wide-eyed, they sucked in the sight. Mesmerised by the bustle, the incessant noise and the medley of vibrant images. People were congregating at the base of One Times Square.

The Square was a mass of heaving humanity. The adjacent ring of skyscrapers loomed menacingly over it. Their facades, adorned by massive, garish, neon lit, technicolour billboards, promoting the latest Broadway shows, upcoming films, or advertising items such as; Panasonic, Yahoo, Bud light, Ricoh, W pharmacy, Toshiba, MacDonald's, Sanyo, etc.

A network of traffic filled streets, intersected the square. They were crammed with; cars, taxis, motorbikes and buses.

The sidewalks of the Square was a sea of hustling, cheerful, people, as was the Square. However, here and there, some people occupied, small foldout chairs and tables They were mainly dressed in non-descript casual; T-shirts, jeans, casual jackets and trainers.

Numerous roads, ran into the Square, and disgorged more traffic and pedestrians. It was energetic. It was in your face. It was New York. This was the big league.

It was a bright spring day. The New Yorkers, had shed their winter grey and rushed about. They were some scattered dots of bright colour, amongst the otherwise, drab looking, pedestrian streetscape. This identified the, occasional Woman, who had dressed up, in vibrant colours and high fashion. While the occasional Man, was dressed in a smart suit and a few wore Fedoras.

Alberto and Dov strolled in with suitcases. They were dressed in Mid-American casual; shirt, jeans and cowboy boots. They drank in the scene: the feverish activity, the landmarks, the vibrant energy and the people. They put the suitcases down and just stared. Awestruck, blown away, Dov shouted. "Wow! Far out," Alberto was thrilled. He loudly shouted. "Watch out New York, the Amigos' are here," eyes wide, he nudged Dov, as a gorgeous creature approached. She was svelte and dressed in a couture gown, with an impressive décolletage. Alberto was completely smitten and couldn't take his eyes off her. Excited, he indicated her, to Dov, as he sang;

ALBERTO (GET TO THE TOP.)

Check out the sights.

Dov, cut in and tried to get Alberto focused, on their planned objective;

DOV

Names up in lights. We're going to be hits.

Alberto was distracted, by another lovely. Awestruck, he indicated a buxom young woman, in a tight top. Her breasts were large enough, to comfortably shelter under, in a rainstorm. Alberto was irrepressible. He nudged Dov, as he sang and mimed, huge breasts;

ALBERTO

Look at those-

Dov again, vainly tried to keep Alberto focused on their goal. He cut him off with;

DOV

Not gonna stop.
Till we get to the top.
Get to the top.

Dancing and singing. The New Yorkers, encircled the stunned pair and began to enthusiastically sing; as they danced around the startled pair.

NEW YORKERS.

Got to, got to, give to till you drop.
If you want to, want to, get to the top

At the end of the song, Alberto and Dov, jubilantly slapped each other on the back. Meanwhile, the New Yorkers had dispersed. The boys looked around, but their cases were gone. Alberto exclaimed. "Christ! Some New York bastard's pinched, all our stuff." Aghast, horrified. Dov shouted. "The demo tape!"

Panicked. They frantically rushed around the Square and checked the feeder roads. Finally, in the distance, down one of the Square's tributary roads, Alberto spied a man, as he struggled with two large cases and a small one. Alberto screamed. "Stop thief!" They gave chase. The Man turned and increased his speed, but battled to keep ahead. Eventually, he abandoned the cases and ducked down a side street. Reassured, the boys rescued their cases and carried them away. Dov reflected on their first day in New York, it had certainly been, a roller coaster experience. Relieved, they sat on their cases, while they calmed down.

Still recovering from the chase and his fright. Dov ignored the army of scruffy teenagers, who bustled around like pesky blowflies, as they eagerly handed out flyers. The teenagers, wore an assortment of tattered T-shirts, torn jeans and brand-name sneakers. They had a vague sameness and seemed to represent, a United Nations of different countries, plus a significant number of African-Americans.

While Dov ignored them, Alberto took a flyer and avidly read it. Bemused by events, Dov wondered, what awaited them in this huge, sophisticated, frenetic metropolis. His reflections were rudely interrupted, when Alberto nudged him in the ribs. His friend was itching to get started. When Dov still hadn't moved, Alberto impatiently urged. "Come on, we've got lots to do." Dov was surprised, at the sudden change in his friend's attitude. He asked. "What's the rush?" Silently, Alberto thrust the flyer under his nose and with a finger, decisively stabbed at an item. Dov read. 'Announcing. The Premier of, 'Journey To The Centre Of The Earth'. Today at the Sheen cinema Centre, complex New York. Starring James Mason, Pat Boone, Ariene Dahl'. Dov mused, Pat Boone again; his persistent karma, who had initiated his journey New York. Now seemed to be here, waiting for him. What next, Dov wondered.

Impatient, at the delay, Alberto exclaimed. "We have to find a pad, then there are sights to see and people to meet. We need to kick start your career," Dov smiled at Alberto's enthusiasm and energy. He was delighted he had him on his side.

Chapter 23

New York. The Initiation

It was unusually clear and warm in New York. Dov and Alberto made the most of the good weather and explored the area near their basic, rented bedsitter.

As they strolled along, a Greenwich Village street. Dov gaped wide-eyed at the surroundings, and explained to Alberto." It's just like the film. Angeline Dubois, in Tease Queen," Alberto was silent. He remained single-minded and finally announced. "The Musos on the train said we should head to Bleecker Street, in Greenwich Village."

Dov was puzzled." Why?"

"That's where they all go for news about gigs," Alberto smugly replied. On the train to the New York, he had made friends with a local New York Band- the Searches. They told him Bleecker Street was the place they could learn about any upcoming gigs. Impressed by his homework. Dov agreed to the visit. However, he made it clear. He would not do just covers. He had not rushed away and risked losing Jane, to masquerade as a pale imitation of an established artist. Dov had come here to establish himself as a singer-songwriter in his own right.

Chapter 24

New York. First Step

Catching a taxi, they were soon in Bleecker Street, in Greenwich Village and quickly located the Club. 'The Bitter End', had a prominent blue awning, announcing its presence. It was frequented by musicians. Taking advantage of the good weather, they had spilled onto the pavement, chatting, smoking and drinking. Alberto started a conversation with a long-haired man in his late 30s. This Muso, seemed to know the scene.

Alberto broke off, indicated Dov standing nearby, as he teased out a few chords on his guitar. The Muso idly checked him out. Then, Alberto walked over and quietly spoke to Dov. At Alberto's urging, he eventually, performed one of his songs on the sidewalk. He began a subdued rendition of, 'Look Out World.'

DOV (LOOK OUT WORLD)

Heey Janey heey Betty-Lou School is out

Some of the Musos,' paused their chatting and casually listened.

So pack your bags There's plenty more things to do. Heeey teachers! Time to close your books It's over now, your time is past So keep your dirty looks.

The Musos' started to clap along.

So grind your teeth
Were out of reach
It's time to be free Buckle up with me Now hang on tight
Roller coaster ride
You're trapped and we're free We have earned our liberty

When Dov finished. The Muso turned to Alberto. "Not bad," then called out to Dov. "Got anything, anyone's heard of?" Dov replied. "I'm a singer-songwriter." The Muso wryly responded. "Listen my friend. Clubs only want songs they know," but Dov remained adamant. " I only want to do my own stuff." The Muso wryly countered. "Do you want to be on Social Security, the rest of your life? I'm telling you. The clubs only want songs they know," somewhat deflated, the hopeful duo, journeyed home. Once home, they revisited their old argument regarding, Dov performing covers. With the same result. Dov remained insistent, that he wanted to do his own songs and establish himself as an original singer-songwriter.

Chapter 25

New York.
Doing the Rounds

etting no leads, in Bleeker Street. Over the next
few weeks; they tried to make themselves comfortable, in their basic bedsitter and explored the local
neighbourhood.

By now, they were getting short of funds, and had been
reduced to short rations. Their evening meals were now,
restricted to sharing, a hamburger with the lot. So, over
the next few days. With their resources dwindling. They
had to check out other options. They were forced to hustle
around New York, as they tried to land a gig. It was desperate times.

They decided to approach a range of Clubs. At first.
The Boys attempted to do their pitch to the Receptionist.
Unfortunately, she barely listened, remained idly chewing,
then shook her head. At the next. The Boys managed to
see the Manager. Again, they repeated their pitch. But the
bored Manager, was also not interested. That made two

strikes. At the third Club. As they approached the entrance. Alberto held his hand up and announced. "Hey! Let me do this one, on my own," shoulders braced, he strode in.

Dov shrugged and strolled along the street, he stopped and gaped at the tempting food in the window, of a Delicatessen shop. It had been quite a while, since they had a decent meal.

After a few minutes. Alberto bounded out and gave Dov, a jubilant thumb up. " You've got a gig! " Dov was ecstatic. "Great!" Until, Alberto hesitantly added." There's just one thing," Dov's enthusiasm now dropped and his suspicion rose, he snapped. "I'm not doing other people's stuff,"

Dov was adamant, but conceded Alberto had a convincing argument. Currently, they were broke and had no prospects. If he stuck to his guns and ideals, about only performing his original songs. He'd have one hundred percent of nothing. Conversely, covering an established artist may give him some exposure and anything could happen. Finally, he conceded, Alberto's most telling argument, had some validity. Covering any Elvis hit, was not demeaning, but a privilege. And this would give him a chance to get his songs and talent out there. He decided, all be it unwillingly, he would do it.

Chapter 26

Not long after. A reluctant Dov was on stage in a small Club. In the Spotlight, he sang a low-key version of; Heartbreak hotel.

DOV (HEART BREAK HOTEL)

Well, since my baby left me.
Well, I found a new place to dwell

Concurrently; back in Denton. Jane had despondently, made the long train trip to Kansas City. Forlornly, she stood outside an imposing, two storey brick building, not far from the Kansas City, CBD. She stared at the sign. 'Kansas Teachers College.' Several bright, cheerful, chatting, young students passed her and strode inside. Sad-faced, she finally entered. The next day she was back home in Denton. That night, in their living room she was trying to study. But her thoughts were elsewhere, she gave it up as a hopeless task and began to despondently sing a song she had recently received (by mail), from Dov;

JANE (IT'S YOU THAT I NEED)

When the champagne bubbles sing
When peals of laughter ring.
Look at all the people dance.
I'm so lonely.

Concurrently, In New York. Dov was missing Jane and also feeling miserable. He was, in their bedsitter, attempting to write a letter. Nearby, there was an open diary with Jane's pressed Rose. Unable to continue the letter, Dov started to dejectedly sing;

DOV (IT'S YOU THAT I NEED)

When leaves fall from the tree.
When swallows flying free.
Morning's ear light says I'm lonely

Simultaneously, in Denton. In the Cornhucksters' eating area. Jane tearfully, signed a letter, she had just finished, then began to sing;

JANE (IT'S YOU THAT I NEED)

I don't want anyone It's you I really need
I beg and plead do any deed
To get you back please come back to me

The next night. In a third rate club, Dov was on stage in the Spotlight, with guitar and singing.

Unbeknown to either one. Their moods were in sync and they were singing the same song, which Dov had written and posted to Jane. Except, Jane was in Denton, on her porch, singing, while Dov was on stage in New York. Though they were kilometres apart, their moods, were completely in tune.

JANE and DOV (IT'S YOU THAT I NEED)

I beg and plead
Do any deed
To get you back,
Please come back to me.
You fill my soul, with happiness
When you're gone, there's emptiness.
You're the air that I breathe.
The blood that I need.
You lift up my soul, to the sky
It's you that I need
Baby come back to me

DOV

I can't live I can't breathe
Begging you on my knees
Without you I die

JANE and DOV

Come back to my life
It's you that I need

It's for you that I bleed
It's you that I need.

Several weeks later. In the Manager's office, of a swanky private Club, in New York. A middle-aged, snappily dressed Manager, regarded Alberto and his small gaudy, "Carry – on," case, with disdain. In the background, there was a wall of photos, of past headline Club, acts, the Manager snapped. "What are you selling"? Alberto handed him a 10 by 8 of Dov. "He's a headline talent," he entreated. Then he opened his Case and lifted out the Mullins' magnetic tape recorder and turned it on. They listened to Dov singing;

DOV. (DESTINY'S PRIZE)"

Too long I've been burdened by other's aspirations
Their alien hopes and false expectations
Worn ill-fitting dreams, their fears and expectations.
But no more I've shed this load
It's time for me
To find my destiny.
Dreams delicate thread's easily broken
Unravel the web of promises spoken
Have I the will, the courage, the fire?
This is for me
This is my destiny

During Dov's singing. The Manager barked." What the hell's this?" Alberto was taken back, he hurriedly replied. "He does his own material," the Manager's response, was terse. 'Goodbye!" Alberto hastily added. "He's got some great songs," the Manager conceded. "The voice is okay. But the punters only want stuff they know," Alberto was desperate, he pleaded. "Listen. They didn't know the stuff they know before they knew it. Look, just give him one night! Your members don't like him, you don't pay," the Manage was unyielding. "Like I said. Just stuff they know," disappointed, Alberto put the Mullins' magnetic tape recorder away and turned to leave. Stopped, stared at the wall of Photos; then swung around, for a last try and declared. "When he's a star you'll be proud, to have him on your wall. What have you got to lose?!" The Manager was firm. "Only stuff they know. But maybe, we can work out a compromise?" the relieved, Alberto, put down his case and prepared to negotiate.

Once again, Alberto and Dov argued the merits of doing covers of established artists. Again, Dov, all be it reluctantly, agreed to do it, but only as an interim, temporary measure.

The next night. Dov was on stage, in a small club. As he straddled the stamp sized Stage, in the spotlight. He struck the first chord and began to sing an energetic cover of, 'Heartbreak Hotel'.

DOV (HEARTBREAK HOTEL)

Well, since my baby left me
Well, I found a new place to dwell
Well, down at the end of lonely street at heartbreak hotel

Alberto was in the wings. The snappily dressed Manager was in the Audience and observed with interest.

Where I'll be-
Where I get so lonely, baby
Well, I'm so lonely I get so lonely,
I could die although it's always crowded
You can still find some room
For broken hearted lovers
To cry there in the gloom
And be so, where they'll be so lonely, baby
Well, they're so lonely they'll be so lonely,
They could die.

Dov finished to loud Applause. The Manager caught Alberto's eye. He smiled and gave Alberto, a thumbs up sign.

Soon after. In the rundown dressing room. A jubilant Alberto bounded in and faced a depressed and worn out Dov, and announced. "I've got us a top gig at the Athenaeum," Dov was guarded. "That's a great venue. What's the catch?" "No catch! You can sing your stuff, but for every one of yours, you have to do two they know," Dov looked thoughtful.

Still considering the proposal. The next day Dov and Alberto were walking along a street, in Greenwich Village. Suddenly, they both spied, something. They stopped and studied, a brightly-coloured wall poster, which displayed: 'Variety acts at the Bitter End Club. Host, Woody Alan.

Featuring; Bob Dylan, Arlo Guthrie, Frankie Vaughan, Billy Crystal, and Angeline Dubois,' Dov exclaimed." Jane would love her autograph" "Yeah. Plus, she'd be a great contact," Alberto added. Dov had reservations. "But how do we get to see her?" Alberto remained undaunted, he declared." I'll think of something."

Chapter 27

The next day. Alberto visited a Recording studio, in Downtown New York. It was a super high-tech, glitzy, impressive, large space. A long-haired, middle-aged man, with a neat ponytail, was engrossed, as he listened to a track, on his headphones. Bill, reluctantly faced Alberto, as he was ushered in, by a slim young Receptionist. Bill, was annoyed by the interruption, took his headphones off and impatiently scowled at Alberto.

"What?!"

Alberto had done his homework, he exclaimed. "You're Angeline Dubois's Record Producer."

"So what?" Bill replied, disinterested.

" I manage a great, young singer-songwriter, Davey Gold", Alberto anxiously, pitched. Bill was dismissive and curtly retorted. "Never heard of him,"

Alberto, enthusiastically replied. " He's just starting out. But he's going to be huge."

"Yeah. Of course, he is," Bill sarcastically responded.

Alberto announced. "He's about to appear at the Athenaeum."

Bill was not impressed and growled. "So?"

"It would give Davey, a huge boost if Angeline came along to hear him", Alberto pleaded.

"She's not in the charity business," Bill retorted.

"It could be worthwhile."

"Guess who for?" Bill, derisively mocked.

Alberto offered. "It could be great for her image. A huge star, discovering young talent." Bill wasn't buying, he growled. "Hey. This isn't British TV, with Opportunity Knocks. And she's not Hughie Green in drag."

Alberto persisted. "Look. He's got some songs that would be great for her. Get her back in the charts," now he had Bill's guarded attention, he barked. "What?!"

"She hasn't had a hit since Tease Queen," Alberto brashly declared.

This was, too close to the bone. Bill was pissed. He got up, and snapped. "What the fuck do you know. Get out!" Alberto scurried for the door, turned and offered. "Deep down, you know I'm right."

Outside, in the Street. Dov was patiently waiting. As the despondent Alberto came out. He saw the waiting Dov. He attempted to hide his dejection and announced. "Looks like plan B."

Chapter 28

Although, it was only a brief subway ride and a short walk by the time they arrived at the 'Bitter End Club'. It was already evening. Dov and Alberto waited in the Laneway outside the Stage door. They mingled with a few fans. Dov was in an overcoat and had his guitar. After a moment of puzzled scrutiny, a fan approached him and tentatively asked. "Are you anyone?" Dov shook his head and the fan lost interest. Several Musicians arrived, knocked on the door and entered. Dov and Alberto tagged along, behind them.

At the door of the Bitter End Club. A burly, uniformed doorman, guarded the entry. Alberto approached him, and politely enquired. "Excuse me. I've got some comedy material for Frankie Vaughan. Where would I find him?"

The doorman replied. "He's always in the Bar across the road until 7.30 PM." During this exchange. Dov slipped by, with his guitar and started to check the names on the dressing room doors. No luck. Turned a corner out of sight, he now moved briskly along. Finally, hit pay dirt. Rapped on a door with Angeline's name and waited anxiously.

Then, he faintly heard. "Come in," Dov cautiously stepped, inside the Dressing room. He stopped and stared dumbfounded, at the sight of a gorgeous, semi-naked woman.

Angeline Dubois, was wearing, a near- sheer dressing gown, panties, bra, and high heels. Dov had never seen anything, so beautiful and sexy, in the flesh and close enough to touch. She was sitting, with her back to him, preoccupied at her makeup mirror.

Disinterested, without turning, she asked. "Who are you?"

"I'm a big fan, 'Dov managed to eventually mumble.

"I see fans at the stage door, after the show. Please go," she said curtly, without turning.

"Can I just-," he desperately offered. But Angeline cut in. "Go! Do I have to call the-" This time Dov, urgently cut in. "Please," she grabbed a phone and barked. "Angeline.

George! Get down here- now!" Dov hurriedly held his guitar- up, and desperately added. " I'm a musician," she turned-stood and now actually saw him. She liked what she saw and softened. "Haven't seen you around. Who are you backing?"

"I...I...I've actually got a gig down the road," he responded

"What? Busking?!" She asked.

"I've got a gig at the Athenaeum Club, for a week, I'm Davey Gold!" He hurriedly replied. Angeline was quite impressed and exclaimed. "Oh, really?" Dov took the opportunity and added. " The thing is, a friend of mine's a huge fan. It would mean a lot, if you'd sign something for her?"

"No problem," she promptly replied. Dov pulled out Angeline's autobiography from his coat pocket. Angeline picked up a pen and looked questioningly at the waiting, nervous Dov. Getting no response, she finally asked. "Who to?" Somewhat surprised, Dov eventually managed. "Um-Jane! Make it out to Jane," Angeline smiled teasingly. "Your girlfriend?"

Dov was taken back. "Oh – Yes," Angeline took the book, signed it and offered. "She's a lucky girl," then passed the book back. Dov on a roll added. "Be fantastic if you could catch my act one night," she fobbed him off with. "I can't promise," Dov offered her a card from the Club. Angeline reached out and ever so slowly pulled the card free. Suddenly, there was loud Knocking at her door. Then, a booming voice asked. "Miss Dubois! Are you okay?"

"It's okay George. My mistake," she shouted back.

Chapter 29

The next night. Dov was on the small stage. In the extensive entertainment area, of the Athenaeum Club. He belted out, "Blue Suede Shoes"

DOV (BLUE SUEDE SHOES)

Well it's one for the money
Two for the show
Three To get ready now go, cat go
But don't you step on my blue suede shoes
Well, you can do anything
But lay off my blue suede shoes

The Patrons clapped along.

Well, you can knock me don't step on my face
Slander my name
All over the place

A group of chattering, latecomers arrived at the back of the room. With the Spotlight in his eyes, Dov couldn't distinguish individuals, but was aware of their noisy entrance.

He was unaware, that standing out in the middle of the group, was Angeline Dubois. The group, included; Bill and two attractive, slim, Latin looking young men, Alfonse, and Marco, her back-up singers. They were, slim, in their 30s, with olive skin and jet black, slicked-back hair and smart ponytails. Completing the Group were two giggling young couples, obviously high.

Well, do anything that you want to do, but uh-uh
Honey lay off my shoes
And don't you
Step on my blue suede shoes
Well, you can do anything but lay off my blue suede shoes

When the song ended. The Patrons clapping turned to loud applause.

The Manager escorted the latecomers to a dance floor table. The Group checked out the venue, noting: the substantial dance floor, made up by different coloured light panels, the hanging flashing, huge Disco ball. And the large Wreath on an easel, on one side of the prominent, raised Stage.

Dov stopped singing and earnestly addressed the Audience. "Thanks. It's a pleasure to be here", he indicated the Wreath." It's clear someone's recently left a big gap in your lives. I didn't know them. But I know, for those left behind, how much it hurts. My mother died, not long ago. This song's dedicated to her. I hope it means something to you, as well," Dov reached down the top of his T-shirt, lifted the dangling chain with the large shining Star of David. Then, he began to sing;

DOV (NOW YOU ARE GONE)

Your loving shadow has passed on
As has the sunlight, all the fun light, and the song.
A dark black hole is now my home
Since you are gone.
A debt repaid, to promise made
Brings me to this place, light-years from home
An outsider in a foreign land Isolated, so alone.

Angeline's full attention was now on Dov. Bill whispered to her. "Got to admit. He's not bad," Angeline gave him a look, which said what did I say!

You were my compass,
My homing beacon.
Without you I feel rudderless and lost
But somehow I must carry on.
You were my rock
The bosom I could cry on
My protective shield And now you are gone

The noise continued at her table. Dov attempted to ignore it.

If only you could be with me
Enjoy my success, console and cheer me

I close my eyes, and sense you near me
So I carry on You were my rock
The bosom I could cry on
My defensive shield

Eyes moist, Angeline was caught up in the song. She glared at the two noisy young couples and hissed. "Listen. This guy's putting himself, on the line. If you haven't the courtesy to keep your traps shut, you better piss off!" Subdued, the young couples shut up and sheepishly left... Dov had gratefully observed the proceedings.

And now you are gone
Now you are gone
Now you are gone.

He finished the song to scattered Applause, mainly driven by Angeline and the Manager. Dov approached Angeline's table. Alberto had entered from the Wings and trailed him. Angeline offered a bright, welcoming smile. As he came closer, he was pleasantly surprised, when he recognized her and exclaimed." Miss Dubois! Thanks for coming," Angeline remained seated, casually offered her hand, and suggestively said. " I like your work," and paused. The pause was loaded with sexual intent. But Dov didn't read the voltage. Guileless, he replied. "I...I like your work," Angeline still held his hand and huskily said." That number really got to me".

"It's kind of personal." He naïvely replied.

"Do you have any other kind of personal songs?" She asked. This was Alberto's cue. He jumped forward and cut in. "He's got a drawer- full. They'll break your heart"

"I'm always looking for good material,' she offered. This was Bill's prompt. He extracted a card from his jacket and offered it to Alberto, and barked. "Send them over," Alberto grabbed it. Meanwhile, Dov and Angeline had maintained torrid eye contact.

Chapter 30

Backstage. Soon after. The glum faced, Dov stared into a cracked mirror. Slowly, he removed his make-up. Clapping his hands and bubbling with excitement, Alberto bounded in and asked. "Hey, why the long face? That was a mutual admiration society going on out there," but Alberto realised, Dov wasn't thinking about her and adjusted his strategy, he suggested." Jane will be thrilled, when she hears about this connection," Dov responded. 'Will she ever." Alberto cautioned. "But watch it with this lady".

Dov was confused. "What?" Alberto was happy to explain. "She is after your bod amigo," this was foreign territory for Dov, he exclaimed. 'She's a big star. She's not interested in me," Alberto wasn't so sure. "Are you kidding? She almost had your pants off out there," Dov reminded him. "You know who I want." Alberto attempted to warn his friend. "Good. Because, this one's got way too much mileage, for a guy like you," Dov nodded and ruefully replied. "At least, we agree on something, " Alberto decided to focus on the main game. "I'll get the demo over to them in the morning." Dov reached across to grab a towel and revealed his large Hasidic (Shtreimel), Hat. Alberto saw it and picked it up. "That's cool! Can I try it on?" Dov nodded. Alberto put it on. It slipped over his eyes, like a cowboy hat gone wrong. He posed, hands poised over imaginary holsters. In a John Wayne imitation asked. "Wanna see the fastest draw in the West?" He didn't move. And again asked. "Wanna see it again?" Dov obligingly smiled and muttered. "Sure." Alberto indicated the hat. "Hey! I thought you turned your back on religion?"

"You thought right," Dov adamantly replied.

"So what's this doing here?" Alberto asked. This question caught Dov, off-guard.

" It's... It's, in memory of my Parents," he replied and the chastened Alberto replaced the Hat on the cabinet. Feeling awkward he said." Anyway. Tonight was a great contact. Said you could bet on me," and began to sing.

ALBERTO (BET ON ME)

Fate and karma's in our view
Don't hesitate stop pondering
Don't let chances pass you by
Have the balls stop wondering
Bet on life and not on horses
Fate is just a lottery. Death n' taxes are for certain

Alberto faced the preoccupied Dov.

Take a chance and bet on me

Dov had more pressing matters on his mind. He checked his watch and hurried out into the backstage corridor. Meanwhile. In the Cornhucksters' living room. Jane was grading papers.

In the backstage corridor. Dov griped a wall phone and rang Jane. As he listened, he idly fiddled with his neck chain. On the Phone, he said. "Yeah...I'm going to send you something, you're going to love... Wait and see... We're doing great, "then louder...."It's going well!" Jane on the other end of the phone focussed, as she tried to hear. Her hand blocked the other ear, she shouted. "What?!"

So, Dov said it louder. " Well...We're doing great!" Jane, still struggled to hear and comprehend. She shouted. "What about your mate? Is Alberto OK?" The Operator. In a broad New Jersey accent, cut in. "Your time is up. Do you wish to pay for further time?" Dov snapped. "Yes! Hang on! Hang on! " Desperate, he fumbled in his pocket for coins. Found none. He shouted urgently, into the phone. "I love you!" No response. Only the sound of a loud dialling tone. Jane listened puzzled, she strained to hear. Dov listened frozen, waiting. But got no response. Glum-faced, he hung up. Belatedly, Jane spoke loudly, into the phone, and announced. "I love you!" She held her breath, waited. Heard only the Loud Dialling tone.

Desolate and lost, she also hung up. Fate had played a cruel, sick trick, on our forlorn, lovesick lovers.

<h1 style="text-align:center">Chapter 31</h1>

In New York. Dov loitered, outside, the Gimbels Department store, in 32nd Street. He sauntered along the sidewalk. Suddenly, stopped, something had caught his eye. In the window, there was an opulent display of exclusive Hampers. He wandered in.

In Denton. Jane picked up a book and settled into an armchair. Marge entered, carrying the shopping and saw Jane reading. "Oh sweetheart, it's such a lovely day. You need to get out sometimes," Jane, slowly, laid her book down and wearily said. "When I feel like it."

In Dov's Bed sitter. He was dejectedly labouring over a letter. Alberto bounded in, excited. He registered Dov's morose expression. "Cheer up. I've got you something that will take your mind off Jane for a while."

Dov hopefully asked. "What? Has Angeline got back-?"

"No. But while we're waiting, I've got you a gig." Dov was guarded. "Oh yeah. What's the catch?" Alberto was affronted. "Hey trust me. I'm Mr. Magic."

Chapter 32

First Real Gig

In the Performance area, of the up-market Eden Club, in Greenwich Village. The generous space, had a raised substantial stage. Dov was on stage, at the upright Microphone with his guitar, singing;

DOV (DESTINY'S PRIZE)

Too long I've been burdened by other's aspirations
Their alien hopes and false expectations.

Six Nuns with veils over their face, sedately glided on Stage. They stood demurely in a line behind Dov and swayed to the music.

Worn ill-fitting dreams, their fears and expectations.
But no more,

Defiantly, all the Nuns. Ripped their veils and their Head Coverings – off. And revealed, glamorous hairdos and faces caked with provocative makeup.

I've shed this load
It's time for me to find my destiny

The Nuns paired up and started dancing, a sedate Waltz.

DOV (DESTINY'S PRIZE)

Dreams delicate thread's easily broken
Unravel the web of promises spoken
Have I the will, the courage, the fire?
This is for me
This is my destiny

The Cyclorama at the back of the stage lifted, and revealed, a glitzy Las Vegas, Casino Ballroom. It had a raised Stage, occupied by a small band. Above the stage, there was a prominent banner with; 'World Championship. Welcome strippers'.

From gentle stream, to raging river.
A rolling wave, engulfs my soul.
It cannot be denied,
This dream that sweeps me, on to my goal
On to my destiny
Golden thread, precious dreams.

The Band members, stood, held onto the ends and threw Rolls of Yellow Streamers to the Nuns. They clumsily caught them and seductively wound up the Streamers until they were also, on the small Stage.

Destiny is within my reach.
This is my dream, it's worth any price.
If I succeed, I'll have destiny's prize.

Once they reached the raised Stage, the Nuns-began to strip. The Audience began to whistle and clap. The Band started to play, as they accompanied Dov.

A long, long journey, and no end in sight.
But if I succeed, I'll have destiny's prize.
If I succeed, I've got destiny's prize.
Yeah, yeah, yeah, destiny's prize.

The Act got an enthusiastic ovation.

After the show. Back in the dressing room, at the Eden Club. Dov had the space to himself. Alberto sensing a possible issue, adopted a cheery bluster as he entered. "Did you hear the crowd. Great show." Dov was not diverted and snapped. "What the bloody hell were you thinking?" Alberto tried to justify his booking and exclaimed. "Look. As I told you. It's great money and it's a three-month contract. We had no other option," Dov wasn't buying it, he barked. "This is bullshit. This is not for me. It's not-" Alberto concerned about Dov's rising anger, cut in. "Are you kidding? Guys are queuing up and paying big money to watch these girls," took a deep breath, stared at Dov and added. "Plus, you get a front-row view every night, not to mention a shared dressing room. I call that a bonus."

"I didn't leave Jane, disrupt my life and come all this way, to sing in some strip club," Dov angrily retorted. Alberto attempted to deflect Dov's anger and changed the subject. "How about making up a foursome?" Dov was startled into silence, by the proposition. But Alberto was not deterred, he offered. "Mother Superior thinks you're cute. You could get lucky," he leered. Dov was still thinking about the Angeline opportunity and asked. "Have you had any-?" But Alberto remained on point. "She's the stunner, second on the left." Dov shook his head. Alberto nudged him and winked. "Time you put it about," Dov ignored this and remained focused.

"How about-?" He hopefully asked.

"Keep her happy and I think I've got a shot with her friend," Alberto exclaimed.

"Have you heard from Angeline?" Finally, Dov asked directly.

"Her people are still looking, over your stuff," the subdued, Alberto replied. Dov patted him on the back and strode out. Alberto slumped into a chair. He looked up startled as Cleopatra, a petite, well-endowed young woman, breezed in, and offered a cheery. 'Hi!" Alberto was pleased and taken back, he exclaimed. "Hi. It's not going to be a foursome." She shrugged, sat on his lap and gave him a wild kiss.

Chapter 33

The next morning. In their dingy, bed sitter. Dov was having a meagre breakfast. He looked up surprised, as a bedraggled, but jaunty Alberto staggered in. Dov asked.

"Where have you been?"

"I've been to heaven," Alberto joyfully replied.

"What?"

Alberto, jubilantly announced. "I'm in love."

Dov wryly replied. "Now you know how it feels."

Alberto remained up-beat and exclaimed. "But, this is real. Hot, sweaty, passionate. Not some soulful Barbara Cartland relationship," Alberto was jubilant. One of the driving forces for his New York adventure, had just been experienced. It confirmed he had made the right decision.. There was no way he would have had this experience in Denton. Granted, he liked and was attracted by Betty Lou, but Cleopatra was in another league. She was movie star attractive and super sophisticated.

DOV was not convinced. "You'll understand when you've finally met the one." Alberto was adamant. "Just have. And it's awesome."

Chapter 34

Meanwhile, back in Denton. Betty- Lou and Jane were in Jose's. They were sitting at a table, catching up. In the background. The other tables were occupied by chattering students.

Hesitantly, Jane offered. "I tried to call you last weekend. Your mum said you were out. With me."

"She doesn't approve of Rip," Betty Lou explained.

"How could you?" Jane gasped.

"I didn't think you'd mind," Betty- Lou responded.

"I'm talking about going out with Rip," Jane explained

Betty- Lou, defiantly, retorted. "Alberto's there. I'm here. I can't live like a Nun for the rest of my life," Jane threw her a disappointed look. Betty-Lou replied. "It's all right for you. Dov keeps in touch."

Jane became choked up and announced. "Check, what he has sent me," took Angeline's Biography from her handbag, put it on the table, and emotionally added. "Look at the Title page." Betty- Lou checked the Title page and saw, 'To Jane, best wishes Angeline Dubois,'

Betty-Lou was impressed, and exclaimed. "Angeline Dubois. Wow! He's a Prince... So, what are you going to do about him?"

"I wish I knew," the doleful Jane replied.

Betty-Lou, insisted. "Shouldn't he be told?"

Chapter 35

One night. Weeks later (1959). Jane was in her bedroom, fretfully, tossing and turning. Finally, she got up. Sat at the dressing table, fighting back tears, began to laboriously write a letter. She finished and slipped it, inside an envelope. It was too much for her and she buried her head in her hands.

The next day. A teary-eyed, Jane dragged herself along a street in Denton. She stopped at a Post Box. Slowly, pulled an envelope from her handbag. It was addressed to, "Mr. Davey Gold. Post restante, c/o PO Box 82. King Road, New York." About to slip it into the slot, she hesitated. Finally, she let it go. Dragged herself away and trudged home. It was evening, before Jane eventually, shuffled into their eating area. The downhearted Jane was greeted by, an upbeat Marge and Clem. Marge indicated, a large gift-wrapped box and announced. "Now you're here. We can finally open it," she handed Jane an envelope. Mystified, Jane opened it and took a card out. Stared at it and broke into tears. Written on the card; 'with love and appreciation to Jane and family, signed Dov'. Marge hugged her.

In the background. Clem took off the gift wrapping and revealed a large, smart looking hamper. He eagerly opened it and began to remove: exotic groceries, bottles of wine, exclusive biscuits, special teas, mustards, and jams.

Chapter 36

Some weeks later. Dov was in his rundown dressing room. He sat motionless, glum-faced, as he stared unbelievably, at Jane's Letter. Tearful, he began to sing;

DOV (BRING ON THE NIGHT)

How can she not see?
My heart's on my sleeve.
How can she not, notice my yearning?
How can she not hear, my heart?
How can she not notice it's breaking

He crunched the letter up and threw it into a nearby rubbish bin. Paused, retrieved it and dragged himself to his feet, lumbered into the corridor, and over to the call box. Holding the Phone and still clutching the crumpled letter. He talked on the phone. "I see... I see... Thanks, operator," despondent, he replaced the phone.

Back in the dressing room. Dov stared blindly at the Letter. Alberto bounded in, bursting with news. He announced. "Guess what?" Registered Dov's obvious misery and asked.

"What's up?" Dov held up the letter and exclaimed. "Jane's called it off." Alberto was dumbfounded. "What?!" Dov lamented. "It's over. She won't even take my calls."

Alberto was totally bamboozled. "But all those cards, letters and stuff,"

Dov bemoaned. "She wrote, she's tired of the long-range romance. Wants to get on with her life. Claimed, I should do the same, "

Alberto, eagerly jumped in. "What have I been telling you. Listen, I've got some good news to start the New Year,"

Dov was too preoccupied, to register and just kept smoothing the letter, disinterested. Finally, he casually said. "Yeah. I heard on the radio. Castro's taken Cuba,"

Alberto could hardly contain his excitement. "Better than that. Angie loves your song, 'but Dov was offhanded and preoccupied, as he replied. "Oh yeah,"

Alberto was understanding." Look, I know it's tough, but hey! Earth to Dov! Angeline, wants to record, one of your songs," Dov got up and again hurried into the corridor and to the wall phone. He was tagged by Alberto. Alberto watched frustrated, as Dov picked the phone up and stared at it. Alberto was irritated and snapped. "This is the break we've dreamed about. A G-d sent opport –" watched silently, exasperated, as Dov dialled.

Chapter 37

Concurrently, in the Cornhucksters' house. Clem, in a dressing gown picked up the ringing phone and barked. "Operator, can you please tell him to stop phoning," he jammed the receiver down.

In New York. In the theatre dressing room. Alberto entered and saw Dov was fixated, by the open diary, with Jane's pressed rose. Alberto demanded. "You got to make a decision, or this Angeline deal will fold," Dov casually shrugged. Alberto barked. "I thought you had a dream!" He finally, had Dov's attention. He waited, impatiently, while Dov mulled it over, then Dov exclaimed. "I did!" Paused, then grabbed the Rose, crunched it in his fist and hurled the fragments into the air. As he watched the fragments float down. He pensively sang;

DOV (DESTINY'S PRIZE)

From gentle stream, to raging river.
A rolling wave, engulfs my soul.
It cannot be denied,
This dream that sweeps me
Alberto, was overjoyed and joined in.

ALBERTO

On to your goal,
On to your destiny
Together, they began a rousing chorus.

DOV and ALBERTO

Golden thread.
Precious dreams.
Destiny is within my (our) reach.
This is my dream, it's worth any price.
If I succeed, I'll (you'll) have destiny's prize.

Chapter 38

Meanwhile. It was midday, back in Denton. Marge opened the front door and greeted a smiling, nervous Bob. He had a large, bunch of flowers, and cheerily announced. "Hi Mrs. C. Just seeing if Jane's ok?"

"Hello Bob. Thanks for the flowers. Come on through," she ushered him into the lounge room. Jane looked up from her book, surprised and wary. Bob offered a smile. "Hi. Heard you were a bit off colour" Jane nodded and offered. "A bit."

"Well, I'm testing a new car. Came by to see if you'd like to come for a spin?" Marge cut in.

"That would be lovely. Jane, some fresh air would do you-" a glare from Jane stopped her mid-stream.

Jane offered a low key. "Thanks, I'm not really up to it," but Bob persisted. "Thought it might be good for you. Get you out a bit," Jane graciously declined. "Maybe, another time," Bob offered her the flowers. She accepted. "Thanks," Bob hung in. "Sure, you won't change your mind?"

"I'm a bit tired," she replied. But, Bob still persisted. "Any time you want company, ring. Bye Mrs. C. Bye Jane." Finally, Bob left.

Now, Marge faced Jane and cheerily commented. "Such a nice boy. And from a good family. You could do worse," this set Jane off, she emotionally announced. "I had better. I–" Marge cut in." Your health was our priority," Jane was not appeased, she emotionally responded. "But Dov was the one. And I've had to lie to him. - Twice!" Broke down and started to cry.

Chapter 39

n her New York Recording Studio. Angeline stood behind an old-fashioned upright microphone and sang;

ANGELINE (OUR LOVE)

From that first glance,
You overwhelmed my heart.
You ignited something, that's burning deep inside.
Glowing brighter than...

She stopped. Shook her head, frustrated and swore. "Shit!" Lights came up in the elevated, glass-walled Sound room and revealed her backup singers, Alfonse and Marco. Bill stood nearby and watched anxiously. Angeline shouted to Bill, "Where is he? I want to see him, now!"

Bill was nervous, as he responded. " They're here." Angeline was curt. "Well get them in for Christ sake," Bill hurried out. Alfonse and Marco entered the Studio. Angeline paced up and down, clicked her fingers. Alfonse passed her a cigarette. Marco whipped out his Zippo and lit it. Angeline took a deep drag.

Bill entered. He was followed by an exuberant Alberto, trailed by a wary looking Dov. He thought it, had been too good to be true. Now he nervously waited for the set-back. The reality check. Angeline turned, full voltage on him. "Loved this number on your demo. So what the Hell's gone wrong?" Dov and Alberto waited puzzled. Angeline explained. "It's just not working," Alberto jumped in and breezily announced. "If anyone can fix it, Dov can, "now he turned to Dov and growled. 'Fix it!"

Dov asked Angeline. "Who's singing it, with you?"

"What do you mean?" She asked. Dov was apologetic. "I'm sorry, I should have made it clear. It's not meant to be a solo".

Chapter 40

After a short break. Angeline and Dov were back in the Studio but on separate microphones. They were ready to record.

ANGELINE (OUR LOVE)

From that first glance
You overwhelmed my heart.
You ignited something, that's burning deep inside.
It's glowing brighter than a hundred stars.
Much sweeter than a thousand guitars.

Dov joined in. During the song. It became obvious, Dov was falling under Angeline's spell. He watched her mesmerised. The song invoked tender, romantic memories, her glamorous proximity and alluring perfume rekindled, unbidden, desires and inflamed him. Despite himself, he couldn't prevent himself from staring, as he guiltily remembered, how, attractive and sexy, she had looked in her brief, lacy underwear.

DOV

Never felt this way, but you stole my heart.
Can't believe this feeling, you elevate my being.
I'm floating high, way up above the clouds.
Feel my spirits soaring, no longer earthly bound.

Dov gestured to Angeline. She enthusiastically joined in, on the chorus.

DOV and ANGELINE

Our love's brighter than Haley's comet.
Sweeter than a Shakespearean sonnet.
More uplifting than Gandhi's marchers.
Stronger than all of the Eifel's arches.

Angeline indicated, to Alfonse and Marco. They joined in.

DOV, ANGELINE & BACK UP SINGERS.

That's our love.
Aaaahhh!
That's our love.
That's our love.
Aaahhh!
That's our love.

DOV.

Sharing thoughts with understanding ears
A harmony of dreams, that no one else can hear

Bound together, so that we become.
A melody of moments, uniting us as one.

DOV, ANGELINE and BACKUP SINGERS

Our love's brighter than Haley's comet.
Sweeter than a Shakespearean sonnet.
More uplifting than Gandhi's marchers.
Stronger than all of the Eifel's arches.
That's our love.
Aaahhh!
That's our love.
That's our love.
Aaahhh!
That's our love.

During the next vocal exchange, it became evident that Angeline was totally into the song and Dov. She appeared to be captivated. As she exchanged the lyrics with Dov. She reached out and grasped his hand. Similarly, the combination of the song and her alluring proximity, had totally entranced Dov. He edged closer and stared intently into her eyes.

DOV

It's overwhelming, ever present

ANGELINE

Omnipresent incandescent

DOV

Effervescent enhancing

ANGELINE

Entrancing

DOV

Enchanting

ANGELINE

Exciting

DOV

Inciting

ANGELINE

Astounding

DOV

Abounding

ANGELINE

Soul-Lifting

DOV

Soul-Gifting

ANGELINE

It's Celestial DOV
Extra-Terrestrial

They all sang together, for the final, rousing finale.

DOV, ANGELINE and BACKUP SINGERS.

Our love's brighter than Haley's comet.
Sweeter than a Shakespearean sonnet.
More uplifting than Gandhi's marchers.
Stronger than all of the Eifel's arches.
That's our love. Aaahhh! That's our love.

Fired up, Angeline turned to Dov. She gasped. "Wow!" Dov enthusiastically, nodded. Put an arm around her shoulders and enthusiastically exclaimed "Works for me!"

<h1 style="text-align:center">Chapter 41</h1>

Some weeks later, back in Denton. Jane was in the Cornhucksters' living room. She sat riveted, as she listened, to the Radio. It played, Dov, Angeline and the Backup Singers version of, 'That's Our Love'. When it finished, the excited Radio Announcer cut in. "You heard it here. The newly released single by Angeline Dubois and newcomer Davey Gold, will go boppo. Angeline's Pop career, after 'Tease Queen,' was tired, but this will certainly kick start it."

Chapter 42

Success At Last.

Dov felt as if he was riding in, an out of control space-ship. Suddenly, his career had meteorically blasted off. He found it hard to adjust to his changed circumstance: one night, he performed in a large department store, packed out with fans. Then he'd be whisked to an Auditorium or a large Club to perform. After he performed, he'd sign countless autographs. This was all the stuff of dreams.

However, the cream on the cake, was the one-on-one time he spent with Angeline. After their gigs, they would go out and have dinner and drinks at places like the Langham, the Waldorf Astoria, and the New York Marriott. The opulence and luxury of these surroundings, were totally foreign and mind-boggling. Often they would go for intimate drinks at the Conrad New York.

He clearly remembered, one particular evening, as if it was yesterday. They were sitting in a secluded alcove. Nestled on a seat, holding drinks. As they chatted and laughed. Dov held up his champagne glass, for a toast.

"To harmony,' they clinked glasses. Angeline exuberantly responded. "I'll drink to that," she took a big swig. Leaned forward and kissed him on the lips. Guiltily, he liked it, kissed her back and was turned on.

A short time later, they ended up, back in her apartment. It was in central New York, near the Theatre district. Outside, the busy traffic sped past. But the double glazed windows, repelled most noise. Later that night. An empty champagne glass, lay on the floor next to the bed. While Angeline and Dov sprawled naked on it and shared a joint, oblivious to the passing, heavy traffic.

Dov stared, mesmerised at the naked Angeline. He marvelled at her voluptuous, undulating hills and was lured and beguiled, by her inviting, seductive valleys.

Uncomfortable, with his unblinking scrutiny, she demanded. "What is it? What's wrong?" Somewhat abashed at being caught out, embarrassed, he hurriedly replied. "Nothing! Nothing is wrong. You are perfect and I can't stop looking at you."

Although she was flattered, by his infatuation, she felt uneasy. What had she created? She hurriedly, lifted the sheet to cover herself. He went to stop her and hurriedly pleaded. "Please don't. I want to burn your image onto my brain." Angeline was no stranger to compliments, but Dov's abject devotion was unnerving.

After their recording studio duet. Their relationship had changed, he now viewed her with different eyes. He still pined for Jane, but now it was tolerable. There was no denying it, he was attracted and addicted to Angeline.

She also seemed to like him. He rationalised, it would be ungentlemanly, impolite, if he didn't reciprocate. After all, she was a talented, gorgeous woman and he felt a strong bond with her. She had helped make, all this possible. He felt a growing attachment. He managed to subdue any lingering guilt regarding Jane. He rationalised. She had expressly, called their relationship-off. Why should he feel guilty, about moving on? After all, she had specifically suggested it.

Angeline had opened up new worlds for him: five star hotels, sophisticated bars, and nightclubs and tried to introduce him to Coke and pot. These latter two weren't his go. He was wary about indulging in them. She appeared to have no such qualms. She also introducing him to foreplay and sex. These were experiences, he was more than happy to experiment and indulge in. She was an excellent and patient teacher. He had no idea there were so many erogenous zones, in the human body and was happy to fully explore each and every one, under her expert tutelage.

He had never realised how fulfilling and erotic, a kiss could be. Or the beauty and intoxication, of a woman's body. A complete novice, under her expert, coaching, he developed a huge appetite to experiment and learn. According to her. He was an avid and energetic pupil, who had rapidly gone from a terrified, trembling, inept, novice to a more than accomplished lover. For Dov, it had been a liberating, exhilarating, life-changing experience. He would be forever grateful to her for her patient and knowledgeable guidance.

He continued to marvel at her seductive, voluptuous slopes and her appealing, enticing vales and dales. He could happily spend hours studying her naked body. Occasionally, she would catch him gawking. Uncomfortable, by his intense scrutiny, ignoring his pleas to stop, she would hurriedly cover herself. He found her modesty, and vulnerability, surprising and somewhat endearing.

Chapter 43

Some weeks later. One lazy, midday. After they had spent a torrid, sensual night in Angeline's Apartment. Dov emerged from a deep sleep and noticed, daylight had managed to bypass the drawn curtains. The bathroom door opened and Angeline came out. She was made up and looked gorgeous. Dov was now, fully awake and lecherously reviewed her. He sat up and patted the bed. "Come back here. Angeline obligingly smiled, but walked towards the door, as she said. "I've got to run."

"Tell them a problem has suddenly, come up. And only you can fix it," he suggestively replied. Angeline swayed across and kissed him. As he attempted to grab her, she sidestepped and headed for the door. Over her shoulder, casually said. "See you later," then she was gone. Dov was left, frustrated, suspicious and disappointed.

That evening. Alberto was reading the newspaper, in their apartment- He looked up surprised as a dejected Dov stumbled in, the worse for drink. Alberto said." You're early. What's up?"

"No idea. But this is not the first time, she's done it."

"Done what?"

"Just taken off. No explanation. Nothing."

Alberto made a suspicious sound. "Mmmmm!"

"What does that mean?" Dov guardedly asked. Alberto shook his head. "Nothing." Dov gave him a look of utter disbelief. Alberto relented and explained. "Okay. Maybe she's got some guy stashed somewhere. "

Dov was aghast and in complete denial. "No way! We've... We've got a genuine connection. "

Alberto elaborated. "It sounds like she's giving you the run around." Dov felt insecure and was unsettled by the suggestion. Alberto persisted. "We need to find out, what's going on," Dov asked. "We?" Alberto responded. "I'm not only your manager. I'm your amigo. We're in this together."

Dov mulled it over, he was sorely tempted and tentatively asked. "How could we do it?" "Get a private Dick to follow her." Alberto smugly offered. Dov instinctively, shook his head, He couldn't do that. Alberto tried another tack. "Okay. We'll follow her." Dov was emphatic. "No! Definitely not."

Alberto pushed on. "Do you want to know what's going on?" "Sure," Dov promptly replied. Alberto closed the trap." Is she likely to tell you?" Dov had to admit. "No. That's unlikely," Alberto, was on match point. "Then, there's no option," Dov looked thoughtful.

Chapter 44

Some days later. In a street in the Lower East Side of New York. A glossy limousine pulled up outside a small dilapidated two storey terrace. Several Street kids appeared and ogled the car. A group of three, aged between eight and 10. They looked scruffy and were dressed in grubby, short-sleeved shirts and shorts. The neighbours,' were also observing. The Chauffeur chased the kids away. Nearby several husky 'African – Americans,' lounged in doorways, smoking.

The claustrophobic narrow street was lined with a long row of one and two storey dilapidated, rundown New York terraces, on both sides of the road. The gutters were littered with a cocktail of rotting debris. The neighbourhood had the feel and smell, of progressive, depressing decay.

Dov and Alberto's taxi pulled up at the end of the same Street with a view of the parked Limousine and the Terrace. Dov and Alberto observed events through the windscreen and saw; Angeline bounce out of the Limousine, carrying a parcel. Aware of the locals watching, she put on a show and swayed towards the old Terrace. Spotting the African – Americans', she affected a brief vamp pose and waved to them. In the Taxi. Alberto dug Dov in the ribs, as he indicated the 'African – Americans' and yelped. "See! She's got them lined up."

Content with the 'African – Americans,' stunned reaction, Angeline continued to the front door and knocked. It was opened and she swayed inside. As she entered, Angeline offered a cheery. "Hi," a frail-looking woman in her late 60s saw the parcel, and moaned. "What are you wasting your money on now?" Angeline closed the front door and followed the lady into the small family room. Inside, the table was set for two. Angeline replied. "You know. I wouldn't come here empty-handed. Enjoy," she put the parcel on the table. The lady looked her over and enthused. "You're glowing. What going on?" Angeline was taken back and played all innocent. "What?" But the lady, knew her, too well, and persisted. "Come on. There's a man in your life."

"When have I got time for a man?" Angeline replied, then looked around the dingy room and bemoaned. "What do I need to do, to get you out of this slum?" The lady retorted. " Don't forget, you were born and bred here Miss Toffee Nose."

"That doesn't mean you've got to stay here. Let me get you somewhere half decent," Angeline replied.

"I'm happy being plain Marge Wood, thank you very much. Just because you've become all hoity-toity, Miss Angeline Dubois. Doesn't mean I have to, "the lady snapped back. "That's show biz. And it's not hoity-toity, to live somewhere with an inside toilet," Angeline countered.

Her mother dug her heels in. "Told you umpteen times. This is my home. All my friends are here," then she, indicated the nearby phone. "Don't know why you had that thing put in. Who do I know who's got one?" Angeline silently, stared at her and she quickly added. "Apart from you," then her mother started to pour the tea and tentatively offered. "Now tell me about your man friend. It's time you started a family." Angeline had no desire to explore this subject, she lamented. "Oh G-d!"

Shortly after. Angeline left the house, stopped and looked back. She mimed making a phone call. Waved goodbye and moved towards her Limo. The Chauffeur opened the door, she got in, and shortly, it drove off.

Chapter 45

Dov was eager for information, he jumped out of the taxi and strode to the terrace. He was trailed by Alberto. Dov started to pound on the front door. Stopped, when Alberto grabbed his arm and shouted. " Hey! Slow down. This Guy could be bigger than both of us," Dov judiciously decided to tap on the door. Three inquisitive Street kids gathered and watched Dov and Alberto. Now, they excitedly nudged each other, as they pointed at Dov. Street kid # 1, was a 10-year-old grubby, small urchin, with the chutzpah of a teenage mobster. He cheekily faced Dov and announced. "Hey! You're Davey Gold." Alberto confronted him, and snapped." Piss off small fry," the kid backed away. Dov again tapped on the Door and impatiently waited. Meanwhile, the Street kids stared at Dov and began another, deep conversation. Finally, the door partially opened. The lady peeked out and hesitantly asked." Yes?" Dov was taken aback and hurriedly explained. "Oh. We're looking for Angeline Dubois," the lady was suspicious, and snapped." Not the bloody press again. Push off, or I'll phone the police, 'went to shut the door, but Dov jammed his foot there and hastily explained. "I'm a friend of hers." the lady was not convinced, she sceptically responded." Says you."

"You wouldn't be her Mum, would you?" Dov tentatively asked.

" What if I am?" She guardedly replied. The Street kids gained courage, crossed and began to sing a parody version of the chorus of, 'Our Love,' to Dov and Alberto.

STREET KIDS. (That's Our Love.)

Aaaaaaaah
That's our love
That's our love
That's our love

Suddenly, the lady stared at Dov with new eyes. She smiled brightly and exclaimed. " Hang on. You're the guy on her new hit, " then she faced the Street kids and belligerently yelled. "You lot. Piss off, or I'll tell your parents, "the Street kids beat a hasty retreat. She again faced Dov and pleasantly asked. " Are you her new man?" Dov was put on the spot, he finally responded. "I--I guess I am," he appeared to pass muster. " About time she found someone half decent," she enthusiastically responded.
Dov stared at her and loudly mused. " I can see where she got her looks."
She enjoyed the flattery and wryly responded. "Get away. You're full of it."

"No. I swear," he replied, then he checked the neighbour-hood, and offered. "I've read she came from around here. And now she's a big star. That is amazing!"
" Steady! We might not have had much, but we looked after each other and our neighbours," she retorted.
"And she hasn't forgotten her roots. Always comes to see you?" He asked, fishing.
"Two or three times in the last few weeks. She's a good daughter," she replied, reflected, and then added. "I'm lucky. The only thing missing, is a grandchild, "she stared intently at Dov, as she added. "But who knows?"
Dov was bewildered and embarrassed. "Nice to meet you. But we must go," he hustled Alberto away from the door and they headed towards their taxi.

Chapter 46

After they left. The lady hurried back inside. She quickly picked the phone up and dialled. She waited impatiently. But there was no answer. Frustrated, she hung up.

Meanwhile. The source of her calls were about to meet in a plush stage dressing room.

With success, there had come some fancy perks. A plush stage dressing room was one of them. After his afternoon show. Dov was back in his dressing room, sitting at the mirror removing make up. Alberto bustled in with a bottle of champagne, and breezily announced. " Great show. With the record taking off, we're booked for the year," Dov nodded, then smiled, as he said. "You're a slave driver. But thanks," Alberto smugly replied. "What did I tell you. Stick with me and I'll make you a star," just then, Angeline sashayed in, dressed to kill. She was trailed by, Alfonse and Marco. She slinked across to Dov.

Up close, fluttered her long eyelashes and lasciviously, licked her lips. It was obvious, Dov was smitten and turned on. She enjoyed his reaction, Alberto's discomfort, was an added bonus. Dov was aroused, he huskily implored. "Let's split," Angeline teased. "What do you have in mind, my cute, cuddly, sexy, K..i....ke?"

"One guess, "Dov suggestively replied. Alberto looked from one to the other, and announced. "I'm taking a cold shower," he hurriedly departed. But it hardly registered, to the preoccupied couple. They maintained torrid eye contact. Pause. Then Angeline, snapped her fingers. Alfonse handed her a Joint. She waited for Marco to light it, took a deep drag. Held it in with obvious enjoyment, then slowly exhaled. "Aaah! That's so good," she exclaimed and performed some eye popping bumps and grinds. Offered Dov the Joint. He held up his champagne, shook his head and declared. "Thanks. I'll stick to this."

Chapter 47

Soon after. They were both at a lavish Art Deco Nightclub, in the Theatre District. Angeline, was in the Spotlight, on the small Stage, holding a glass of champagne. Marco and Alfonse were on Stage, behind her. The select, elegantly dressed Audience applauded Angeline. She faced them, smiling, then announced. "The next number's something that's close to all our hearts,' the Venue was packed with, a select, patron list. Men in bespoke, tuxedos. Women in couture, lavish gowns, draped in expensive jewellery.

Dov was near the Stage, he stared infatuated at Angeline, as she held her champagne glass, up and began to sing;

ANGELINE (MARY JANE)

Champagnes fine, so refined
A taste acquired, so rarefied
Old malt whiskey,
Makes you tipsy
It's sublime

The audience swayed to the beat and listened intently

ALFONSE AND MARCO

So sublime

ANGELINE

But the one that tops them all
The one that I adore

ALFONSE AND MARCO

Je 'adore, Je 'adore.

Marco and Alfonse took the glass and slipped her a Joint.
Fondling it, she teasingly, sang;

ANGELINE

Is a lady,
Oh so shady
One sniff, one whiff, one drag, one hit
Your life will change,
You'll know that's it.

ALFONSE and MARCO

That's it, that's it, that's it!

ANGELINE

Honey Bunn
Smoke these honey blunts
Will drive you crazy
Make you lazy, warm n' hazy make you feel so good

The Patrons commenced an enthusiastic Charleston type Dance, on the brightly polished dance- floor.

ANGELINE (cont'd)

Indian hay
Blows those blues away
Your pain will ease
Brain in deep freeze
Life's a breeze
Make you feel so good

ANGELINE and the BOYS

Come blow a stick
Bite your lip
Suck on that joint
You'll get the point
Come feel no pain
You'll go insane
Embrace n' hold, sweet
Mary Jane
Oh sweet Mary Jane
Her many devices
Her infinite disguises
Will test your soul

ANGELINE

Rasta weed
Sweet black
Ganja seed

Will make you glow
Your head will blow
Your juices will flow

ANG and the BOYS

Make you feel so good

A number of the patrons had furtively, extracted and lit up joints. They offered them around. Taking deep puffs, the patrons enthusiastically swayed, to the music, enveloped in scattered clouds, of marijuana smoke.

ANGELINE

Come blow a stick
Bite your lip
Suck on that joint
You'll get the point
Come feel no pain
You'll go insane
Embrace n' hold, sweet Mary Jane

ANGELINE and BOYS

Sweet Mary Jane
Her many devices her infinite disguises
Will test your soul
Columbus black real fine wack
Love a pinhead
Try the big red
What's in a name

It's all the same
Embrace n' hold sweet Mary Jane

ANGELINE

Oh Mary Jane
Oh sweet Mary Jane
You drive me crazy
You make me lazy
You unforgiving witch
You sweet seductive bitch
You're an unforgiving witch, Mary Jane
You're an unforgiving bitch, Mary Jane

Still holding the Joint, she stepped down from the stage and tempted Dov with it. Smiled in satisfaction, when he eventually, accepted it. Oblivious to the crowd, she gave him a lusty kiss.

Chapter 48

After her gig. They hurried back to her Apartment and straight to her bedroom. Soon, they were dressed in bathrobes and snorting Coke. Dov was high. They kissed wildly and fell onto the bed.

Suddenly, the phone rang. Irritated at the interruption, she grabbed it and growled. "Hello?!"... Became startled and exclaimed. "Mum! What's wrong...? What are you doing up after midnight? ...No!... No! Call at any time. Use it"...stared at Dov, while she continued to listen on the phone, with rising anger, then snarled. "Oh! Did he?... Yes, he is... What! ... Okay. Talk soon," replacing the receiver, but still holding the phone confronted Dov, and screamed. "Who the hell, do you think you are, Mike bloody Hammer?" Picked the phone and the handset up, and hurled the lot at Dov. He ducked. It smashed against the wall. Now, she confronted Dov and angrily yelled. "It's bad enough the press prying around. I won't have you doing it," Angeline picked up an ashtray and hurled it at Dov. He dodged and it also smashed against the wall. Dov attempted to explain. "You wouldn't say, where you were going."

She wasn't buying it. She bluntly rebuked. "I don't have to."

He pleaded. "Can't you understand? I couldn't bear the thought of you with anyone else," she had no sympathy, she snarled. "Oh grow up!"

"It was driving me crazy. I had to know."

She was like a rock, she snapped. "No you didn't!"

He was desperate and lamented. "I have never experienced anything like this."

"Honey. It's called sex," was her curt, mocking response.

Dov was out of his league. Desperately, he went for the last roll. "I've even written a song about us."

She remained unimpressed, as she snarled. "Who gives a shit. Piss off," defeated, Dov trudged from the room and closed the door behind him. She poured a drink and then impatiently, listened to his singing, through the closed door.

DOV (Off. THIS IS THE BEST.)

Above Romeo and Juliet,
This is the best Beyond Napoleon and Josephine.
This is the best
It's as good as it can get.
This is the best yet.

In another room. In her Apartment. Dov continued to play the guitar and sing,

DOV. (THIS IS THE BEST).

Anthony and Cleo-

Suddenly, the door was flung open. The steamed up Angeline, straddled the doorway and barked. "Fuck you!" Dov's initial, welcoming smile, was wiped off. But then she reluctantly added. "It's not half bad," a reprieve and he was delighted and jubilant.

Soon after. The ebullient Dov, skipped onto the pavement, outside Angeline's apartment. Several drunken Entertainers, in tuxedos, lounged outside. Startled, they looked up when Dov burst out, then returned to their chatting and drinking.

Dov jubilantly yelled. "Yipeee!" As he bounded up and down the sidewalk and began to sing;

DOV (THE BEST YET)

I was a poor boy from the sticks
Headed west to follow my dream.
She was an icon a Hollywood star
A glamorous movie queen.

The drunken, Entertainers stirred by his passion and by the song, enthusiastically joined in.

ENTERTAINERS.

She saw the yearning in his eyes
A kindred soul she met
Ignited a feeling lost long ago.

This is the best yet.
This is the best
Above Romeo and Juliet,
This is the best
Beyond Napoleon and Josephine,
This is the best
It's as good as it can get.
This is the best yet.

Dov was touched by the Entertainers gesture, he now sang with renewed gusto.

DOV.

A collision of stars,
Venus and Mars
Our stellar romance, lights the sky
Two heavenly bodies a cosmic light
Two comets flashing bye
This is the best
Above Romeo and Juliet,
This is the best
Beyond Napoleon and Josephine,
This is the best
It's as good as it can get.
This is the best yet.

DOV and ENTERTAINERS.

This is the best
Above Romeo and Juliet,

This is the best
Beyond Napoleon and Josephine,
This is the best yet.

DOV.

Anthony and Cleopatra

ENTERTAINERS.

This is the best

DOV

Ava Gardner, Frank Sinatra

ENTERTAINERS.

This is the best Oh yeah!

Caught up in the song and infected by Dov's fervour. Dov and the Entertainers linked arms around each other and sang a rousing final chorus.

DOV and ENTERTAINERS

This is the best
It's as good as it can get.
This is the best yet.
This is the best yet.

Chapter 49

Meanwhile, back in Denton. Jane and Betty – Lou decided to meet up, one afternoon, after work, at Jose's. Betty-Lou sat waiting, at a front window table. The Jukebox was playing, 'Our Love'. Chattering students lounged at several tables. Jose was kept busy, making coffee and milkshakes. Betty-Lou was reading a magazine. Jose limped over, placed a cup of coffee, on her table and excitedly exclaimed. "The record's gone Gold. The muchachos have made it," but Betty-Lou had a gripe, she growled. "Would that be the same two hot shots, who left here and dropped off my radar?' Jose was confused." I …I …Say something?" She explained. " I thought Alberto and I were an item." Jose beamed and reviewed her with different eyes. "Really?! Has he ever told you about our family?"

Betty- Lou shook her head. José enthusiastically explained." I'm an orphan like Dov.

When I was a boy, I was-" Jane entered, wearing a headscarf. Jose waved. She gives him a weak smile. Jose turned to Betty Lou, and apologetically said. "Another time, "Jose moved away. Jane drifted over and sat next to Betty-Lou.

She grabbed Jane's hand and exclaimed. "Hi, I was getting worried," Jane remained silent. Betty-Lou fidgeted, finally had to ask. "How?...How did it go?" Jane glumly replied. "Could be better,"

Bob entered. He wore a flashy suit and a broad smile. He swaggered across with a folded newspaper and offered a cheery greeting. " Hi Ladies!" Betty-Lou was not impressed. " Jesus Bob, you look like a used car salesman," Bob replied. "I am a used car -?" gave a false laugh, realised he'd been had, waved the newspaper and announced. "How about our singing Dove. Always knew he had something." Betty-Lou sarcastically, shot back. "Yeah! Leprosy! You tried to run him out of town," Bob countered. "Come on! I was just kidding," Betty-Lou wasn't buying it, she disputed. "What about him being a reffo dip stick?" Bob retorted. "But, now he's a successful reffo dip stick," Betty-Lou had enough and snapped. " We're trying to have a private conversation, if you don't mind," Bob still didn't get it, he announced. "I've got my new wheels outside. How about all of us burning rubber," this was the last straw for Betty-Lou, she turned to him and snarled. " Piss off!' Then turned to Jane. "So what did the Dr -?" Bob cut in. "Look, if you change –" Betty-Lou suddenly, stood and eyeballed him. He stumbled back. Then, tried for a graceful exit, made a gun action with his thumb and index finger and offered. "See you later alligator," Betty-Lou snapped. "Make it a while crocodile," she shook her head as she watched him exit, then turned to Jane. " Once a jerk," sat, again faced Jane and demanded. "So, what did Dr West say?"

"It's...It's not responding." Jane mumbled. Betty-Lou tried for optimistic and emphatically responded. "Then they'll try something else. It will be okay," Jane was unconvinced. "Absolutely," she hesitantly announced. Betty-Lou gripped her hands and forcefully declared. "It...Will....be... okay," waited for a beat. Then insisted. " You must tell Dov." Jane was definite. "No way!" Betty-Lou persisted. "I think you should call him."

Jane, categorically declared. "No!" Betty-Lou pressed on. "Why ever not?" Jane explained. "He's happy. A success. I'm the last thing he needs, he should focus on his career," Betty-Lou had sudden, startled comprehension, she exclaimed. "Oh my G-d!" Choked back tears, as she gasped. "You love him - that much!" Holding back tears, just stared at the now silent Jane, then affectionately hugged her.

Chapter 50

Distraught, and miserable, Jane rushed out of Jose's. She was tormented and depressed. By the impact of her decision not to tell Dov and to remain in Kansas. It was proving too much for her to cope with. She hurried home, went to her bedroom and tearfully, started to leaf through her photo album. It was filled with photos of her and Dov. She selected several and began to mournfully sing;

JANE (Just Me And You)

Can't believe that I lost you
If only I stayed true
You told me not to stay
But I couldn't go away

During the song, she reviewed a series of photos of her and Dov in happier times.

JANE

Destiny has sealed our fate
I want to go but it's too late

I'm trapped by life that has no key
My history keeps following me

She looked at a Photo of her and Dov, joyfully jiving at the Graduation Dance. This was probably her favourite memory.

When I look back into my mind
I sit in silence wondering why
Why I ever let you go
As I look back I can't hide
Feelings locked up deep inside
And the tears that beg to flow

She looked at a Photo of her and Dov, arms around each other's waist, admiring the Roses in the front garden. She faltered – and started weeping, as she sang;

When harmony is sung by two
Just me and you
Life takes on a different view
When it's me and you
Destiny has turned the page
I want to go but, it's all too late
We're trapped by life that has no key
My memory keeps haunting me.

Now she reviewed a Photo of her and Dov, holding hands, as they walked by the local river.

When I look back into my mind
I sit in silence wondering why
Why I ever let you go
As I look back I can't hide
Feelings locked up inside
And the tears begin to flow

Finally, she stared at a Photo of her and Dov, laughing on the front porch.

Should have left but couldn't go
Should have gone and simply
followed through.
Should have spent those times with you
Should have known when love was true
Memories keep me up all night
I try to hide my feelings
When harmony's sung by two Just me and you
When harmony's sung by two Just me and you

In hindsight. She now bitterly, realised. Although, not telling Dov the truth, was an unselfish, noble act. Eventually, it had sabotaged, their new found love. A love that she sorely missed and would probably never experience, again. This realisation, left her devastated. Sobbing, Jane bowed her head and hid her face in her hands.

Chapter 51

Months later. In New York. Outside Carnegie Hall. There were Long queues of Fans rugged up in full winter gear, as they braved the falling snow, and chilling wind. Inside. The venue was packed, with excited, expectant Fans. There was an eager buzz and palpable energy from the crowd.

Finally, inside Carnegie Hall. The stage Announcer, resplendent in a tuxedo, appeared, in front of the curtain, and excitedly announced. "Ladies and gentleman. Let's have. A warm Carnegie Hall welcome, for an exciting new talent. His debut solo single with his newly formed band has gone Gold! Davey Gold and the Gold Tops!" The crowd erupted with loud applause. Some stood and stamped their feet. The noise and excitement continued on and on.

After a moment. The curtain was drawn back, the scrim lifted. And revealed the Stage. This initiated further loud applause and stomping. On Stage, the crowd saw: Dov on an elevated rostrum, behind him the Gold Tops with two female backup singers. (Band and Singers, were in all gold outfits). In addition. 8 Dancers in tight gold costumes stood in the background. Dov faced the audience. The noise gradually settled and he began to sing;

DOV (DESTINY'S PRIZE)

Too long I've been burdened by other's aspirations
Their alien hopes and false expectations
Worn ill-fitting dreams, their fears, and expectations.
But no more I've shed this load it's time for me.
To find my destiny.
Dreams delicate thread's easily broken
Unravel the web of promises spoken
Have I the will, the courage, the fire?
This is for me
This is my destiny
Golden thread precious dreams.
Destiny is within my reach
This is my dream, it's worth any price.
If I succeed, I'll have destiny's prize.
If I succeed, I've got destiny's prize
From gentle stream to raging river.
A rolling wave engulfs my soul.
It cannot be denied, this dream that sweeps me,
On to my goal
On to my destiny.

All the Fans jumped ,to their feet and began a deafening, rhythmic clap. The Hall reverberated with the sound.

DOV and the GOLD TOPS

Golden thread
Precious dreams.
Destiny is within my reach
This is my dream, it's worth any price.
If I succeed, I'll have destiny's prize.

Standing in the wings. Alberto smugly reviewed the scene and nudged the 50 something, well-dressed man beside him and announced. "I told you, he'd fill the whole venue and set the place alight."

ENSEMBLE

Destiny's prize, destiny.
Destiny's prize,
Oh my destiny

DOV and ENSEMBLE

Golden thread
Precious dreams.
Destiny is within my reach
This is my dream, it's worth any price.
If I succeed, I'll have destiny's prize.

ENSEMBLE

Golden thread
Precious dreams.
Destiny is within my reach
A long, long journey and no end in sight.

DOV

But if I succeed,
I'll have destiny's prize
If I succeed, I've got destiny's prize yeah,
yeah, yeah, destiny's prize

The Fans erupted, they jumped to their feet and began loud cheering, stomping, and clapping. Dov and the Gold Tops had definitely arrived.

Chapter 52

Some weeks later. Dov and Angeline held a celebratory gathering, in her Hudson- side mansion. The grand ballroom was meticulously prepared for this special occasion. It was a plush black tie affair. The space included a magnificent curved, marble staircase, and lavish chandeliers. The guests and Alberto burst into enthusiastic applause, as Dov entered. A pause. Then Angeline dramatically made her entrance. She chassed down the staircase, slinked across and stood beside Dov.

When they embraced, the Guests again erupted into applause. PK lounged in the background, he appeared completely, out of place in this gathering. The muscular hard case, was in his early thirties and looked imposing, in a tight black leather outfit. Arm around Angeline, Dov waited for silence, before he formally addressed his Guests. "Thanks for helping us celebrate my Gold record. Enjoy the night," Angeline faced Dov, moistened her lips and breezily offered. "Congrats. We do make a good team," Dov quipped. "Like Eddie Fisher and Debbie Reynolds?" She smiled as she replied. "You are so sweet"

"You're sweet, too," he shot back.

Angeline, gently held his face and offered a bittersweet smile, and gently said. "You're such an innocent,"

Dov responded. "You're great, "then indicated PK, and growled. 'You don't need all that stuff."

Angeline responded with a hollow laugh. "I'm fine," looked about, got PK's attention, clapped her hands, and loudly addressed him. "Let's party," she patted Dov on the cheek, then swayed towards PK. Meanwhile, Alberto had strolled up to Dov with two champagne glasses and handed him one.

At the same time, in the background. Angeline and PK, had their heads close together, whispering. Alberto lifted his glass, for a toast. "Mazeltov! Read the press? You're the next young Elvis," but Dov seemed underwhelmed, he mumbled. "Doesn't feel like it. I know this was my dream, but"...In the background, PK had whipped out a joint, lit it and handed it to Angeline. She inhaled with obvious enjoyment. Dov watched with a pained expression, as he addressed Alberto and lamented. " Angie's getting into more and more shit," Alberto snapped. "So get her to stop," Dov heaved a weary sigh. "You're kidding," Angeline approached. Dov hurriedly pasted on a smile and darted a warning glance to Alberto. Angeline announced. "That was so good," turned and checked the scene, faced Dov and announced. "Darling, it's a lovely party," tempted Dov with a pill, and invitingly offered. "Try it honey, it's fabulous," Dov hesitated. But she persisted." Come on Baby, they're great," with that. Alberto grasped Angeline's wrist and barked. "Very clever, with the press all here." Angeline wrenched free and snapped. "Butt out, you no talent, Cuban gnome," Alberto lamented. "Not my week. First the Bay of Pigs. Now the baying bitch," then he strode off. Angeline confronted Dov. She was furious and her accent frayed. "Keep your school buddy on a leash, or I'll forget I'm a fuckin lady, "then Angeline crossed to PK. They chatted. She blatantly accepted another joint. Sucking on it, she slinked across and also offered this to Dov. She pouted and said. 'I love it when you're high." Dov backed away and hesitantly replied. "Got to be in the mood." She snapped. "Get in the mood, or you may find I'm not," there was a long pause. Finally, Dov accepted the joint. And took a deep drag.

Chapter 53

Soon after. They appeared in the dark street, outside her Hudson side mansion. Sharing the joint, they wandered along the pavement. While they walked, they became increasingly uncoordinated. Suddenly, they were bombarded by popping lights. They reeled back, besieged by a mob of shouting, paparazzi. Paparazzi # 1, shouted to Angeline. "Hey Angie, you settling down?" Receiving no answer. Paparazzi # 2, shouted to Angeline. 'Six months with the same lover boy. How come?" Paparazzi # 3, shouted to Dov, in unison with #1. "Hey Davey, is this a career move?" Again no response. So, Paparazzi # 1, shouted to Angeline, in unison with #3."Darling, he's looking pretty peaked." Paparazzi # 2, shouted to Paparazzi #3. "How long has he got?" Paparazzi # 3, shouted back to Paparazzi #2. "Will he last another six months?" Then he tauntingly shouted to Angeline. "When are you going to get yourself a real man?" Laughed and added. "I'm available," performed a Pelvic thrust. Fighting through the throng, our couple weaved away and disappeared in the darkness.

Chapter 54

The invitations for Dov to appear kept flooding in: concerts, opening stores, clubs, you name it. Alberto efficiently handled them. One of the strangest involved, The New York campus of New York University. Dov decided to reconnoitre the location, before his appearance. On the evening, of his appearance, he arrived early at Josie Robertson Plaza and gaped at the iconic Lincoln Centre and the David Geffen Hall, with its massive wall of brightly lit glass. He cautiously entered the spacious lobby and marvelled at the display of prominent art work that included; Roden's bust of Gustav Mahler and Dmitri Hadzi's sculpture The Hunt. Unsure where to go, he approached a Security guard, showed him his invitation and identification. The guard spoke on his earpiece and shortly a polite, uniformed, young usher arrived. The young man, briefly reviewed the paperwork, then brusquely said. "Let's go," without waiting for an answer, he strode off. Dov hurriedly followed. They strode through a series of maze like corridors and passed by a series of wall-mounted, lights and a row of gold framed pictures, of past distinguished Lincoln

Centre artists. Finally, they arrived near the stage of the Auditorium.

Dov could now, faintly hear, a speech from inside. "That concludes the formal part of the evening. Now, for the Post Graduation entertainment," Dov hurried to the wings. From there, he reviewed the Auditorium.

It was a massive, three storey, balconied Auditorium, painted all gold. The lower-level was packed with graduates and their families. From the wings he could see: several rows of Lecturers, wearing formal gowns as they sat on the raised stage. A distinguished looking man, in his late 60s, in full regalia, addressed the audience, from behind a lectern. The Chancellor continued. " So without further ado, let's welcome Davey Gold!" This was met with enthusiastic applause. It was his cue.

Dov stumbled on stage with his guitar, to the accompaniment of more applause.

He stood behind the upright microphone and nervously address the audience. "Some years ago, I wrote a song... to ...to mark my graduation, please don't scoff, from High school. And...And... My first public performance. Can I humbly suggest that... the sentiments in this.... This song also applies tonight."

DOV (LOOK OUT WORLD)

Heey Janey heey betty Lou
Uni's out
So pack your bags
There's plenty more things to do

Hey lecturers
Time to close your books
It's over now, your time is past
So keep your dirty looks

The audience started to clap along. The Lecturers and the Chancellor remained stoic, unsure how to react to the sentiment in the song.

Were out of reach... (Fumbled for words)
So... so grind your... teeth... it's time...
...It's time. . .

Dov stopped. He sheepishly faced the audience. "Sorry about that, I've got to cut back on my medication," gave a fake laugh. Then with bravado, added." Let's try again, " performed a loud bass rip on his guitar and began again.

DOV (cont'd)

Were out of reach
So grind your teeth
It's time to be free
Buckle up with me
Now hang on tight
Roller coaster ride (indicates lecturers)
They're trapped and you're free
You've earned your liberty
Look out world you're standing up
You've got lots to prove

Look out world your time has come
You're all on the move
Look out,
AAAAAAHHHHHHH(YELL)
Look out world!

He received. A loud standing ovation from the Audience. Dov took a bow and stumbled off. Two male Graduates, in the audience, looked at each other and commented. Graduate #1, offered. "What a Jerk!"
Graduate #2, replied. "I wouldn't throw him out of bed. "

Chapter 55

Dawn. Next day. Dov was back, at the Hudson- Side Mansion.

Unable to sleep, after a late night gig. He had travelled back to the mansion, somewhat the worse for wear. He stumbled into the semi-darkened spacious Ballroom and found it was littered with party debris and revellers.

The centre of attention was a drug-laden coffee table. Alfonse and Marco, popped Pills and passed a Bong around. Angeline and PK hovered around the coffee table.

Dov wore an old, shabby overcoat, was unshaven and looked washed out. He cautiously approached Angeline, and nervously tried to get her attention. "Hi…Hi Angie, we have to talk," Angeline was offhanded when she replied. "Sure Baby," she was more interested in checking the circulating drugs. Dov was emphatic, he insisted.

"Somewhere private." PK and the Group took it personally and loudly exclaimed." Oooh!" Dov was persistent. "Please," he attempted to pull Angeline away. She finally, submitted with bad grace and they moved some distance from the group, she dropped anchor, confronted him and snapped. "Ok, ok. This will have to do," Dov tried to explain. "You know what happened in New York?" Angeline remained irritatingly indifferent, she casually replied. "Darling, whatever happened in New York, stays in New York," Dov realised he had to be more specific and spell it out, he exclaimed. "No! It's nothing like that I... I forgot the words. A song that I'd written. Performed, I don't know how many times. I...I forgot...the words. I've got to get off all this stuff," Angeline had lost interest in the conversation. She performed a mock yawn and bleakly commented. "G-d you can be so boring."

Dov was apprehensive, but it was obvious he had to explain it in detail. *"Alberto thinks I* should book into detox." Now he clearly, had her attention, she exclaimed. "What?!"

Dov was uncertain and fearful how Angeline would take his suggestion. He was nervous and tentative, as he outlined it. "Maybe... Maybe you should too?" Angeline was pissed, she snapped." So that's what the boys' club decided," It was as bad as Dov had feared. He hurried to explain. "Alberto's just trying to help," Angeline wasn't buying it. She barked with derision. "Help! He's part of the problem. Your small-time buddy, can't hack it in the big league. Get rid of him," Dov was astounded, he gasped. "What?!' He desperately hoped, she didn't mean it. But Angeline wasn't kidding. She clearly outlined it, in detail. "Give him the boot. Sack him!" He realised, she was serious. But it went against everything, he believed in and stood for. Reflexively, he announced. "No! No way!" Still fuming, she ignored his comment and continued to vent her spleen, she barked. "I won't have that little parasite, bad mouthing me."

Dov attempted to calm her down, he pleaded. "He's just looking out for us," it was pointless, she ignored his comments, continued on and barked. 'You can't cope, you book in," she went to leave, but Dov grabbed her arm. He was adamant. "We both need help," distressed, he hoped his song would calm her down. He began to sing;

DOV (COME WITH ME)

Come with me
Jump off this ride to hell
Leave the lost souls and temptation.
Degradation and sure damnation.
I'm offering hope and salvation.
If you come with me. (more)

Angeline broke free. Strode to PK and demanded a joint. The desperate, Dov trailed after her, while he continued to sing.

DOV (cont'd) COME WITH ME

I can't go on like this
come with me
We can't be doing this

Dov was ignored, he gripped Angeline's arm, as he continued to sing. She tried to break away, but couldn't.

DOV (cont'd)

This all-night party scene.
This booze n' drug pharmacy.
An addict's crazed fantasy
This is now a nightmare to me.
So come with-

PK suddenly - wrenched Angeline free. Then shoved Dov. He fell. PK towered over him and snarled, in a broad New Jersey, accent. "Fuck off! Leave the lady alone," Angeline wrapped an arm around PK's waist. They stared down at the still sprawled and humiliated Dov. Angeline grimaced and said. "You're becoming so boring. And get rid of that Desi Arnez wanna be," she laughed, arms around each other Angeline and PK watched, as Dov struggled to his feet. Then, they moved away. Dov remained immobile, as he watched them disappear. Hung his head in despair, then as though he was dragging a heavy chain, the depressed, and shamed Dov, exited.

Chapter 56

Days later. Dov was still distraught and depressed, about what had happened. In his stage dressing room. He sucked on a Bong, on the dressing table. On the table next to him, there was a Hookah and next to it, a full 'water bottle'. Dov tried to disguise his actions as Alberto bustled in. But Alberto saw and all too clearly, understood what was going on. He snapped. "Are you crazy? You're on in five minutes," Dov weaved about, slurred his words, as he lamented. "What is it with me and women? First Jane, now Angeline," turned away from Alberto, and sucked hard on the Bong. Alberto had seen enough and barked. "I'm cancelling the major cities Tour." Dov was startled. "What!" But Alberto hadn't finished. "And booking you into Detox, 'Dov snapped. "The fuck you are!' Alberto grabbed the Hookah from the Dressing Table and added. "And you're not fooling anyone with that vodka," he lunged for the 'water bottle'. But Dov was too quick. Alberto shrugged, still holding the Hookah, turned to go. This made Dov ballistic, he screamed. "Hey! Don't you walk away!" Alberto kept walking. Now Dov completely lost it.

Angeline's threats were still ringing in his mind. "I carried you, all these years. You know what? You're finished!"

Alberto stopped and stared uncomprehendingly at him and hesitantly asked." Are ... Are you saying I'm sacked?" Dov snarled, mockingly. "Do you want me to sing it?" Alberto was shocked and incredulous but managed to retort. "You must be kidding. This is such a movie cliché. Drugged star, boots out his trusty, old friend."

"I'm glad you got the message," Dov responded and cringed, even as he said it. He could hardly believe he had been so cruel and unfaithful, to his trusty, loyal, buddy.

Alberto knew him and cut to the heart of the matter, he exclaimed. "Don't kid yourself. This won't bring Angeline back." This comment hit, like a bulls' eye and totally, set Dov off. He screamed." Go! Get out! Get out!' Alberto with impressive dignity left. Dov shrugged. Took a big swig of his 'water bottle' and sat down.

Chapter 57

At dawn, the next morning. Unable to sleep, after a late night gig. Dov hurried back to the Hudson-side Mansion. He stumbled into the Ballroom. Dishevelled and out of breath, he gaped as he registered the scene. In the gloom. Angeline and PK giggled, as they shared a joint. They ignored Dov. He waited expectantly, but was still ignored. Finally, he announced. "I've sacked Alberto. " Eventually, Angeline looked up, with world-weary indifference and exclaimed. "Good. Now, you fuck off too," blew Dov an air kiss. Then turned back to PK, and accepted a joint. Smoking joints, they wandered out.

Dov was left behind, isolated and excluded. He stood, like a statue. He felt drained and utterly miserable. Finally, he hauled himself away. The anguished Dov, began to sing, with total despair: as he dragged himself through the, deserted, dark, empty, gloomy, Mansion.

DOV (LOVE SURVIVES ANOTHER DAY)

Flowers bloom then wilt, then die
Lover's passion slowly fades slips by
For all things there is a season

But what can be the reason?
For you to act this way
If love is dead, why do I stay?
Loving you was a fool's delight
Deceived me with innocent eyes
Seduced my soul, then stole my heart.
Why do you tear me apart?
You drown me in your lies.
Is joy received worth the price?
You're a drug I can't do without
It hurts to stay, but much worse without.
I accept the shame, swallow my pride
Why fight and stay, stay here by your side?

Clearing away the extensive, thick layers of cobwebs. He entered the dusty, dark, musty Music room.

Because, because the moon will glow.
The tides will flow, the sun will climb the sky.
And despite the pain and all the lies.
Despite a love that daily dies.
I still can't turn and walk away
So love survives another day.

Dov dragged the mouldy, heavy curtains, back and a beam of light struggled, through the dirty windows.

We're actors on an empty stage
A love song with a sad refrain.
Two ships passing in the night.

Why has love turned to spite?
I'm no stranger to this pain.
That I suffer time and time again.
You're a drug I can't do without.
It hurts to stay, but much worst without.
I accept the shame swallow my pride
Why fight to stay, stay here by your side?

In the gloom. Dov slowly trudged down the long, curved, marble staircase.

Because, because, the moon will glow.
The tides will flow, the sun will climb the sky.
And despite the pain and all the lies.
And despite a love that daily dies.
I still can't turn and walk away
So love survives another day
So love survives another day.
I'm in pain, I can't walk away
So Love survives another day
So love survives another day.

Having reached the bottom, of the stairs. Dov hung his head and leaned against the wall. Wryly, he thought it was symbolic. He had now hit his lowest point. It was only later, he realised he had much further to fall.

Meanwhile. Back in Denton, Jane was teaching at the local school. She was in the classroom at the blackboard. Behind her, the packed classroom was filled with cheerful, laughing, young children.

Chapter 58

Some weeks later. Dov had a sell- out, major gig, with over 10,000 excited fans attending. It was at the Louis Armstrong Stadium at Flushing Meadows, in New York. He was on stage, behind the microphone. Beside him there was, a stool with, a 'water bottle', over the backrest, there was a draped towel. Dov was sweating freely, he frequently swigged from the 'water bottle'. Behind him, but unseen, were the Gold Tops.

Dov faced the audience and announced. "Great to be back in New York. One of my very favourite cities. Right Guys?" He made a swift downward hand gesture to the unseen Band. This initiated, a brief Drum Roll, accompanied by a loud Chorus from the unseen, Gold Tops. "Yeah!' Then, Dov began to sing and accompanied himself on guitar;

DOV

Great town, New York is,
Great town, New York is.

Then he yelled. " Yeah. The best beer!" His downward hand again initiated a brief Drum Roll. On stage, the girls responded. "Great!" Then, Dov's downward hand, initiated, yet another Drum Roll.

Confused and halting, he continued. "And the Coke - A Cola is unbelievable!" His downward hand, initiated a bigger Drum Roll. Accompanied by; a louder Chorus from the unseen, Gold Tops. "Yeah. Right!"

Dov added. "Only joking," he swigged from the 'water bottle'. Then sarcastically announced. "This song's dedicated to my ex Lady."

DOV (COME WITH ME)

On a downward speeding spiral
A spinning whirling, whirlpool
Nothing's certain, nothing's real
Can't tell day from night
Can't tell wrong, from right.
I can't go on,
I can't go on.
I can't go on,
I can't go on

Mentally, Dov, drifted off. Forgot the lyrics and desperately improvised.

Can't go on,
I can't go on,
I just can't go on
This all-night party scene,
This booze n' drug pharmacy

An addict's crazed fantasy
This is now a nightmare to me.
It's a fuckin nightmare

The Band faltered and petered out. Distraught, losing it, Dov struggled to continue.

Come hit me I need to get a fix
Desperate for some LSD.

Stage staff hurried on stage and tried to shepherd Dov off, but he kept singing.

Get this monkey of me.
Get a hit, get more shit
Get high, get stoned
Get near overdosed.

Dov began to scream. "This is a nightmare. A fuckin nightmare," Stage Staff manhandled the struggling, screaming Dov off Stage, as he loudly yelled. " A nightmare. A freakin nightmare... A freakin- "

Meanwhile. Back in Denton, Jane had her own issues and problems. It was bedlam in the schoolyard, at the local school. Some of the students were screaming, others were active: playing, touch football, hopscotch and skipping, during their lunch break. It was bedlam. Jane on yard duty, was beside herself, as she attempted to supervise. Futilely, she repeatedly, loudly, blew her whistle.

Chapter 59

Days later. There was a hurriedly convened meeting, in the Boardroom, at the Mega Records HQ, in New York. The room reeked of money and success. Windows overlooked the Theatre district and the panelled walls, were littered with a framed assortment of gold and platinum record sales of a list, of eminent artists. The MD, the Chairman, a distinguished looking elderly man, and the six, formally addressed, cigar smoking, Record Company Directors; were present. They were all seated around a massive, mahogany, boardroom table. They were absorbed by the image on the huge Projection Screen. On the Screen, there was a recorded replay, of Dov's breakdown.

When it finished, the screen, went blank. The impeccably dressed, middle-aged MD nervously, faced the Board. The Chairman asked him. "What do you intend to do?" "Cut him loose. He's damaged goods, "the MD promptly, replied.

Chapter 60

It was now October 1962. Late one evening, Alberto arrived back in Denton, and headed directly, to Jose's. When he entered. The Radio was playing, 'Destiny's Prize,' softly. The Café was empty except for Betty-Lou, reading at a table and nursing a milkshake. When Alberto strode in, wearing a snappy outfit. Betty-Lou jumped up startled. Once he saw her, he screeched to a halt.

They stared at each other for a moment, then Alberto strutted over and joyfully exclaimed. " Hi! You look Fab," Betty-Lou regained composure and jabbed him in the chest, with a rigid index finger. He reeled back, in pain and surprise. She snapped." Why didn't you tell me you were coming?" Alberto was taken back, he nervously offered." I…I…It was a spur of the moment-" stopped, when he received another jab and gasped. She snapped. "I hadn't finished, Mr. Showbiz Manager, who's too big time, too busy to keep in touch with his High School girlfriend," Alberto was indignant, he barked. "I rang!" Betty-Lou strode up to him and retorted. "Once! In the middle of the night. I get more communication from your dad," Alberto asked. "Has he been bending your ear?" She rebuked. " At least, he communicates."

" Is that, what you call it?" He sarcastically responded. Betty Lou nodded.

Alberto, mimicked Jose when he added. "Must be thirty years. I was in the Havana Jewish quarter, wid the Epstein's, they took me in. No matter I'm an orphan and not Jewish. Jacob a great guy. Sara whad a lady. Her heart, "he extended his arms. "This big, then much later my poor Rosa died. I promise, to look after our son. If she was still here, she'd be muy proud of him," Betty Lou was touched and kissed him on the cheek.

Alberto was disappointed, he had hoped, for a more passionate welcome. He lamented. "What's this, a Doris Day movie? How about a lusty home town welcome," he stood straight, arms wide apart, head back, lips pursed, eyes closed and waited. Just then, Jose entered. He saw Alberto standing, with his arms wide apart, rushed over and embraced him. It wasn't long before, Alberto sensed something was wrong. He opened his eyes and saw the beaming Jose. Betty-Lou had observed the warm embrace. She shook her head and strode out.

Jose regarded his son, and inquired." Great to have you back. But why aren't you in New York with Dov?"

" Do I need an excuse to see my father?" Alberto promptly responded. He wanted to hide the real reason. But Jose was still suspicious, he persisted. "Is something wrong?"

"As if," Alberto, promptly replied, then got solemn, as he confessed. "There is a big problem in Cuba," José realised his son was serious, he nervously asked. "What?...What is it?" "It's major. Hang on," Alberto replied, then strode over to the radio and tried various channels. Finally, found what he wanted and turned the volume up. The Radio Presenter solemnly announced. "Tonight, President Kennedy revealed, surveillance of the Soviet build up on Cuba, has found evidence of offensive missile sites."

Alberto was unimpressed, and casually said. " It's no big deal. " But Jose was apprehensive. " Hold on. This could mean –" The Radio Presenter relentlessly continued." The President claims the purpose of these bases, can be none other, than to provide a nuclear strike capability against America's Heartland."

Alberto dryly commented. "It's America's fault. And can you believe it, they're crying foul," Jose paced agitated, and barked." Caramba! I've raised an imbecile," Alberto explained." They cut all aid and the imports of Cuban sugar," but Jose didn't accept this. He snapped. " Castro nationalised all the American companies. They had to do something," but Alberto wouldn't concede this point. He tersely countered. "Yeah! They wrecked the Cuban economy. Castro was forced to turn to Russia for help," Jose realised, it was pointless to argue and backed off, he retorted. " Whatever. This is serious shit. Those two hombres, have their fingers, on the H Bomb button. Testing each other's cojones, " he switched the radio off. Deeply concerned, he faced Alberto and began to sing;

JOSE (THIS IS THE BEGINNING)

This day may forever, change our world.
Could destroy and shatter, our universe.
Bring an end, to our innocence.
Leave us grieving and questioning.
Is this the beginning of the end?
Or is this the beginning?

Alberto, had become progressively apprehensive, as he listened. He now faced the agitated Jose and commenced to sing;

ALBERTO

Can we survive this savage blow?
Has fear replaced, our certainty?
Are we now ruled, by tyranny?
Caught in a web, of insecurity.
Is this the beginning of the end?
Or is this the beginning?

Arms around each other, seeking reassurance. Father and son, despondently wandered out.

Chapter 61

Meanwhile. In Denton. In the local school. Jane was in the foyer, greeting parents as they arrived, for the parent/teachers night. She had a different hairstyle and nervously, faced the long queue of expectant parents.

After she finished, her meetings. The exhausted Jane went home. She collapsed on a couch, in the living area. Then went into the kitchen, sat at the kitchen table, and began to mark exam papers. The Radio was on, the newsreader, gravely reported the news. "Russian ships are on a collision course with the American ships blockading Cuba." Jane was startled. She stopped marking and looked up. The reader continued. "There is grave fear that this confrontation, could result in an all-out nuclear war," suddenly, there was loud knocking at the back door. Jane turned the volume down and shouted. "Come in."

Alberto in Sacks 5th Avenue chic, bounded in. Jane embraced him with surprised pleasure. "Alberto! Great to see you," he exuberantly responded. "Caramba! "Stood back and regarded Jane. "Pretty as ever-and a new hairdo," Jane played it down." I felt like a change." Alberto checked her hands and exclaimed. "No ring, "with an exaggerated Cuban accent, cheekily asked. "Darling, is there no romance in your life?" Jane gave a hollow laugh and pointed to the papers. "My students keep me too busy," she studied Alberto." Wow, look at you," Alberto preened. Gripped the lapel of his jacket, posed and declared. " Sacks 5th Avenue."

"What are you doing back here?" She asked. Alberto was uncertain how to address the issue, he tentatively asked. "How...How do you feel about Dov?" Jane was taken back. This was a topic, she was reluctant to re explore. "That's... That's ancient history," she mumbled.

Alberto persevered, he announced. "But you were our Romeo and Juliet," Jane offered a smile and wryly said. "And look what happened to them," Alberto pressed on. "Seriously,"

Jane shrugged it off." That's life. Same as you and Betty-Lou,"

Alberto shook his head and exclaimed. " But you two. Those phone calls, cards, and letters. Then Bam! All over," for Jane, this subject, was an emotional minefield. It was still too painful and dangerous, for her state of mind. After an awkward pause. She pointed to the papers on the table and offered. "Look. I have to mark this stuff," she started to usher Alberto, towards the door. Alberto grudgingly complied, then dropped anchor, faced her and bemoaned. " I saw it coming. Should have stayed and cancelled the Tour. Could have stopped it," he now had her full attention and she apprehensively asked. " Stop what?!" Alberto was relieved to get it off his chest, he exclaimed. " His melt down. You must have seen it. It's been on every TV Channel," Jane was stunned, silent. She realised, she couldn't deny her enduring, strong, emotional bond with Dov. Alberto continued." He completely lost it. I can't get through to him,"... he beseeched her with a long enquiring look. Waited for her to take the bait. Jane was surprised, as she realised what he had implied. "We haven't talked in years," she desperately offered and hoped he'd accept it and forget his request.

" Come to New York. Just speak to him," Alberto, directly pleaded. There was no way she could face Dov right now. She had too many secrets. "I can't. I just can't," she tearfully implored.

But Alberto was desperate and showed no mercy. "I wouldn't ask, if I wasn't frantic," although she couldn't face Dov. Jane was conflicted. She was apprehensive about what Alberto had implied and deeply concerned for Dov. She pleaded. "You don't understand. I just can't," but had to know how Dov was. She tentatively asked.

How?...How is he?"

" He's on a cliff edge... If you ever loved him," Alberto paused. But when Jane remained silent, he added." "I'm leaving in the morning," paused a second then desperately continued. "If you change your mind," Jane remained immobile and silent. Alberto waited head bowed, for what seemed an eternity, then dejectedly, when she still didn't move or speak. He left. In the ensuing silence, the music from the radio seemed magnified. Jane looked up startled. Her face paled, almost haunted as she recognized, 'Our Love,' just then. Marge hurried in, flustered, and loudly announced. "Better hurry dear. You'll be late for your Chemical thing." Jane was extremely brittle. She snapped. "It's Chemotherapy Mum!" Marge hugged her, they held their embrace, as the music seemed to build and build until, it was consuming, overpowering.

Chapter 62

After his stage meltdown. Dov couldn't get out of the theatre quickly enough. He was appalled and devastated about what had happened. How could he have jeopardised his career, particularly, at a time when things were going so well? He couldn't face anyone, especially the media. Why had it happened? How could he explain what he'd done? When he couldn't understand it himself. Why did he self-destruct his whole future?

He needed to get away and try to sort himself out. He just wanted to drop out and disappear. He looked for a safe, discreet, bolt hole. After several days of scouring the New York CBD. Eventually, he found a small, discreet, run-down B&B, in a narrow, out of the way alley. He moved in and was prepared to stay there, as long as it took, for everything to settle down and until, he was in a more stable place mentally.

After several days of solitary confinement, the room almost began to feel like home. He was comfortable, in his isolation and privacy. It gave him a chance to gather himself and try to heal. Even though the room looked like a pigsty. He refused to allow, the cleaner access to clean it.

He wanted no distraction, or disruption, to his self-imposed solitary, bereavement. After two weeks, he felt somewhat better, but remained a mess mentally and now he also looked it physically. He had not shaved or showered since he arrived and spent each day in a torn singlet and boxer shorts. He sought refuge in a smorgasbord of drugs, which he managed to acquire from the local dealers, with the assistance of the obliging, knowledgeable Concierge. He would spend hours hunched over the coffee table, sucking on a Bong, or smoking a joint.

After two weeks. The coffee table was, now near covered by a big mound of discarded joints and a large Hookah/Water pipe.

Dov had a final suck, on the dope. He stood, straightened up and swayed about. Suddenly, there was loud incessant knocking at the door. Dov was startled, by the unexpected interruption and reluctantly stumbled towards the door. Speaking to himself, irritated, he muttered. "What the Hell!" He flung the door open and revealed Alberto. Dov gladly exclaimed. "Hi buddy! Great to see you," Alberto pushed past him, looked around and was disgusted by what he saw, he exclaimed. " Holy Jesus!" Then, he hastily whipped, the curtains back. Sunlight, exploded into the musty, gloomy, room. Dov stumbled back, shielded his eyes, and barked. "Hey! You can blind a guy. Have you come to share the glory?" Gave a bitter, brittle, sarcastic laugh, then added. "You're more than welcome, to twenty percent," then he recommended sucking on the Bong. Alberto grabbed the Hookah. Dov tried to salvage it. They began to struggle over it. Dov was outraged, he snapped. "Hold on! That's expensive shit and bloody hard to get," Alberto confronted Dov and exclaimed. "Don't you read the press?! You're dead, busted, wiped out. You committed showbiz suicide in front of an International audience," but Dov was in denial. He blithely responded. "Lighten up amigo. Desi's back. You're Mr. Magic, you can fix it," Alberto forcefully responded. "This time, you need to get it together," he confronted Dov and began to desperately sing;

ALBERTO (NOW IS THE TIME)

There's a mountain to be climbed
A challenge to be met
The fear in your heart
Cast aside, reject
The sound that you hear
Is the starters' gun
The fear in your soul
Weighs down like a ton
Now is the time
The battles begun
Tomorrow is here.
Make it day one

Alberto's attempt to engage and motivate Dov, fell on deaf ears. Dov, aggressively pushed, his face close to Alberto's, and barked. " Bullshit! A few days and the bastards will be begging me back."

Alberto stared back dejected. It shocked and saddened him, how out of touch, Dov was. Alberto paused, then walked to the door. Dov remained immersed in his own misery, as he lit, yet another joint. Then gaped transfixed, as Jane appeared in the doorway and slowly edged in. Immobile, he watched her approach. Their eyes locked. Dov was dumbfounded. He stared at Jane and huskily croaked. "My G-d!. I..I... I've –" he was silenced by Jane's gentle finger on his lips. There was a long, pregnant silence. Their eyes remained fused... Then, Jane began to softly sing;

JANE (NOW IS THE TIME)

Give up your fear
Fear on the run
Dreams burning bright
Burning like the sun.

Jane held her hand out and offered it to Dov. He blatantly ignored it. Meanwhile, Alberto remained immobile and apprehensively observed. Dov retreated, while Jane still advanced towards him and continued to tearfully sing;

Now is the time
The moment is here
Victory is yours
Victory is near
Stare it in the face
Feel it in your heart
Lay it on the line

Don't stand apart

Suddenly, Dov brushed past her, to Alberto. Then swung around shamefaced and faced the now close-up, and still advancing Jane, he implored. "I can't do it. I just can't," Jane gripped his arm and emphatically, urged." "Yes you can! " Dov shrugged her hand away. Now he became emphatic and bitter. "No!" Jane urged. "You can do it." Dov was immersed in self-pity and bemoaned. "How would you know? You've always had it easy," he tried to break free. But Jane hung on. They struggled, for some moments. Finally, she had his full attention and direct eye contact. Maintaining it, she reached up and with a slow, considered movement, removed her, Hair/Wig. She was completely- bald.

Her revelation was greeted with astounded, immediate and unbearable silence. She stood rigid, as she tried to hold it together and suffered their amazed, horrified, inspection. Finally, she managed, a halting, tearful. "I...I... I'm waiting on the latest results." Dov was devastated, he emotionally pleaded. "I'm sorry ...I- -I didn't know... I'm so sorry," he felt such a thoughtless, self-centred fool. Then, he had a lightbulb moment and wondered whether, Jane's revelation, was the reason for her decision to stay in Denton? He had imagined all sorts of bizarre reasons, but never this. If this was the reason, then she had been selfless, in not revealing it and spared him the agony of deciding whether to stay or go. He'd like to think he would have stayed. But now, they would never really know. In retrospect, his paranoid speculations had been absurdly wrong. Ironically, her silence turned out to be, the pivotal key, to his subsequent success. He owed her more, than he could ever repay.

But would he ever have the chance, to make it up to her? He needed to demonstrate his love. The fates had been cruel. The full consequence of her revelation, now sank in. He was shattered and inconsolable. He attempted to choke back tears and covered his face, with his hands. Jane and Alberto stared at him for a moment. When he began to weep, they slipped out.

Dov broke down and sobbed, he tearfully begged. "Please dear G-d. Her students worship her. You can't take her from them," heartbroken, he began to sing, with utter despair;

DOV (IT'S YOU THAT I NEED)

She fills their soul, with happiness
If she goes there's emptiness
She's the air that they breathe
The blood that they need
She lifts up their soul, to the sky
She's the one that they need
Don't ever take her from them.
Please don't take her from them.

Dov got down on bent knees. Took a handkerchief from his pocket, placed it on his head, looked skyward and continued to sing.

DOV

Begging you on my knees
Please don't let her die
Let her live out her life

Dov decided to make a sacred commitment to G-d, regarding Jane. It was the least he could do, given what she had done and experienced. He stood, looked skyward and tearfully vowed. "I swear, I will never touch drugs again. Just don't take Jane."

Chapter 63

Some days later. Early one morning, while the city was still not fully awake. The side-walks were near deserted and there were only a few passing cars. Alberto dragged a reluctant Dov along the sidewalk, in the New York CBD. Dov was annoyed and puzzled, he irritably asked. "Why did you drag me out, at this ungodly hour? What the hell are we doing here?" Alberto smiled mysteriously, as he smugly answered. "Relax. I want to show you something interesting."

They walked along the deserted sidewalk, turned a corner and were confronted by, a massive queue of people, mainly under 25 and alternate looking. They had blocked the sidewalk and spilled onto the Street. The queue snaked along, as far as the eye could see. They were forced to stop. They crossed to the other side of the road and curiously walked parallel to the queue. Dov was intrigued and asked. "Is someone handing out money?" Alberto remained smugly silent. He grabbed Dov by the arm and they began to jog towards the head of the queue. Finally, they arrived, near the head of the queue. It was now evident, that the queue's target was, a massive Record store. Alberto pointed and released a loud, cynical Laugh, then he jubilantly, announced. "Since your stage rant, you've become a teen antihero. A megastar!"

Chapter 64

Some days later. Back in New York. In the Boardroom, of the Mega Records HQ. The Record Company Directors and Chairman, were again, sitting around the large, mahogany, boardroom table. There had been a hastily rescheduled emergency meeting of the board.

They were absorbed with the MD's slide presentation. He was outlining, Davey's recent record sales with a long pointer. "As you can see. Since his meltdown, his record sales have gone ballistic. This guy's become huge!" The Chairman confronted him and snapped. "But his contracts void. What are you going to do?" The MD backpedalled, quickly responded. "Everyone deserves another chance. Currently, I'm in discussion with his manager," the Record Company Directors and the Chairman remained silent but exchanged cynical looks. The MD was astute enough to notice, but too smart to comment. He fidgeted and shuffled silently.

Chapter 65

Alberto was pleased, but not overly surprised when, he received an urgent call from the Mega Records MD. They arranged to have a meeting at the Mega Records HQ, the following week. By a bizarre twist of fate, it seemed that Dov's career and to some extent his own, had been given a new lease of life, a second chance. Instead of being washed up, and blackballed. As a result of the bizarre public reaction, Dov had somehow become, hot property, a teen antihero and in big demand.

Alberto was optimistic about the upcoming meeting. Especially, when the MD offered him a return Business class tickets to get to New York for the meeting and a five-star hotel accommodation for his stay. Alberto was jubilant. It seemed, as if another item on his wish list was about to be kicked off. His decision, to leave Denton, had proved to be an excellent one. He couldn't wait to share the good news with his father, José.

Alberto, considered the situation and decided, he had to be astute with future arrangements and any future contracts. He must maximise this golden opportunity. Excited about their future and bursting to share it with someone.

He elected to ring José. It was a fortunate choice and a most opportune timing, since José also had some news. News that could definitely help, to further kick-start Dov's comeback.

José reminded Alberto, that this year marked Denton's Centennial. José was on the committee planning, the proposed Centennial Celebrations. A number of proposals were before the committee, but the one that resonated with most, was to have a nationally televised Centennial concert. But this proposal had got bogged down, by arguments, on who would headline the event. José naturally suggested Dov, as a local boy who had found national, perhaps even international success. However, he was howled down by the other members. They claimed, Dov's recent stage meltdown, made him, "Too risky, plus, he was not a big enough name, not a drawcard,"

Alberto jumped at this potential opportunity and hurriedly briefed José. He documented Dov's recent, staggering record sales. Plus his recent, long-term highly lucrative, new Mega Record deal. Emphatically, he pointed out that Dov was now hot, a major drawcard. He would be ideal for this gig.

When José raised the issue of Dov being, "too risky," Alberto snapped. "Judy Garland, was risky. But she still had packed live shows and massive TV audiences. They all wanted to witness her, walking the tightrope," José was sold. He pleaded. "You must come to the next meeting and tell them what you told me," Alberto was taken back, he retorted. "Why don't you do it?" José responded. "You're much better at this. Anyway, you are his manager. Plus, this is what you do and you do it so well."

Some weeks later. After arriving back from New York. Alberto attended the Centennial committee's meeting. It was held in the front section of Jose's. Two tables had been pushed together near the front window, to accommodate the five committee members and the honorary committee 'recorder,' Marge. The meeting was chaired by Mitch, the president of the local bank. The rotund, puffed up, 50 something man, thought it was his birthright, to act as chairman. He chaired the meetings, with autocratic distain sometimes, verging on the point of insulting. But the other members tolerated it. Grateful, to delegate the responsibility. Despite his lack of social graces, Mitch proved to be, an effective chairperson. The rest of the committee included; Clem Cornhuckster, José, Bert, the Principal of the local high school and Dr West. Clem had coaxed Marge to become involved and act as the honorary, official note-taker. A task, she had come to enjoy, after her initial trepidation.

Alberto did a slick presentation, and also tabled a substantial cheque, from Mega Records, to help bankroll the event. After a short debate. Dov was voted as, their headline act for the Centennial celebration and Alberto was asked, to arrange the national TV coverage. All in all. It had been a very successful night for the two friends.

Chapter 66

Alberto couldn't wait to tell Dov the good news. He quickly rang Dov's New York B&B to check he was still there. He didn't fancy having to trace him down again. The memory of his initial exhausting search were still fresh in his mind. The days of incessant calls to any and all hotels, bed and breakfast places in the New York CBD, before he finally located him. Still plagued him. He was relieved when he confirmed that Dov was still at the same place. He rushed back to New York and hurried to the run down hotel in the New York CBD.

When he arrived, he found Dov was still in his boxer shorts, torn singlet and was still dejected and depressed. It was obvious, he had continued with his high-level drug use. He and the room stank with the pungent aroma. As Alberto regarded his friend. His buoyant, jubilant mood, suddenly deflated. Nonetheless, he bounded in and embraced the surprised, guarded Dov.

Alberto knew he had to shake him out on his and his self-destructive depression. He stepped back and jubilantly announced." Listen, amigo. You have been given a blessed second chance," Dov was drowning in self-pity and his misery, so the announcement, hardly registered. "What?! . . What do you mean?" He mumbled. Alberto realised, he had to connect with the 'old Dov,' he gripped his shoulders, waited until he thought he had his full attention, then emphatically declared." The G-ds must be looking after you," he held up one finger." First, after your meltdown. The public by some weird, unexpected response, suddenly regard you as a teen antihero," he now held up two fingers." Second. This coincided with this year's Denton Centennial celebrations," he paused, then, he held up three fingers." Third. To mark the event Denton had decided to have a nationally televised concert and were looking for a headline act," now held up four fingers." Fourth and finally, they voted you, for the spot!" Dov was speechless, trying to absorb what he had just heard. Eventually, it all sank in and he gratefully embraced Alberto. Then, stood back embarrassed." I... I. .. I...Am sorry about the sacking. I... I don't know what got into me?" Alberto was relieved, he had his old friend back, he said casually." Forget it. We all go crazy sometimes," but Dov was reluctant to skirt over the issue, he lamented." I'm so embarrassed and ashamed of what I did. Can you forgive me?"

"It's done and dusted amigo," Alberto promptly replied and warmly hugged him. Dov wanted more information about Alberto's announcement, he demanded." So how did all this happen? Tell me all the gory details," Alberto was happy to oblige. "When I spoke to dad about your anti-hero resurrection. He mentioned the Denton Centennial celebration and told me about their search for a headline act," paused and studied Dov, to see if he had connected the dots. He had and gratefully hugged Alberto." Amigo. I still don't know how? But somehow you did it. You are a hell of a Manager. You have managed to turn abject defeat into a stunning victory,"

Alberto discarded any false modesty and addressed Dov, he proudly announced." The opportunity was there. I did what any good manager would do. Took it and ran with it," Dov was still puzzled." But how?" Alberto smugly replied. "Simple. I attended the next Centennial meeting and convinced them, there was only one choice for that gig. They eventually agreed and as a plus, I got the job to organise the National TV coverage for it," he now stared fixedly at Dov and emphatically outlined." This is our first step back. Let's do it and do it right," Dov nodded, but deep down he still had doubts, he hesitantly offered." I...I...I'm not sure. I'm up for it? This isn't some small-no account club gig. This is a huge, nationally televised event," Alberto jumped in. He wasn't going to let Dov miss out, on this golden opportunity.

He stared intensely at his friend, and firmly announced." Step one. You have got to stop taking all this shit and get yourself clean. If you do. I'm convinced you can do it," Dov was grateful, but still uncertain, he tentatively asked. "Really?" Alberto responded firmly." Definitely!" But Dov still, looked doubtful. He needed more reassurance. Alberto forcefully added." I have not the slightest doubt. But the drugs stop today. It's cold turkey, as of now!" Dov went to speak, but Alberto cut him off, he snapped." No buts or maybes. Today, is day one, or I walk," he turned towards the door and took a step. Suddenly, Dov shouted." Stop! I agree," Alberto stopped, turned and smiled, as he approached Dov, with an outstretched hand. They firmly shook hands, for some moments, like true friends. Then the emotional Alberto, stepped back, confronted Dov and firmly said. "Step two, we need to get you out of this drug den," Dov wen t to speak, but again, Alberto held his hand up and snapped. "A new start, needs a new and appropriate accommodation," he made a sweeping gesture encompassing the room.

Dov, still had questions and went to speak, but once again Alberto held up his hand, he demanded. "No buts. "We need to do this, right and do it straight away," he strode to the phone, checked the nearby menu and punched up. "Reception. . . Good. , Room 31, we are going to checkout in five minutes. Could you send someone to pick up the luggage?...Thanks," Alberto replaced the receiver, grabbed a rubbish bin and ignoring Dov's protests, swept the joints and drugs into the bin. When the first was full, he found several more and continued with his housecleaning. During this process, he faced Dov and barked. "While I'm doing this, pack your things ASAP. Alberto continued with his drug project until, all the drugs were in a number of full bins.

A few minutes later. The hotel Bell boy arrived. He took Dov's luggage to the elevator and they silently descended to the Lobby, where Dov and Alberto checked out.

Dov was still bemused, by the rapid sequence of events. He docilely asked. "What now?" Alberto, satisfied by the situation, self-assuredly replied. "We book you into a decent, first-class hotel, that's more appropriate, for an upcoming megastar," Dov was left speechless. Alberto bustled him and his luggage, out the main entrance and to the taxi rank. He found a vacant taxi and addressed the driver. "To the Conrad New York Downtown, thanks," the Bell boy put their luggage into the boot and Dov and Alberto got into the taxi.

<h1 style="text-align:center">Chapter 67</h1>

After a few minutes. Their taxi pulled up outside the Conrad New York Downtown. Several hotel Bell boys converged and took their suitcases to Reception. Dov and Alberto trailed behind. Dov was open mouthed as he viewed the stylish, cavernous, 10 story high, plush Lobby. A stunning, massive skylight flooded the space with welcoming light. The ground floor was littered with numerous green, luxuriously looking sofas. Dov hesitantly asked. "Can we afford this?" Alberto complacently replied. "Easy, with your new record deal, we got a substantial sign-on fee and an attractive slice of the royalties," Dov was pleasantly surprised, but Alberto had more. "Your upcoming televised Centennial performance, will also be a nice little earner and most importantly, will also give you extensive national exposure,"

The receptionist quickly completed the formalities and gave them their room keys. Her assistant offered to show them their room. The Bell boy would bring the luggage up later. They rode the elevator up to the fifth floor and after a 15-meter walk, from the elevator. They arrived at the door of their room.

It was a bright, large room, with two single beds and had stunning views of the Hudson and the New York skyline. It oozed luxury and style. Alberto, looked around contentedly. "This is more like it. Just the place to get you back to your real self. No drugs, good food, no alcohol, lots of fresh air and regular exercise," Dov was taken back, by Alberto's proposal, and nervously asked. "Are you planning some sort of boot camp"? Alberto complacently nodded. He brought out an exercise book and showed Dov, a page filled with a detailed timetable. Dov scanned it, then incredulously asked. "I don't believe this. Are you serious?" Alberto replied self- assuredly. "Hundred percent!" Dov wouldn't accept it, he grabbed the book, opened it at the time-table page and incredulously, began to read out loud. "Wake up at 7 am, followed by 20 minutes of exercise, in the gym, or walking around the park. Then we have breakfast of fruit juice and muesli?" Alberto smiled and nodded. "It's a detox and health program to get you in shape. I consulted several experts," Dov retorted. "It is torture and punishment, that's what it is," grudgingly he reviewed the stylish, bright room with views of the adjacent Hudson River. From the roof they could see the adjacent Rockefeller Park. Dov mulled it over and added. "But, have to admit. If I'm forced to undergo detox, this is not a bad place to stay," Alberto was pleased that Dov had become more compliant. He patted him on the back and nudged him towards the suitcase. "Come on, unpack and let's settle in," he grabbed his suitcase and plonked it on the bed adjacent to the window, zipped it open and began to unpack. Dov started to do the same on the adjoining bed.

At 7 am the next morning. They were both woken, by the shrill ringing of the bedside phone. Still half asleep, Dov groggily answered. "Yes?" A bright male voice replied. "Your morning call Sir. It's 7 am," Dov replaced the phone, confronted the smirking Alberto and growled. "It's too bloody early for breakfast," Alberto nodded, grinning, he retorted. "I know. But you need to go for a half-hour walk around Rockefeller Park first. After that, you can have a shower, get changed and then we'll go down for breakfast," Dov vigorously shook his head and barked. "If I'm going for a walk. You're coming too," Alberto shook his head. "No. I'll sit on the roof watching, to make sure you do a decent circuit," ill-tempered, Dov clambered out of bed. He gathered Alberto's purchased exercise gear and went into the bathroom to get changed.

After a few minutes. He returned in his exercise outfit. Alberto gave him a mock wolf whistle and announced. "You look very nice. Quite macho," Dov went to hurl a pillow at him, but decided not to. Instead, he grabbed his room key, strode out and slammed the door, on Alberto's loud laughter.

He returned half an hour later. Red-faced, sweating, gasping for breath and exhausted. He was, greeted by the beaming Alberto. "I think I am going to have a stroke," Dov breathlessly, gasped. Alberto patted him on the back and announced. "Relax. I've got you a pick me up," Dov beamed. "Great. Just what I need. Hand it over buddy," he expectantly held his hand out. Alberto strode to the mini bar, fossicked around and returned with something behind his back. Suddenly, he plonked it into Dov's waiting, outstretched hand. Dov reeled back, surprised, utterly pissed off and exclaimed. "Cripes! Bloody Tomato juice. You're really trying to kill me," he slammed the small bottle of Tomato juice on a nearby cabinet and stormed out.

Dov had a quick shower. He got changed and they both went down to breakfast. This set the pattern for the rest of Dov's two weeks stay.

Dov followed, the same ritual over the next two weeks, he found, his walk around Rockefeller Park, had gradually become comfortable, even a pleasant outing.

Dov became one of the early morning 'regulars'. He was acknowledged by the young children and their parents, or Nannies, on the several playgrounds, scattered through the Park. Similarly, by the regular early morning walkers, joggers and bike riders. He welcomed the camaraderie and enjoyed being in this select 'fraternity.'

Although, his muscles initially protested, gradually they adjusted, to his routine as did his mind.

He welcomed, the feeling of taking, some degree of control, of his life. After a few days, he found the exertion easier, something he could do automatically, while he switched off, it almost fell, like a period of meditation.

He enjoyed, the early morning, crisp, fresh air, the light frost on the grass, the small puffs of steam which accompanied, each laboured breath and the associated sense of inner peace, and tranquillity.

Gradually, Dov felt his energy and his enthusiasm for life slowly returning. What surprised him most, after a week of this regimen. He had no major craving for drugs and little interest in alcohol.

On the 14th day, Alberto faced him and proudly announced. "Amigo, you're back. Ye of little faith. I said you could do it," Dov nodded, hugged his friend and declared. "I'm lucky to have such a loyal and caring friend and as a bonus, such a great manager," he felt he was ready to face the world, even the media.

Chapter 68

One evening. Weeks later. Dov and Alberto were back in Denton. Dov nervously entered Jose's. He was smartly dressed and looked healthy. He was trailed by Alberto. The Café was near-empty. Dov had a feeling of extreme déjà vu. He couldn't get over it. After all that had happened, here he was back in Denton. Not just back, but the headline act, for the upcoming Centennial celebration. Talk about a comeback, from the brink of, utter defeat. He was excited and also terrified. He remained, apprehensive, how he would cope with the pressure. Would he be able to perform, on this huge occasion? He couldn't mess up this golden, second chance. He had massive doubts.

He checked Jose's. Everything looked the same, except Jose, was now clean shaven. He stood on a stepladder, as he took the Che Guevera photo down.

Dov looked around and musingly commented. "Looks smaller."

Alberto advised." You should be having an early night."

Jose turned to Dov. "You're always welcome, but Alberto's right. This Concert... is... it's stupendous," he crossed himself and added." I have been praying for weeks."

Dov was self-deprecating, when he replied. "You're not alone. Who'd have thought? Here's Little Richard, leaving the Seminary. But both of us, trying for a comeback," Jose gave him an encouraging wave and left.

Dov sauntered to the jukebox, checked the song menu and exclaimed. "Even the songs haven't changed, there's - Oh shit!" Clasped his Head, in agony as he moaned. "My head!" Extended, shaking hands, towards Alberto and muttered. "Look at my hands," doubled up. "I think I'm going to throw up," Alberto tried to reassure him, he casually snapped. "You'll be okay".

"No way I can do the show like this," Dov lamented

"It will be ok. You've been dry for over two weeks," Alberto wryly replied.

" No wonder I feel so great," Dov sarcastically, quipped.

Alberto faced the trembling, scared Dov and tried to lift his spirits and motivate him. He began to emotionally sing;

ALBERTO (NOW IS THE TIME)

There's a mountain to be climbed
A challenge to be met
The fear in your heart cast aside, reject
The sound that you hear Is the starters' gun
The fear in your soul
Weighs down like a ton.

Alberto, gripped Dov by the shoulders and confronted him. " It's all up to you. It's not the alcohol. Not the drugs. It's you. Just do it."

ALBERTO.

Now is the time
The battles begun
Tomorrow is here.
Make it day one

Alberto draped an arm over Dov's shoulder. Arms around each other, the two friends left.

Chapter 69

Now, it was the big day. It was night time. October 23RD, 1962. The High School, Basketball Arena, was packed to the rafters. It was filled by all the locals and many visitors from interstate, plus some, even from overseas. The High School, Basketball Arena, had become the Concert venue, for the Denton, Centennial celebrations.

With seeding funds from the Government and from Mega Records. It had been converted into a High-tech Concert venue. The stage had been enlarged and elevated. Extensive lighting and a sophisticated sound system had been installed. The seating had been steeply banked towards the high ceiling, in order to accommodate the expected 1000 fans, plus the hordes of media and celebrities. Above the stage, a massive TV screen had been installed. Currently, it was showing, 'Welcome to Denton's Centennial celebration'.

In the on-site TV booth. A middle-aged, TV presenter, earnestly faced the camera and enthusiastically intoned. "Good Evening. Print media and News crews from around the world, have converged on this sleepy town, for David Gold's comeback. It was in this very auditorium, only a few years ago, Davey Gold made his show biz debut. Tonight's live performance, launches Denton's Centennial celebrations," suddenly there was a blackout, in the TV Booth.

Meanwhile, in the Basketball Arena. On Stage, the spotlight focussed on Jose, behind an upright microphone. He jubilantly announced." Folks, the moment we've, all been waiting for. The return, of Denton's prodigal son. A chart-topping Rock and Roller, the one, the only Davey Gold!" Beat. The Spotlight swept onto Dov, as he strolled on with his guitar. He began nervously. "Thanks... Thank you for the warm welcome. It's good to be back, " then offered a self-deprecated, laugh." Back anywhere, but great to be back in Denton" I ..I... I'd like to sing an old favourite," a nervous pause, then, began to sing hesitantly. His fingers fumbling on the guitar.

DOV (DESTINY'S PRIZE)

Too long I've been burdened by
Other's aspirations
Their alien hopes and false expectations
Worn ill-fitting dreams...
Fears and reservations.
But no more...
I've shed this load...
Time for me find my destiny.

Dov coughed, stopped singing and nervously offered. "Sorry. Too much healthy living," recommenced. But again faltered. Tried to correct himself, but eventually lost it.

DOV

Dream's delicate thread...
Easily broken...
Unravel the web...
Promises spoken...
Have I the will...the courage...
The fire... this...this is for me...
This is my...this is my...destiny.

Dov stopped and stood immobile. He was like a rabbit caught in a headlight. Head down, mute. He withdrew into himself. After an eternity. The Spotlight focussed on Jane, as she tentatively stepped on Stage. Eyes just for Dov, she strode to him and took his hand. It was only then, Dov realised who it was. Startled Dov faced Jane "I... I thought they were keeping you overnight?" She smiled and jubilantly responded. "There was no need," Dov was fearful, he anxiously asked. "Are.... Are you going to be okay?" He waited, too scared, to even breathe. Jane smiled and softly declared. "I... I'm in remission," there was a pause as Dov computed. Finally, the results came in. He gripped the Star of David around his neck, looked skyward and silently mouthed. "Thank you!" Then he turned to Jane and joyfully exclaimed. "Thank the Almighty.. You're okay!" Next, he shouted to the Wings, "Alberto! You know what I need."

Jane, beamed as she turned to the Audience and announced. "Ladies and Gentlemen. I've been asked to tell you about some breaking news, she jubilantly announced.

"The Russian missile ships have turned back," she shouted, as she added. " No nuclear war!"

Spontaneous, loud cheering and clapping from the Audience and the Stage Personnel. Beat. Alberto slipped on Stage. When he reached Dov, he whipped his arm from behind his back and handed Dov the – Hasidic (Shtreimel) Hat. Dov held it in both hands, then - rammed it on his head. He looked skyward and joyfully shouted. "Now, I'm really back!" Jane and Dov hugged, then holding hands, faced each other and sang their mutual commitment.

DOV (THIS IS THE BEGINNING).

Can our world survive this savage threat?
Has fear replaced trust it in our soul?
Was peace just a fantasy?
Can it resist cruel reality?
Is this the beginning of the end?
Or is this just the beginning?

JANE

I won't allow his dream to die
Won't let him kiss his dream goodbye

Jane and Dov, still with clasped hands, determinedly, faced the Audience.

JANE and DOV

We'll struggle to the bitter end
It's the beginning not the end

This is the beginning Not the end
This is the beginning
This is just the beginning

Pause. Jane gently removed his Hat and gave it to a Stage Hand. Then lovingly, faced Dov. She started singing softly. Initially, hesitant and with no backup music.

JANE (TOGETHER)

Long ago a light filled my life
Foolishly, I let it fade from sight.
But in my heart, a flame remained.
Now fate has brought you back to me again

Jane now sang with more confidence. Dov and Gold Tops joined in.

JANE. DOV and the GOLD TOPS

Your love fills my being and my soul.
Beyond happiness, way beyond control.
You're the missing segment that, I need.
Now the jigsaw of my being is complete.
Together we can face anything.
Defy the lions-roar.
Break the chains of doubt.
Together we're invincible, we soar.
Now fate has brought you back to me, once more.

Inspired, Dov, enthusiastically joined in.

DOV

I have lived the depths of despair.
Even when fame and glory, were there.
Seeking that elusive prize.
Now I know it's right here, by my side.

Dov and Jane reached out and clasped hands. Holding hands, they jubilantly faced the Audience. As they proudly proclaimed their mutual commitment.

JANE and DOV

Your love fills my being and my soul
Beyond happiness, way beyond control.
You're the missing fragment that I need
Now the jigsaw of my being, is complete.
Together we can face anything.
Defy the lions roar,
Break the chains of doubt
Together we're invincible, we soar,
Now fate has brought you back to me once more

JANE.

In my heart, a flame remained

DOV

You freed me from the chains of doubt.

JANE and DOV

Together we're invincible, we soar
Now fate has brought you back to me, once more.
Now fate has brought you back to me once more.

Dov speared Jane with a long searing look and mouthed, Thank you! He picked her up and whirled her around. Put her down, Jane stepped back.

Dov faced the audience and shouted. "Thank you! Thank you!" Waited for silence, then continued. "Tonight we face uncertainty and fear," offered a deprecating smile and added. "Some more than others. I don't know much about politics, but I do know, we cannot surrender to fear," draped an arm around Jane's waist, pulled her close, then continued. "And together, we can face anything," he now started softly, singing solo; without any backup.

DOV (NOW IS THE TIME.)

When fate smiles on you
And you sit out deaths dance
Our world, love, life, and dreams
Gets a reprieve, a gift second chance
Answer the call, make sure you advance.
Thank fate you've been granted, a gift second chance.
There's still mountains to be climbed
More challenges to be met
the fear in your heart, cast aside, reject

The sound that you hear
Is the starters gun
The fear in your soul
Weighs down like a ton.

Jane, Gold Tops and Backup Singers, all joined in.

DOV, JANE, GOLD TOPS and BACKUP SINGERS

Now is the time the
battle's begun
Grab second chance
make it day one

DOV

Give up your fear
Fear on the run
Dreams burning bright
Burning like the sun

Dov held his hand out to Jane. She eagerly took it. They joyfully sang together.

DOV and JANE

Step to the line
Together as one
This is the start
The start of our run

Holding hands Alberto and Betty-Lou skipped on Stage. Followed by Jose, Marge and Clem... The GROUP joined the singing.

DOV, JANE, and GROUP

Now is the time
Time to advance
The moment is here
Grab second chance
Victory is near
It's in your face
It's in your heart
Lay it on the line
Don't stand apart
Now is the time
Time to advance
Line in the sand
Grab second chance
Come take a stand
Now is the time
Now is the start
This is the time
Don't stand apart
Divided we're doomed
United we stand
This is the time
To put up your hand

the Graduates of 57 in their old high school uniforms -surged forward. Bob and Rip in their football jumpers, surged on Stage. Followed by the 'Jocks' and 'Jocketts'. The ENSEMBLE joined the singing.

DOV, JANE, the GROUP and ENSEMBLE

Now is the time
Get fire in your gut
Grab second chance
Time to advance
Snap out of your rut
Now is the time
Now is the start
Don't stand apart
Now is the time
Time to advance
Now is the time
Grab second chance
Now is the time
Now is the time
Now is the time
Now is the time
Now is the time
Now is the time
Now is the time
Now is the time!
CURTAIN DOWN.

Chapter 70

After the show. Jane, Dov, Alberto, the Band and all the Cast were gathered, back in the Dressing Room. The Basketball Arena's, change room had been converted into a large, stylish Dressing Room. The mood was triumphant, and jubilant in the crowded space.

Alberto faced Dov and declared. "I kept my promise and made you a star – twice," he boasted. Dov was buoyant, but more by Jane's announcement, then the show, his principal feeling regarding the show, was-utter relief. He had done it, all be it, by the skin of his teeth. Was it enough? He wondered. He cautiously offered. "Let's see what the critics write, before we get too carried away," however, Alberto would not be deterred, he shrugged and offered. "Okay. Let's check the papers tomorrow. But I'm betting, they'll give you a resounding thumbs up," Jane joined in and enthusiastically added. "It was great. You heard the audience!" Dov faced his friends, the crew and emotionally exclaimed. "I couldn't have done any of this without you", then indicated Jane and Alberto and added. "Especially you two", touched Alberto and Jane hugged him. For a moment the trio, relished a group hug amidst, the laughing, loud, cheerful chatter. Finally, Dov stepped back, faced Jane and nervously asked. "Are you really all right?" Jane touched by his concern and emotion, emphatically nodded and kissed him on the cheek.

Early next morning, the trio were joined by the Cornhucksters and José, at José's. They had pushed two tables together and were crowded around it. The tables were covered by a huge pile of assorted newspapers.

The group eagerly leafed through them checking the items. Finally, Alberto triumphantly announced. "Listen to this," he began to elatedly read the review. "If you didn't see last night's Denton's Centennial Celebration. You missed a wonderful concert. It was magical. Dov Goldstein, is well and truly back. What a great talent," Alberto faced the group and declared. "The rest of the reviews are much the same," this was greeted by loud cheers, clapping and prominent table thumping. He waited for the excitement to subside, faced Dov and added. "Amigo you are definitely back and better than ever," Dov offered a grateful nod, but seemed more focused on Jane. He affectionately embraced her and tenderly kissed her on the cheek.

Hesitantly, Dov dared to wonder. This all seemed, like the stuff of fairy tales. Too good to be true. But then, sometimes fairy tales do come true? He hoped and prayed, this was such a time?

PART 2.
24 YEARS LATER.
1981.

South Williamsville, Buffalo, New York State

Jane and Dov lounged on the window seat of the prominent bay window in their South Williamsville, lounge room. The window overlooked the small, back garden, with a lush green lawn, bordered by alternating, pink and light violet, flourishing hydrangea bushes. The winter sun streamed through the window and with the aid of the wood-burning open fireplace, made the room comfortably cosy.

Along one wall, there was a tall, near ceiling height bookcase, crammed with an assortment of leather bound and hardcover books. The opposite wall was dominated by Marge's, retrieved and lovingly restored large side dashboard minus her beloved Moorcroft pottery. Replaced by an assortment of small framed photos. In the middle of the room, there was a large oval mahogany table, big enough to seat eight people. It was decked out in white linen and set for two. The decorative, China dinner plates and the silver cutlery, clear evidence of a recent meal. At the end of the room, the wood-burning open fireplace, crackled and filled the room with warmth and a delightful aroma.

Dov and Jane nursed a glass of red wine, while they contentedly leaned against each other on the window seat. Dov raised his glass and clinked it with Jane's, as he offered a toast. "To us," Jane eagerly responded. "To us", then reflectively added. "My goodness how time flies. I can't believe we're planning our 18th wedding anniversary," Dov put his glass down, embraced her, tenderly kissed her on the cheek and emotionally whispered. "I'm an extremely lucky man," Jane was touched and responded. "I'm lucky too. But how so, for you?" Dov ardently continued. "Not only was she," quickly corrected himself. "Is she beautiful," indicated the dinner table and continued. "She is a superb cook and astonishingly she happened to love me," Jane was moved, but offered a question. "How could you tell?" Dov willingly explained. "Despite your parents' objections, you were willing to leave Denton and live in New York State, with a penniless ultra-religious Jew and a wannabe singer–songwriter," Jane smiled at his fervour and teasingly countered. "But does that prove love?" Dov conceded. "It goes a long way, but the clincher was your willingness to convert to Judaism, despite your parents and your own upbringing", now it was Jane's turn to concede. "The two-year intensive study, was challenging. But coming from a family with four generations of Cantors, I knew Judaism meant a lot to you and to any of your future children. From my research. I realised Jewish denominations defined "Who is a Jew? Through Matrilineal descent," took a deep breath and emotionally exclaimed. "So yes. I love you very much. But what gave me the confidence and courage to make this major decision, was the story of how, your mother did the same thing, before she married your father. She did it because of her love for him and in view of his long-standing Jewish heritage. I felt, I could do no less," Dov tried, but failed to hide his joy and tears. He jumped up and strode to the sideboard, selected a framed photo, strode back to Jane and showed it to her, as he emotionally said. "You were the most beautiful young woman, I'd ever seen," Jane was deeply affected, but attempted to lighten the mood, as she quipped. "Come on. Who's surprised? You were living like a Monk." Dov was unable to refute this blatant truth, mused, then tentatively sought some personal information. "So what was your first impression of me?" Jane was brutally honest.

"You know. Utter shock and horror.

"Thank you," he ruefully responded.

"My goodness. You looked like some sort of alien," she teasingly, explained.

"So, what changed?" He asked, fishing.

She mulled it over, then replied. "After a while, I saw through the external trappings and fell in love."

"But, with what?" Dov continued to seek information.

Jane knew him too well. She mockingly offered. "You're looking for compliments."

"Of course," Dov confessed.

Jane considered and then confidently responded. "Okay. I liked the way you stood up for yourself. Not to mention your sensitivity."

"I assumed it was because, I was so cool." Dov attempted to keep it light, with some self-deprecation.

"Ditching those clothes, and all that hair helped. Playing a mean guitar didn't hurt either. I always had a soft spot for Elvis," Jane explained.

"What about our first kiss? Now that was something special," he announced, as he continued with his probing.

"Remind me," she teasingly said. He leaned forward and wildly kissed her on the mouth. She passionately kissed him back. He mulled it over, then gazed curiously, at her, then tentatively asked. "Are you having dessert?" There was a brief moment before she ardently replied. "You are dessert," he jumped up and eagerly exclaimed. "Then, let's go," holding hands they bustled out.

Later, they were lying naked in bed, holding each other. As their breathing settled, and the sweat dried, soon, they drifted off to sleep. They were both thankful that despite 18 years of marriage, their sex life remained robust and eminently satisfying. However, neither voiced these sentiments. Both were too shy and reticent.

The shrill ringing phone, rudely woke them. Jane fumbled for it, on the bedside table and softly said. "Hello," a female voice said. "Darling it's me. Just rang to congratulate you, on your anniversary."

"Oh, Mum! That's very thoughtful, but -" her mother cut in.

"Jane, I know what this 18th anniversary means, to both of you. How meaningful, 18, 'Chai,' is in the Hasidic calendar. I—"

This time. Jane cut in "Mum, that's nice but-" Her mother rushed on. "Dov explained that the Hebrew word Chai, translated into English means, life. Within the Jewish faith, the word possesses both numerical and symbolic meaning. The letters of the word Chai, add up to 18. For this reason 18 is a spiritual number in Judaism. I-" again, Jane cut in. "It's all right mum, do you know what?—" her mother was unstoppable.

"Your husband has four generations of Hasidic cantors in his family, so obviously, this is a major anniversary."

"Mum, mum, do you know what time it is here? It's Two o'clock in the morning," the exasperated Jane explained.

"Oh, I had no idea. I'm so sorry," her mother crestfully responded.

Jane replaced the phone, turned to Dov and commented. "Mum's just trying to be nice." Dov grunted, then complained, "Your mother still can't comprehend the concept of the time difference, with Denton."

"Oh, you know Mum. . . She means well. It's a shame, she won't be able to come to our anniversary. I –" Dov cut in. "Her brother needs her. She is his carer. There is no one else. There is no way, she could leave him for several weeks," Jane emotionally responded. "I know and understand. But I and our children really miss her."

"Maybe, at some stage, we could all travel to Denton. Wouldn't that be great?" Dov offered.

"Really? That would be wonderful," Jane eagerly responded. Dov reflected, then commented. "Remember, how lost she was after Clem suddenly died, some years ago. Now, she has found a focus, a role and apparently has met someone else." "Yes. I understand, but the kids loved her when she temporally stayed with us, after dad died. They still talk about her,"

Dov acknowledged her conflict with a gentle kiss on the cheek, then rolled over.

They were both asleep, when the phone rang again.

Jane picked it up, and guardedly asked "Hello?!"

"Jane. It's me. Just want to say how sorry I am for waking you up just now. So silly of me-" Jane brusquely cut in. "Thanks, mum. Try not to do it again, goodnight!" She rang off. Cuddling, they floated off again.

Until, the insistent ringing of the phone, again woke them. Dov heard Jane pick up and snap. "Oh, mum! For heaven's sake," a pause while she listened, then, in a guarded tone said. "Oh sorry. Hold on, I'll get him."

Dov groped for the bedside clock—it was 3 AM. He held his breath. No one rang at that hour with good news. Jane handed him the phone with a terse comment. "It's long distance." Dov's heart was pounding. He anxiously took the receiver and managed to say, "Hello," no one answered. "Hello," he repeated.

A deep, New Jersey sounding male voice, hesitantly asked. "Is this Mr. Dov Goldstein?"

"Yes. What is it?" Dov apprehensively replied.

"This is the New York City Police Department, in Lafeyette Street. I'm Detective Constable O'Reilly. I've been trying to contact you for some hours, but your phone's been engaged. It's in regard to your son Jacob."

Dov listened with mounting apprehension. His whole world focused on the voice. He crushed the phone to his ear and clutched it, like a lifeline.

"He was found in his flat, in a coma," the voice said. After the word coma, Dov found himself choking. His senses now amplified, as he fearfully waited for each, subsequent word. Relentlessly the voice continued. "The ambulance personnel tried CPR, but he couldn't be revived. At present, he's in ICU on life support." Dov gasped, "Oh no!"

"I gave the hospital your details, in case there's any change in his condition. Have you got a pen? I'll give you their contact information," the voice added.

Dov wrote it down, while the fearful Jane watched and anxiously asked, "What is it?" Dov replaced the phone and told her what he had just heard.

"Oh, Dov!" Jane tearfully gasped, then driven by a desperate need, apprehensively asked. "But?... But, he'll be all right?" Sobbing she added. "Please pray to G-d."

Dov was shaken by her obvious grief. Devastated, he couldn't give her the reassurance she so desperately sought. So he did the best he could, he offered. "He's in a top hospital, under expert care," Jane wasn't fooled, she knew him too well. After a moment, her fear turned to anger, she growled. "I told you he shouldn't go. How could you let this happen?" Dov reeled back, as though he'd been king hit.

Guiltily, he recalled their argument after witnessing Jacob's, last public gig. Bursting with pride, Jacob had faced them and eagerly announced, "Watch out, New York. Another Goldstein is on his way." Jane had been startled, she turned to Dov, mortified. "He's so young. I can't bear to see him go."

"Come on. I was the same age when I went away," he replied.

"And look what happened to you," she bitterly snapped.

"He's a young adult. We can't keep him locked up."

"Let him be a singer-songwriter here," she pleaded.

"That's not possible. He has to go overseas, to fine tune and showcase his craft," he asserted. Jacob, tired of it all, had determinedly announced, "Mum, I'm going with, or without your permission." Dov had turned to Jane and commented. "Your baby, seems to have grown up."

Struggling with her emotions, Jane now lamented. "I just wanted him safe," then placed a tender hand on Dov's arm. As Jane recalled that event, tears now cascaded and she pitifully, repeated, "I just wanted him to be safe."

Dov took her in his arms. "It's okay. Let it all out." Her crying dwindled. She took several deep breaths and tried to compose herself and announced. "We'll have to go there, as soon as possible."

-"Yes," Dov emphatically replied, on autopilot, but then as an afterthought added. "What about the children?"

Jane, ever practical, took a moment to embrace him then offered an affectionate smile, as she said. "Don't worry, love. Uncle Rueben and Aunt Ruth would be happy to look after them," he felt blessed. Despite the tragedy, she had harnessed her practicality and resolve.

The phone call left them devastated. The death of his parents a lifetime ago, introduced Dov to pain and grief. But that was no preparation for this dreadful doubt. This was his son!

Arms still around each other, they robotically, made their way to Jacobs's bedroom. After he'd left. Jane had made it soldier barrack neat and tidy. It had taken on the aura of a shrine. Bed made. Clothes folded. Shelves arranged. On one, his sporting trophies. On another, his musical awards. A third was lined with photos. Together, they comprised the bare-boned, bitter plot points of a promising life, cruelly paused. Nothing for them there, except more grief and bittersweet memories.

Dov's eyes were drawn to the row of photos, each triggered a series of memories. Each one, a needle driven into his already bleeding heart.

Photos of Baby Jacob cradled by a glowing Jane and the fulfilled, excited Dov. He recalled how Jacob had cuddled up, his delightful baby smell.

Photo of Jacob aged two, laughing in the stroller, pushed around Buffalo by his proud parents, doing the rounds of friends. In the background, the Buffalo Movie theatre. When Jacob was in his teens, Dov would take him there, to see the double features. They would sit in the dark, entranced by the images on the screen. Sometimes, during a tense, or a romantic scene, they would hear a loud clatter as some kid rolled a handful of Jaffas' (thumb-nail sized round, hard, sugar-coated lolly with a chocolate centre) down the wooden aisle. Then, they would refocus on the film and concentrate on their treat. Jacob would unwrap the paper from his Fantale, with slow deliberation and keep the wrapping for a later read. He would hold the chocolate in his mouth and let it slowly dissolve. If he resisted temptation and didn't chew the hard-caramel centre, he could make three fan-tails last a whole feature.

Dov felt, a sense of crippling dread. Maybe, he would never know the joy of watching Jacob become a man. Maybe, never experience the bliss of sharing milestones: marriage, children and a host of other events. One phone call had imperilled that and left a gaping void.

Dov recalled when he was 11, he accompanied his father to the synagogue. Years later, Jacob would tag along with him and seemed to look forward to these visits. He claimed the synagogue, was an ideal place for quiet reflection. As Jacob stood and listened to the soft melodic chant of the rabbi and the cantor, without thinking, he would mimic their side to side swaying and seemed to drift into a state of near meditation.

Jacob's upcoming Bar Mitzvah, failed to interrupt his new-found musical passion. He spent hours, listening to pop music, rather than rehearsing his Bar Mitzvah text. Even then, he had craved to be a singer-songwriter. Dov remembered at around the same age, he had attended the Yeshiva, a traditional Jewish school, devoted to the study of rabbinical literature. But Jacob couldn't be coaxed to attend.

The Photo of Jacob aged 12, with Dov's old guitar. Reminded Dov, of the golden hours, they had spent together, as Dov taught him. Those times were priceless. Dov treasured their shared enthusiasm, when Jacob got it right.

Photo of Jacob, now aged 13. He looked so smart dressed in his new suit, relieved and smiling, taken just after his Bar Mitzvah. Dov recalled Jane crying, in the upstairs, women's section, of the synagogue and his own proud tears as his son, an upright little figure, in his new, dark blue suit and matching yarmulke, had flawlessly sung his Torah section.

Photo of Jacob, aged 17, at his last public gig, in a popular local venue. The tall, good-looking teen, with a small pony-tail, had a stage presence. The stark small hall had been converted into a trendy dance venue. Dov and Jane struggled to stand near the stage, like a couple of groupies. They were blown away, by Jacob's last gig. His son deserved to get his shot. As he watched, it was like reviewing a film of his own career.

Jacob finished to loud applause. He bounded off stage and approached them. Again, Dov had a sense of déjà vu, as Jane rushed to Jacob. She stopped and stared at this, somehow different young man and enthused. "Jacob. You look, that was just great!" They all hugged.

Jacob's final photo. Nervous at the airport, about to head off on his big adventure. Now aged 18: a good looking, vibrant young man, with an engaging bright smile, his long black hair, tied in a neat ponytail. He towered over his mother. In the background, his younger siblings Abe, aged seven and Sara, aged five. Everyone was sad as they waved him goodbye. A bittersweet moment for the family.

They dragged themselves to Abe's bedroom. By the light from the corridor lamp, they could see him sleeping in his football jumper. Thank G-d, he was okay. They conducted a brief reassuring check of the small football-poster-covered room.

Then, they stumbled to Sara's bedroom. She was sound asleep, in her floral pyjamas. Her walls were covered with posters of young film and pop stars. As Dov gazed at his two children, he was moved by tenderness and love that he had never imagined.

Unable to sleep, he rang New York and paged Jacob's doctor. Eventually, he managed to contact the doctor and was told there was no change in Jacob's condition. The doctor suggested that while Jacob's condition remained stable, there was no point in Dov rushing to New York. However, Dov insisted, he needed to be with his son. Dr. Goldberg, promised he would immediately, ring if there was any change in Jacob's condition.

The next morning, the distraught Dov, sought refuge, in a series of mundane pointless tasks: he trimmed the hedges, cleaned his studio, and washed the car. But had no peace from his thoughts. Meanwhile, Jane kept busy making arrangements for their two children, while they would be away. As Dov stared at her, his heart still seemed to beat faster. The years and three children may have had an impact, but to Dov, they were like smile lines, an expression of inner beauty, of life, loved and well-led. Even, amidst this crisis, he could still catch a glimpse of, the girl he fell in love with, as she attempted a brave smile and murmured. "Hold me," he warmly embraced her, felt her holding him and knew he was home.

Over the next few hours, Dov was desperate to know how Jacob was. He contacted Dr. Goldberg again. Jane lingered nearby, fearful, as he was again informed, there had been no change. Frustrated, he felt impelled to be at Jacob's bedside. He attempted to book them a flight, but was unsuccessful. Similarly, he had no luck booking them, a train seat to New York. However, he managed to get two coach ticket to New York, even if it meant, an over, eight hour trip. He bitterly wondered, why G-d was making it so difficult, for him, to be by his son's bedside? Robot-like, they attended to practicalities, their tight held grief, was a self-protective envelope. Until the phone rang. Jane again grabbed it, while Dov hovered anxiously. "What is it?" He gasped

"It's for me," she said, then hesitantly added. "They want to do more tests." Dov's fragile world was now destroyed. Was there no end, to the bad news? "Why G-d? Why?" He exclaimed. Jane saw Dov's rising apprehension and tried to look confident.

They had almost reached a state of acceptance, regarding Jane's health. Diagnosed with blood cancer in 1957, she was fortunate to receive a pioneering, aggressive combination, of complex chemotherapy.

Her New York specialist, had reassured them that after so many years in remission, biannual checks would be sufficient. Dov realised, her last check-up was just one week ago. He broke out in a cold sweat and his heart began to pound. Jane tried a reassuring smile and offered. "I'm sure, it's not serious. I'll go in and sort things out." Dov volunteered to accompany her, but this was rejected. "Having you around, would just make me more nervous," she explained. Dov insisted, "In that case, I am not leaving until, I know you're okay," he postponed her coach ticket and waited for news about her health.

The next night seemed to last an eternity. Desperate for information, Dov again, called Dr. Goldberg and received the same news. They were in limbo. No change in Jacob's condition and on hold regarding Jane's additional tests. Dov was frantic to get to New York and be with Jacob. But Jane's health was a direct and pressing concern. Each phone call was answered, with mounting apprehension.

The next morning, they both dashed for the phone. Jane answered, while Dov studied her face and held his breath. He noted her anxiety and concerned demeanour, then saw the flicker, of a slight smile, followed by a sigh of relief. She turned, smiled and announced. "The Doctor said you'll have to put up with me a little longer," Dov hugged her and spun her around.

He was stopped in his tracks, when she added, "I need to stay a few days longer. But I will come over soon," once again, Dov's face and spirits dramatically dropped. "Why on earth, do you need to stay?" He demanded.

Jane attempted to comfort Dov and downplayed her situation, "It's their protocol. Nothing to be concerned about. There's no need for you to stay." She managed to convince the fearful Dov that the recent good news was what mattered and staying back a few days, was just a procedural matter. Dov agreed to go on the condition that, she would ring daily, with medical updates. Jane was silent, as she reviewed their situation. Then, she faced him and stated. "I think the children should also come over with me? Keep them involved and make all this, less intimidating, for them," Dov mulled it over and nodded. He rang the coach office to confirm his ticket and asked them to hold Jane's ticket for a later date and ordered two additional tickets for the same date..

Dov said his goodbyes to, friends and tearful goodbyes to his children. He and Jane went to bed after dinner. He had a pre-dawn coach to catch.

The long (over eight hours), traffic cursed, drive to Downtown New York provided too much unwelcome, idle time, to brood about his son's condition. The cheerful, informative, commentary from the coach driver that accompanied, the cavalcade of absorbing, fascinating sights, offered no refuge from his crippling self-recrimination and the sense of pervasive guilt.

Dov sat bookended, by a squirming, overweight woman on his left, near the window and an obese, wheezing man, with flatulence on his right, near the aisle. He felt trapped, like a tethered goat. Easy prey, to his rampaging thoughts, they would be his unrelenting and unwelcome trip companions.

Why didn't he stop Jacob, from travelling to New York? Why hadn't he listened to Jane? Why did he pick this, of all occasions, to disregard her opinion? In his defence, Jacob was well aware of the family history and a natural debater, he had presented a convincing argument. He succinctly, pointed out that after Dov's graduation, he was the same age, when he left to seek success. A point Dov could not refute: nor the argument, that Jacob was much worldlier, and because of Dov's success, would have more financial resources and contacts than Dov had when he went to New York.

Why hadn't he sensed something was wrong, when the letters and phone calls reduced and the tone changed? With hindsight, there were obvious signs of trouble when, the pleas for more money began.

In addition, hadn't Jacob's Godfather, Alberto told him months ago that he was worried; concerned, that maybe Jacob was heading down a similar path, Dov had taken all those years ago. This warning from his schoolboy best friend and manager, who had witnessed Dov's near–disastrous issues, with drugs and alcohol first hand, should have raised a red flag. Why wasn't he on the next plane, train or coach to New York? Instead, he took the soft option and called Jacob directly. During the subsequent long, awkward phone conversation, he allowed himself to be persuaded that everything was all right. Nothing to worry about. Obviously, he must have exaggerated everything, in his own mind. But the truth was, inertia and self-delusion, had won. Now, he had to live with the consequences, an endless series of crippling what ifs? Relentless, they haunted him during the trip and would stay with him for eternity. Dov longed for refuge in sleep. It would be a welcome escape from his confronting thoughts. But he was not gifted, such a convenient haven.

As Dov attempted to freshen up in the cramped coach toilet, he faintly heard an announcement, over the PA. "Please return to your seats and fasten your seat belts. We are about to arrive in Downtown New York. We are approaching the Port Authority Bus Terminal" It was an announcement Dov had dreaded. He was about to face stark reality. Splashing cold water on his face, did little to refresh him. As he picked the flecks of paper towelling from his stubbles, he stared in the mirror at a stranger. Who was this 40 -something -old man, with dark-rimmed, haunted eyes and a sagging face? The few clues to his rock 'n' roll past, were the gold chain around his neck and the small ponytail.

The coach pulled up with a slight jolt. It was mid-May 1981, they had arrived at the Port Authority Bus Terminal. By a bizarre twist of fate, it happened to be on the 23rd anniversary of Dov's last visit. A man not unfamiliar with ironic coincidences, this was not lost on him. This whole event felt surreal.

After collecting his luggage, Dov shuffled glassy-eyed, past the waiting crowd, in the Authority's, waiting Hall. He pulled his case and dragged himself towards the Taxi rank. The once nimble, good-looking 40-year-old, now looked and acted like an old man. Lack of sleep and a guilty conscience had taken their toll. With stooped shoulders, he shuffled mindlessly, through the Hall. He was stopped mid-step by a loud call, "Dov!" His eyes searched the waiting crowd—nothing. He took another step, again heard. "Dov!" He stopped and this time dropped the handle of his case. Making his way through the waiting crowd was Alberto's distinctive, diminutive figure.

In the nearly 4 years since they last met. Dov observed that the years, had added inches to his friend's waistline and played havoc with his once proud dark, lush cowlick hairstyle. Now it had become a wispy shower of grey.

Dov watched, as his friend sidled closer. He studied him with surprise. The usually well turned out, Alberto, had a several day's stubbles and was wearing an old blue shiny suit with scuffed brown shoes. But what struck Dov as most unusual, was that instead of bounding up and enthusiastically greeting him, Alberto was hesitant and unsure. This was completely out of character. When Alberto got closer, he stopped and silently stared. How do you greet an old friend, whose son was in a coma, the godson, you promised to look out for?

Dov gazed at Alberto, overwhelmed by a massive flood of fondness, for his old friend and sympathy for his pain. He clasped his small friend, in a tight hug and marvelled at how tiny and fragile he felt. He choked back tears and mumbled. "Great to see you, amigo." Alberto tearfully muttered into his chest. "Me too," they stood for a long moment. Two silent figures in a tight embrace. An island of quiet grief, amidst the chattering, bustle of the crowded Coach Terminal Hall. After some time, Dov patted Alberto, on the back and announced. "Come on, it's Showtime."

Alberto nodded. Arms still around each other, they headed for the Taxi rank. As the pair passed, several people stopped and stared at Dov, as if they knew him. But after a closer look, decided it must be a mistake and returned to their own concerns.

Downtown New York 1981

Early the next morning, after a disturbed, unrefreshing sleep, in his Manhattan B&B. Dov and Alberto were in a yellow cab, speeding to Mount Sinai Beth Israel Hospital. The taxi navigated, a maze of back streets and soon arrived on First Avenue. It drove to the temporary car park outside the Emergency Department and stopped. They quickly got out and strode inside, to the Information counter and were directed to the ICU unit, on the fourth floor. They hurried to the elevator and Dov punched four.

Dov was nervous as he approached the nurse at the entrance of the Unit. He was apprehensive, as she escorted him to Jacob's bed. His concerns escalated off the chart, when he viewed the: pale, comatose figure, with an IV line attached to his arm, and a tube into his throat, for machine-assisted breathing. Jacob was dotted with electrodes, to monitor an extensive battery of vital signs.

When Dov grasped Jacob's limp hand, the skin felt cold and clammy. On the other side of Jacob's bed, a 50 something man, with glasses and a neatly trimmed beard, looked away from the monitors, reviewed Dov and tentatively announced. "Hi. I'm Dr. Goldberg. I assume you're Mr. Goldstein?" Dov nodded. The Dr continued, "We've spoken several times. I'm sorry. I don't have better news. We have tried everything, but so far no change in his coma," observing Dov's dismay, he added. "But at least he's stable," gripped by a compelling fear, Dov apprehensively asked. "His mother's arriving in a few days. Will he still be ok?" "We will do our best. He's young and healthy and that always helps," but to Dov's ears, he hadn't sounded, overly hopeful. Dov struggled to hold it together, he moved to the head of the bed, bent forward and tenderly whispered to his comatose son, "Jacob. I'm here. Please hang in. We all love you. Bless you, my son." Leaned further forward, kissed Jacob on the forehead and whispered a tearful, Jewish prayer. Dr Goldberg, was somewhat uncomfortable, by all the overt emotion and sidled away. The tearful, Alberto, hugged Dov and shepherd him, from the ICU.

Over the next eight days, Dov haunted the ICU. Each morning, he'd arrive at 8 AM, followed by Alberto. He'd waylay Dr. Goldberg, after he did his ward rounds. Each day, he received the same report. No change with Jacob. After his brief debriefing, Dov would sit at the head of Jacob's bed, hold his limp hand and whisper tenderly to him, for several minutes, while he checked, for any sign of consciousness. Invariably, none would be present. Undaunted, he would softly chant a Jewish prayer into Jacob's ear. Still no response. Deflated, he'd again whisper to Jacob as he squeezed his hand. Finally, a last, tender kiss, then he'd dawdle from the bedside. He'd wave to Jacob's Nurse, then trudge away.

Each evening. Dov would ring, Jane and report, no progress. Helplessly, he repeatedly listened and cringed, at her confronting, overt distress.

Chapter 3

At midday, on the 8th day, following his Downtown New York arrival. After another sleepless night and a fruitless Hospital visit. Dov and Alberto were in a yellow taxi, heading to the NYC Police Department, in Lafayette Street. Still, shell shocked and grossly sleep deprived, Dov didn't register events, until they stopped outside a scuffed brown door, with a brass plate, "DC O 'Reilly." Their escort, a young policeman tapped on the door.

A deep, New Jersey, accented, male voice shouted, "Come in," Dov and Alberto entered a small cluttered office, painted a drab shade of grey. Along one wall, there was a row of three-door, grey Filing cabinets. On another wall, a row of shelves filled with a mix of Police and Legal material. Facing them, sitting with his back to the sun-drenched window, behind a substantial desk, was the vague hunched over shape, of what Dov assumed was a large man? With the light in their eyes, Dov struggled to see his details. The man brusquely gestured towards several chairs, facing the desk and exclaimed. "Sit; take the load off." They both did and now Dov could see details of the big man. He was probably in his mid-to-late 50s, unshaven and appeared so bored, he seemed half asleep. His fingers tapped on the desk, in a mindless fashion. The nicotine stains on them and the liberal cigarette ash on his jacket indicated a poor lifestyle choice.

Dov studied the messenger of his son's coma. He had the look of someone, it would be hard to surprise. He spoke in a deep, accented voice that Dov recalled all too well. "DC O 'Reilly," he said and offered his hand. Dov stood and shook it. "Dov Goldstein, this is my friend Alberto Baca," Dov said and indicated Alberto. Alberto and O'Reilly shook hands. Then, they all sat down.

Finally, after an interminable silence. O 'Reilly, softly muttered. "No matter how long, you're in the force. You never get used to some things," while he leafed through a thick file on his desk, then kindly added. "As I said in my phone call, we found him in a coma. When the paramedics couldn't revive him. He was rushed to Mount Sinai Beth Israel Hospital, admitted to ICU and placed on life support," took a breath and ploughed on. "I heard, there has been no change. My best wishes Mr. Goldstein. But we will need to have an inquest."

Dov surprised himself and cut in. "My wife's due to arrive, in a few days. I would appreciate if we could expedite the formalities," while O'Reilly mulled it over, Dov rummaged through his pockets. Finally, located a crumpled piece of paper. O'Reilly watched bemused, as Dov tried to smooth it out. Satisfied, he offered it to O'Reilly and explained. "This is the contact details for Jacob's New York Rabbi."

The puzzled policeman, took it with the tips of his fingers and carefully placed it in Jacob's, already bulky File. Dov observed his confusion and rushed to further elaborate. "I spoke to him yesterday. He's recently met and spoke with Jacob. It may be worthwhile to interview him," O'Reilly offered a curt nod. "Thanks for the info. No worries."

After a brief uncomfortable silence. O'Reilly stood, stared at Dov, and offered. "Sorry, but I need to ask," craving for it all to end, Dov tendered a casual nod and a terse. "Sure, whatever."

O'Reilly appeared oddly hesitant, then dived in. "Has - Jacob any drug history?" Dov was put on the spot. "No!... Maybe?" O'Reilly looked disgusted. Dov darted a pleading look at his friend. Alberto stepped up and reluctantly plunged in. "He'd fallen in with a bad crowd," O'Reilly stared at Alberto and went for the bulls' eye. "Don't pussyfoot around. What the hell, does that mean?" Cornered, Alberto with one eye on Dov, was hesitant. "He'd fallen hard for an older woman and she got him hooked,"

"Hooked on what?" O'Reilly barked with loaded sarcasm. Alberto was nervous. "Not sure...I...I dropped round one day, darted another cautious glance at Dov and mumbled. "I'd promised his dad, to keep an eye on him."

"And?" O'Reilly impatiently asked.

"He was out to it," Alberto answered, decidedly uncomfortable.

O'Reilly pinned Alberto with gimlet eyes and demanded. "What did you do?" Alberto was drowning in guilt, but attempted to swim. "In hindsight. It's clear, not enough.

I tried talking to him, but he wouldn't listen. Claimed, he could handle it," darted, another glance at Dov, then plaintively continued. "I pointed out his dad's history, but he just shrugged it off," O'Reilly speared Dov with a steel-tipped look and sarcastically asked Dov. "His dad's history?!" Dov was relieved to let it out and vomited his guilt, "He seemed to have followed my lead. Last time I was in Downtown New York, more than 20 years ago. I had the same issues and in the end, almost lost everything." O'Reilly now showed real interest, he demanded. "So what the hell happened?"

As Dov recalled, that chaotic and crazy time, he felt mortified and ashamed. But rationalised, it was well over two decades ago; near to a lifetime, if measured against Jacob's age (19), when he was admitted to ICU. But this thought, gave him no comfort. Instead, it felt as if caustic soda had been poured on his gaping wound.

Confronted by his past. Dov admitted everything and it all- gushed out. "I eventually had a meltdown on stage, in New York. I lost it. Hit rock bottom. Even, had thoughts of ending it all," he looked at Alberto, with gratitude and announced. "He found me and brought my love, back to me." O'Reilly threw his hands up disgusted. Chewed it over as he reviewed the uncomfortable pair and laid the trap, as he innocently asked. "Just one more question?" Dov nodded and nonchalantly muttered. "Sure."

O'Reilly slowly, looked from one to the other, as he slowly intoned. "So given the circumstances, and given," indicated Dov and sarcastically added. "Your history. Why the hell, didn't someone drag the poor son of a bitch, out of town, or put him into Rehab?" Dov had been floundering in guilt. His pent-up culpability and regret had been building, and building, since he received the news- now it cascaded out, like a breached dam. He was drowning, he shrilly acknowledged. "You're right. When Alberto told me, I should have been on the next plane, train or coach." Head in his hands, began to sob. Alberto consolingly, patted him on the back, while he glared at O'Reilly and snarled. "Bastard!" O'Reilly was unmoved and remained silent. Without a word, Alberto guided the still sobbing Dov out of the room and from the Police station.

They hurried from the building, managed to cross the adjacent busy, traffic filled road to the wide, placid centre strip, sprinkled with strolling pedestrians, weaving between the scattered trees and patches of struggling grass.

Chapter 4

It was a rare, sunny day for New York in May, (a warm 16° C). Dov felt drained. He stopped and leaned on a lamppost and wearily announced. "Just need a sec, to steady myself."

"Okay, no problem, we'll take it nice and slow," Alberto replied. They doddered and stopped as bit by bit, they stuttered past, the row of shops and buildings.

Feeling precarious, Dov had to stop again. Alberto studied his friend and anxiously asked. "Are you okay?"

-Dov made an effort to stand straight and admitted. "I'm afraid, it's all catching up with me."

"Let's get you something to eat and drink," Alberto replied, as he supported and guided Dov, down a series of side streets.

At long last, they arrived at their destination, West Broadway. Exhausted; like an athlete pushed beyond his limits and grateful, he had reached the finish. Dov slumped against the building. Relieved to shelter from the May sun, under a red awning, above it, a sign, "Cipriani". Alberto shepherded his washed out friend, inside the low lit, comfortably cool, Italian restaurant.

They were greeted by a jovial, middle-aged man with dentist aided, super white teeth that showcased, a bright white, beaming smile, framed by his thin black moustache and a neat black goatee beard. A vivid white apron failed to hide his protruding belly. Alberto received an enthusiastic hug and an ebullient greeting. "Senior Berto, welcome back. What can I do for you?" It was evident, Alberto was a well-known and well-regarded customer.

"My friend and I would like a nice, quiet table," Alberto responded.

"No problem. For you, anything," the man promptly replied and snapped his fingers. A slim young man, with slicked- back, black hair, also sporting a white apron, bounded up. They were guided through the high-ceil-inged room, past the semicircular bar, lined with tall bar stools, with green leather padding, into the high-ceil-inged dining area. He sat them at one of the rear, white-clothed tables, on elegant, green leather padded chairs. Discrete wall mounted lights, provided a sense of com-fortable privacy.

Dov noted the luxurious interior, with a wry smile. His parents had never dined out. His father had been fash-ioned by his brutal, frugal, early 1900 experience. Why pay for a meal, when his wife could cook, so much better? He scoffed at the notion. Dov inherited his father's attitude and dining out, was not on his social calendar, except for special times. Dov concluded, Alberto must be extremely successful, if he was a regular here.

The waiter bustled back with ice water, glasses and menus. Dov was surprised how thirsty he was. He polished off the jug, while Alberto watched bemused. Partially restored, he sat back and studied the menu. The waiter hovered nearby, waiting for their order.

Alberto noticed his friend's hesitation, over the menu and offered, "I can recommend their veal special, and it's superb." Meanwhile, the waiter had come closer. Dov turned to the waiter and said, "I'll have the veal."

"Excellent choice." The waiter replied and looked questioningly at Alberto. "I'll have the same," Alberto offered.

"Bene. Would the gentleman like something to drink?" Alberto looked enquiringly at Dov. He shook his head. "No thank you," Alberto said, then leaned forward and studied his friend. "Amigo. Stop blaming yourself. It's pointless." "I can't help it," Dov replied and even just owning it, seemed to help – a minute, fraction. The oppressive weight that had dragged him down, squeezed his body and made it hard to breathe, seemed marginally lighter. However, he still had this constant debilitating pain- like a phantom limb. Not a minute passed, he wasn't aware of it and thinking of Jacob.

Up to now, they had both ignored, a delicate, explosive issue, the elephant in the room. But now, Alberto decided to raise it. Selecting his words with care, he skirted it. "I … I'm so sorry amigo. I let you down."

"Rubbish!" Dov snapped. He refused to have his friend take the blame for what he considered, had been his oversight. Seeking absolution. Alberto dived into confession mode. "But you asked me to look after him and I was his godfather." "You had warned me and I am his father. I should have come here. I-I-"Choked up, Dov replied and buried his face in his hands. Alberto jumped in and tried to mitigate his friend's distress and hurriedly announced. "But I was here on the spot, you were many hours away. I should've leapt in," settling for a draw, the two friends became silent, as each brooded about their culpability.

Alberto studied his friend, while he mulled it over, finally had a light bulb moment. Excited, he confronted Dov and began his pitch, he announced. "Look. I've got a great idea," as Dov watched Alberto, he welcomed the return of his friends, buoyant enthusiasm.

Alberto with recharged intensity, confronted Dov and exclaimed. "You need to move on with your life and that's impossible, until you lose all that damn guilt." "That sounds great, but I just can't," Dov admitted. Alberto leaned closer and got set to pitch the clincher. "You need a distraction, to take your mind off all this - even for a few minutes."

"That would be great, but I don't think that is possible," Dov conceded. He appreciated his friend's concern and was prepared to hear him out. He was like a cancer victim, prepared to try anything. Single-minded, Alberto enthusiastically continued. "You know I manage some of the cast members of Cats?" Dov nodded agreeably and Alberto resumed. "I've been allocated, two prime tickets, for their upcoming, reopening. It's in a few days' time. I heard it is incredible. It will get your mind off things."

"I'm willing to try anything," Dov doubtfully replied. "

Good. I'll pick you up at 7 PM on the night. It's a black tie affair," Dov now, had second thoughts. There was no way he could interact, with strangers, at this stage. "Sorry. I haven't any, he announced." Alberto's smile was wicked, as he casually responded. "No worries. It's not far. We'll get you to my excellent tailor. My shout."

Chapter 5

On the 10th night, since his arrival. Dov's world irrevocably changed. He was woken from his restless sleep, by the shrill ringing phone. He felt confused, disorientated and experienced a terrible dread as he checked his bedside clock, it was the dreaded 3 AM.

He wondered whether, this was a recurring nightmare, a Groundhog Day scenario, involving the first phone call, about Jacob. With shaking hands he lifted the receiver and hoarsely answered. "Hello. Dov Goldstein."

"Mr. Goldstein. This is Dr. Goldberg... I... I'm sorry, I have bad news," Dov instinctively, dropped the phone, he couldn't bear to hear the rest. He began to shriek the mourners Kaddish (a Jewish prayer, for the dead), as he rocked side to side. Finished, he felt more grounded, gathered himself, slowly picked the phone up and fearfully asked. "Sorry. Please... Please tell me what happened?"

"As you know, he's been stable. But suddenly, tonight. He seemed to deteriorate, for no apparent reason. We tried everything, but had no success. My... My deepest condolences. He was declared dead, 10 minutes ago," In a daze, Dov tearfully replaced the phone. Collapsed onto the bed and buried his face into the pillow, as he suffered, a crippling repeat of the emotions that hit him, after the first phone call. But now, greatly magnified since, he had just been deprived, of any hope.

After a few minutes. Unable to delay any longer, he got up and called Jane. A few rings, then the phone was picked up. He could hear her fearful voice, "Jane Goldstein,"

"Jane...Jane it's me. Sorry darling, but its bad news. I just-"Stopped and gripped the phone as Jane cut in, shrieking. "No! Please don't say it. I couldn't bear it. Pray G-d, it isn't so!" Dov cringed as he was speared by her pain. But she had to know. He braced himself, as he continued, "Dr. Goldberg just rang. Jacob suddenly got worse, they tried everything, but he died, a few minutes ago," Dov was shaken as he again, heard and felt Jane's grief, "No! Not my son. It's so unfair. I can't-"Jane broke down with loud, gut-wrenching sobs. Dov couldn't bear to listen to her pain. He tried to calm her down, "Darling, I'll come home ASAP and be with you, through this," sobbing, she emphatically announced. "No! You need to bury our son. You must stay there. Dov felt helpless in the face of her grief. He listened as she continued. "I'll be there soon. I-"Again she broke down, couldn't continue and rang off. Dov was desperate to try to alleviate Jane's misery, but was mindful of her wishes.

After a few minutes, of frenzied reflection, he rang her schoolgirl best friend. He informed Betty Lou of the tragic situation and Jane's reaction. Without hesitation, Betty Lou volunteered to catch a plane to Buffalo and provide emotional support. Feeling somewhat reassured, Dov now rang his uncle and also informed him of the situation. Rueben also offered to travel to Buffalo, with his wife and offer their condolences and support.

Tasks completed. Dov decided that there was no way he could get back to sleep. He dressed in his exercise gear and went for a long walk. It was a mild night and a full moon. Fuelled by his overwhelming grief and misery. He strode briskly, through the near-deserted streets of Downtown New York, unnoticed and undisturbed except by several passing police cars. They slowed down, and enquired if he was all right? He waved them away and continued until sunrise was imminent, then he hailed a passing taxi back to his B&B. The night Porter paid for it and put it onto his Bill.

The walk had been helpful. Dov was ready to face the day. He had a quick shower, got dressed, had a coffee in his room and rang Jacob's Rabbi, then Alberto. As he briefed his friend, the lurking pain was reawakened and he had to stop. Alberto volunteered to come straight over. But Dov declared it was not necessary. Alberto insisted, "I'll be there shortly," and hung up. Sure enough, he arrived, soon after. On his arrival, they immediately hugged and both started crying. Their worst nightmare, had eventuated. They would have to live with their guilt indefinitely. There would be no reprieve.

Chapter 6

The next day. Dov and a baffled Alberto, travelled in a yellow cab, along a series of traffic filled, winding streets until they reached Manhattan's Lower East Side and the Bialystock synagogue, in Willett Street. They stopped outside, a two storey Greystone building, with prominent wooden doors breaking up the ground floor facade, while stained glass windows broke up the first floor. The whole building was elevated, but could be reached after mounting several steps.

The Sephardic (Oriental Jew) Orthodox synagogue was an imposing building with a prominent dome.

Dov led Alberto into the empty synagogue. Inside, the sun illuminated, stained glass windows were magnificent. Dov nostalgically looked around. The place felt comfortable, friendly. It reeked of tradition and reminded him of the many other synagogues he'd been in, some with his father and sometimes with Jacob. It brought back a series of fond, reassuring memories.

The countless times, he and his father attended the Friday night service. After the service, his father would invite, any solitary member of the congregation, home for a Shabbat meal. His parents had not only preached charity and doing good, they also lived it. His reflections were interrupted, by a 70-something – year old man, with a bushy beard, he politely asked. "Can I help you?"

"I'm looking for Rabbi Abraham Bassous," Dov replied. The old Caretaker respectfully responded, "The service is over. He's probably in his quarters out back,"

"I need to speak to him. It's a matter of some urgency," Dov announced. "Follow me, I'll show you the way," not waiting for a reply, the Caretaker laboured along the carpeted aisle and out the back door. Dov and Alberto obediently followed him, to the single-storey, brick annexe.

The Caretaker indicated, a cream-coloured wooden door and announced. "He should be in," Dov tapped on it. As he waited, he heard the sound of shouting children. He tapped again. The door was creaked open, by a forty-something, Middle Eastern looking, dark-haired, distracted, slim woman. She was dressed in all black: black headscarf, long-sleeved top, and long black dress. Meanwhile, the shouting and noise had increased. Looking past her, Dov could see four young children, loud and vocal, chasing each other around the room. "Excuse the noise. Can I help you?" she asked.

"My name is Dov Goldstein. I spoke to the Rabbi recently."

"Come in. I'll call him," she said and strode inside. The four young children curiously approached him. In the distance, Dov could hear, her shout. "Abraham, it's for you."

A male voice, with a thick accent, answered. "I'll be there in a minute."

The woman returned and gestured to the living room. "Please, be seated. Can I get you anything?" Dov shook his head and muttered. "No thanks," Dov and Alberto moved inside, sat down and waited, while the four children studied them. Dov noted the congested bookcase, crammed with thick leather bound prayer books. It reminded him, of his father's study.

Dov looked up at the sound of approaching footsteps. A forty-something, Middle Eastern looking, bushy-bearded man, with a prominent moustache and payus, in full Hasidic gear, entered. Dov hurriedly stood and faced him. "Sorry to intrude. We spoke on the phone. I'm Jacob's father." The Rabbi extended his hand. "My condolences on your loss Mr. Goldstein. I remember your son, he sometimes attended here," he looked questioningly at Alberto.

"My friend Alberto Baca," Dov hurriedly added. The Rabbi and Alberto shook hands. The Rabbi stepped back studied Dov politely asked. "What can I do for you?" Put on the spot, Dov was hesitant, he finally offered. "Could the Chevra Kaddisha (Jewish Burial Society), pick up Jacob's body from the police and could you arrange the burial?"

"No problem. We have a good relationship with the local Chevra Kaddisha. They will do a good job," the Rabbi readily replied, in his heavy accent.

Dov was relieved. "Thank you. I gave your details to the policeman in charge. Could you call him? And ask him, when the body will be released," the Rabbi considered the request, then said. "As you are aware, our tradition is to perform the burial, soon after death," Dov nodded. The Rabbi continued. "I will speak to the policeman and ask for the body to be released, as soon as possible," Dov offered a grateful. "Thanks," the Rabbi stared at Dov and inquired. "I suppose you know the Chevra Kaddisha, has a strict protocol?" Dov nodded and replied. "But please remind me and I'm sure my friend would be interested," Alberto, quickly responded. "Yes, I would." The Rabbi nodded. "Good. Please excuse my accent and poor English, it's only a few years since we left Iran," Dov hesitated, then responded. "You speak very well." "Thank you," the Rabbi replied, then formally addressed the two men. "Immediately following a death, according to tradition, the deceased should not be left unattended. This is based on the principle of honouring the dead. A Shomer (a watchman), usually a family member. Should stay with the deceased from the time of death, until burial. Obviously, this was not possible with Jacob. I could arrange someone to serve as Shomereim if you wish?"

Dov nodded. "Please see, if that's possible," he handed the Rabbi a piece of paper. "That's the contact details of the policeman in charge of the investigation."

The Rabbi took the paper and taking care, put it in his pocket, and then said. "Viewing is not a Jewish custom, except for identification by the family," the Rabbi saw they were attentive, and continued. "The Chevra Kaddisha will perform the Taharah (purification). They will bathe the deceased, in warm water and dress them in Tachrichim.

Traditional burial garments, usually pure white linen. A simple garment with no pockets. It symbolises that we are all equal in death. Tradition calls for a simple wooden casket, without metal parts. Like unvarnished Pine or solid plank Walnut," once again, the situation seemed surreal. It felt like, he was in a Kafka play.

No parent should ever be in this position. To plan a child's proposed marriage, or the birth of a grandchild, was natural. What they were doing, was against all the laws of nature. It was perverted. He couldn't believe they had discussed his son's imminent burial, in such a casual manner. Each sentence, was as if another shovel full of dirt had thumped on Jacob's coffin.

Dov was brought back to reality, by the Rabbi, as he asked. "Any ideas, about the cemetery?"

Taken back, Dov tentatively, replied. "I hadn't thought about it. But shipping the body back to Denton doesn't seem practical. Somewhere local I guess?" The Rabbi nodded. "We generally use the Third Shearith Israel, Jewish cemetery, in Manhattan. I could take you there if you like?" Alberto shrugged. Dov nodded and muttered. "Okay," the Rabbi led them out to a 1950s, extensively dented green Chevy. The men got in, while the Rabbi sat behind the wheel.

A short time later, the car lurched to a stop, outside the nearby, Third Shearith Israel, Jewish Cemetery. They staggered, out of the car. The drive had been a white knuckle experience. The dents on the car should have warned them. The Rabbi was a terrible driver. Oblivious to his passengers' reaction, the Rabbi was single-minded and continued to stride along the gravel road that bisected the long Italianate two-storey brick building and led into the cemetery. The building had a prominent tower and a chimney, from the crematorium. As they followed the Rabbi, under a high brick arch that divided the building, he indicated and gave a running commentary. "That building contains two crematorium chapels and a chapel for remembrance."

As they continued along the road, they now faced an extensive five acres garden: with numerous large Tombs: two ponds, a bridge, and a large crocus lawn. A gravel road encircled a central area which was dotted with, a variety of different styled and sized Tombstones. The cemetery was encircled, by a high black wrought iron fence interspersed, by a series of tall brick pillars. In the distance, rising above the fence and encircling trees, they saw the tops of adjacent houses.

The Rabbi led them to an area of manicured lawn that had no Tombstones. He indicated, "He'll probably, be buried in this area," the air was fresh. In the silence, Dov could hear the tweeting birds. They had the place to themselves. It was tranquil. It felt right. He thought Jacob would have approved. He was back in the Kafka play. A parent selecting a cemetery plot for his offspring. A nightmare situation. He took a deep breath and with his voice breaking, mumbled. "This. . . This will do. Please go ahead," the Rabbi nodded and muttered. "I'll arrange it. Now, I'll drive you back," Alberto and

Dov turned and with reluctance, faced the prospect of the drive back.

On their way back, Alberto confronted Dov in the back seat. He whispered urgently, "if you don't go to the Musical, then I can't possibly go." Dov was bewildered and demanded. "Why ever not?" Alberto remained tight-lipped, all he'd say, "I just can't." Dov studied his friend. Finally, he sadly offered. "I'm sorry. But I'm in mourning, there's no way I could attend the Musical, less than a month after Jacob's death," Alberto absorbed this information and mulled it over. He regarded his friend, studied the Rabbi, then he unexpectedly smiled and turned to Dov. "Leave it with me, amigo. I'll sort something out," then, they arrived back at the Rabbi's house. As they went inside, Alberto draped an arm around the surprised Rabbi and guided him away, while he urgently whispered to him. Then he separated from the Rabbi and strode further into the house, leaving the puzzled Rabbi, who, after a moment, followed him. Dov remained behind, perplexed, by what had just happened.

Sometime later, the Rabbi returned. He saw Dov sitting on the sofa sipping tea, uncomfortably enduring, the scrutiny of his four young children. He shooed his children away and reviewed the patiently waiting Dov. "Sorry about the delay, but I was having a productive discussion with your friend." Dov was taken back and uncertain what was going on, but tried to appear offhanded, he asked. "Really. What about?"

"He's extremely disappointed, you refused to attend the reopening," the Rabbi hesitantly explained. Dov straightened, confident he was on solid ground and exclaimed. "Rabbi, it would be less than a one month since my son died. It would be disrespectful to attend. You of all people should understand," The Rabbi rocked back and forth on his feet as he formulated his reply. Satisfied, he began in a polite, measured voice. "You're quite right, in normal circumstances. But this case, as your friend explained, is an unusual situation," Dov was mystified and emphatically demanded. "How so?"

The Rabbi explained. "If you don't go, he can't go. He-"Dov attempted to cut in, but the Rabbi: held his hand up to stop and Dov did. So, the Rabbi continued. "Your friend couldn't bring himself to go, out of respect for you and because of some misplaced guilt about Jacob. Even if it meant, he would lose clients and probably his business. He was willing to risk that, but didn't tell you, he didn't want to unduly pressure you to do something, you weren't comfortable with. Dov struggled to hold back tears and was left wordless, as he digested this information. The Rabbi took the opportunity to mount his case. "In this situation, you are not going for pleasure, or to enjoy the music, but would be going as a mitzvah (blessing, good deed) for your best friend. You would be going, because it's relevant to his work and his livelihood and indirectly to yours as well since you are his client. Considering these circumstances, it would be acceptable to attend. So-"Dov went to cut in but again, the Rabbi continued. "Despite the time factor, of Jacob's death." Dov flopped back on the couch, bereft of any further arguments.

A short time later. Alberto bounded in and curiously reviewed the scene. The Rabbi put him out of his misery, he announced. "I think your friend has something to tell you," as the silence lengthened, Dov took the cue, he stood, hugged his friend and tearfully murmured. "Let's get back to your tailor, I've got a re-opening to attend," Alberto was speechless, they emotionally hugged, for some moments. Finally, the Rabbi patted Dov on the back and exclaimed. "Good choice."

Chapter 7

Several days later. In the early evening. Clean shaven and looking movie star handsome, in his new bespoke suit, shirt, and tie. Dov waited in the reception area, of his Manhattan, B & B. On the stroke of 7 PM, Alberto bounced in, hair trimmed and freshly shaved. He looked very smart in his bespoke tuxedo. He regarded Dov, with approval. "That's more like it. Now you look important," he led Dov out to the waiting Limousine. Dov stared and exclaimed. "Wow! You've pulled out all stops," Alberto gave Dov a gentle cuff and bellowed. "Always first class for my Amigo."

It was a short ride to the Winter Garden Theatre on Broadway, but the traffic jam of limousines, forced them to stop, a block from their destination. The cavalcade of limousines and the searchlights that crisscrossed the velvet, dark sky, were dead giveaways that something major was happening in the vicinity. During their walk, they mingled with a steady stream of highly scented, coiffured people, as they converged on to the Theatre.

Outside the theatre, the well-known and the rich, mixed and mingled. An army of waiters, in black and white uniforms, struggled to hand out drinks. Off to one side; on the red carpet, in the glare of bright television lights, a succession of celebrities, were interviewed, on camera.

A short time later, there was the sound of a loud bell. The signal for the selected people, to start filing, into the theatre. Dov and Alberto mingled with the crowd and soon found their allotted, red padded places. Front row seats, in the upper deck, with a bird's eye view of the stage. The elevation and the steep incline, was vertigo provoking, to anyone uneasy with heights. Dov reviewed the theatre; the semicircular levels afforded great views of the stage. The red seats and red walls, illuminated by soft, wall-mounted lamps, evoked a sense of intimacy and luxury.

Dov sat back, determined to try to stop dwelling on his loss and guilt. Just enjoy the show. For a time, he succeeded, caught up in the magic of the show. The constant pain and sense of utter despair had marginally subsided. It felt as if, he had been given a shot of morphine, for his chronic anguish and pain. The diminished symptoms, were liberating, he felt lightheaded.

He sat entranced through Act One, thankful he was thought free. But at the end of Act one, when the curtain came down to loud applause, it singled his return to reality. As he mingled in the upstairs foyer. It returned in a mounting wave. He tried to reassure, the concerned Alberto, but his friend knew him too well.

At the start of Act Two, he thought he had it controlled. Until, after the Jellicle Ball, old Deuteronomy sat down and Grizabella returned to the Junkyard. She addressed the gathering and sang-"Memory"; then - it all flooded back. It hit him like a Tsunami. Memories of- Jacob- returned as a vivid, crashing technicolour kaleidoscope. He broke out in a cold sweat and struggled to breathe. Alberto sensed something was amiss and anxiously asked. "Are you all right?"

Dov was unable to answer. Instead, he jumped to his feet and whipped, his tie-off. He ignored the disgruntled loud murmurs from the row behind and squeezed his way, to the main aisle. Then raced, to the upper circle foyer. Behind him, he heard Alberto's, urgent, strident whisper. "Wait for me," unheeding, he raced downstairs, frantic to escape his memories.

In the entrance foyer, he realised, like a shadow, his memories had relentlessly followed. He erupted, from the building. Rushed past, the waiting media throng. In the distance, he could still just hear, Alberto's shouted. "Dov! Wait for me," soon even that was lost, as he raced on.

Dov strode, along the darkened, near-empty streets, in a random fashion. He had no specific destination. His main goal was just to escape. But his memories, refused to be dismissed or disregarded. They haunted and hunted him like implacable, vengeful Demons.

Chapter 8

Distraught, overwhelmed and disorientated. Dov found himself by the Hudson. Unsure, how he had got there, he paused and scanned his surroundings. Surprised to find, it was late evening and he was on the Hudson Embankment. He paused in the moonlight. Grateful for the respite, he sucked in the warm evening air, thankful for the unseasonal weather, which he had cursed a few days ago.

Agitated, he took another deep breath and tried to damp down his turmoil. The quiet moment was disrupted by, the sound of running feet and a loud. "Dov! Wait." Dov stared surprised, as a breathless Alberto, stumbled from the shadows. "Hold on, I'm too old for this shit. I-," he gasped. Dov crossed and sympathetically, patted his back, as Alberto pleaded. "Please. Stay here Amigo," though Dov loved his friend. Right here and now, his main desire was to be alone. He needed time to compose himself; and try to come to terms with his issues, without any well-meaning interruption. He stared at his breathless, troubled friend and implored. "Please, I need to be alone," Alberto was torn between Dov's desperate wish and his concerns about him, he haltingly pleaded. "Please... Promise me, you won't do anything stupid," Alberto, was fearful about his friends state of mind. He had difficulty, coping with the guilt of Jacob's death. Two also, loses best friend, would be intolerable. He couldn't cope with that.

Dov was shaken, by the level of his friends fear and emotionally declared. "I promise; I won't. I just need to be alone and try to get my head right," without waiting for an answer. Dov turned on his heels and paced away from his wheezing friend. Soon he had the Embankment, all to himself.

No company on the Embankment; except his memories and thoughts, the occasional passing vehicle, and a few semi-darkened vessels cruising on the river. No distraction as he sought to restore some degree of inner peace. But instead, he was bombarded, by a succession of vivid images on his, 'Thought Cinema.'

The opening scene on his, 'Thought Cinema,' and the one that made him vulnerable for all that followed; had taken place, when he was approaching 13 and preparing for his Bar Mitzvah. That was the first and sole occasion, he ever saw his father cry.

Since that time; every time Dov experienced a vivid memory and he had many. It made him wonder, was it because he'd been traumatised by his father's reaction? Alternatively, was he born with a genetic tendency towards this trait? Either way, there was no denying that memories played a huge part and were a powerful influence in Dov's life.

Dov strode with unremitting intensity, along the Embankment. Trying to put some distance between the present and his thoughts and memories. Hoping his extreme exertion, would act as a safety valve for his intense, high-pressure turmoil and boiling emotions.

It had all started, some weeks before his Bar Mitzvah. Following the required routine at his Jewish school. Dov was asked to prepare a 'Roots' (a genealogical history) of his family. His mother's side of the family was no problem. Elizabeth Goldstein ne Cumming, four generations of Irish Catholics, the last three born and bred in America; the last one in the small Kansas country town of Denton. Their names and dates readily available through, Elizabeth mother's well-thumbed family Bible. In addition. After her death, Dov had found and treasured, his mother's detailed, intimate Journal.

But tracing his father, Miklos (Mike) Goldstein's 'Roots', was a completely different matter. For a start, his father's single, remaining record was an old passport and he claimed he had no recollection of his past or his early years, before World War I. However, he would repeatedly, bitterly, recount, details about the virulent anti-Semitic sentiment that pervaded Hungary in 1920 and eventually, led to his leaving and arriving in France, in the large town of Lyon. He was in his early teens and boarded with a Hasidic family.

He would repeatedly, retell, his arrival in Lyon and the subsequent events, in minute and vivid detail. He often entertained the fascinated young Dov, with details of his great adventure.

Chapter 9

Miklos (Mike), had arrived in Lyon. On a cold, dark night, at the Lyon–Perrache Railway station. The young, weary and fearful teenager, gathered his meagre belongings and cautiously got off the train. Aided by the illumination from several dim overhead lights, he could see, the cold, windswept platform was deserted, apart from a handful of other, just arrived passengers. Despite this, there was a strong lingering smell of cigarettes. Though he had only schoolboy French, he was curious and studied the bright coloured wall posters. Unsure where to go and what to do, he buttoned the top buttons of his thin, shabby overcoat, against the chill wind and sought the Stationmaster.

Miklos left the platform and climbed a set of cigarette-butt littered, concrete stairs to the first floor and explored the building. But the size of the building and the inadequate lighting, made exploration difficult. The semi-darkened empty, long corridors were eerie. His footsteps echoed and reverberated in the empty space, no matter how quietly, he tried to tread. He had no desire to linger. Unsuccessful, on this floor -he sped, to the next and had the same experience. Tired and disappointed. He decided to abandon his daunting search.

He returned to the platform and sought the exit and any official. As he moved towards the exit, he sighted a bearded, sixty-something, chunky, uniformed man sitting on a stool. As Miklos hesitantly walked up. The Ticket Collector, reluctantly, put down his foul-smelling pipe. Miklos tried out his basic French. Aided by a series of imaginative charades, he managed to identify himself as Jewish. Miklos like countless Jews, before him, had settled - on the same plan of action. Arriving in a strange town, where he knew no one. He decided his best strategy, was to head to the local synagogue, especially on a Friday night.

The kindly Ticket Collector, escorted him from the station and mimed the directions. Miklos set off in the quiet moonlight, through the deserted streets. He passed a bright lit, noisy Public House and had to shoo off several curious dogs.

After walking some time, he was thankful, he had just a few belongings to carry. Homesick and nervous, he regretted his choice of Lyon as his goal, when twinkling in the distance, he saw a light and in the silence, faintly heard a familiar chant. Invigorated, he strode towards the source.

As luck, or fate would have it. Miklos was still in time for the Friday night service. After he finally arrived. The bedraggled teenage boy straightened his large Hasidic hat, left his belongings in the doorway and sidled into the synagogue. His arrival caused a ripple of interest. Soon, a forty-something, overweight, bearded man, swathed in a tallit (a prayer shawl), strode up and wished him a hearty. "Gut Shabbosh"(Good Shabbath) and hopefully asked. "Have you had your Bar Mitzvah?"

When Miklos nodded, he was slapped on the back and led further inside. The bearded man was gleeful. "Great. We now have a minyan," (Sufficient numbers- 10, to read the Torah). He introduced himself as Mr. Pascine, the Cantor (leads the singing) for this Hasidic (Orthodox Jewish), synagogue. In slow French, aided by a clumsy charade and halting English, Mr. Pascine explained. In recent times, there had been an alarming exodus of young Jews from the community. As a result, it had become increasingly difficult, to get a Minyan. So he was grateful when an extra, post-Bar Mitzvah Jew had arrived on his doorstep.

Following, the service, overriding Miklos's half-hearted excuses, he was guided to Mr. Piscine's home. There he was introduced and welcomed by the family, his wife, Rebecca, a genial, plump, lady. His two teenage daughters, pleasant, but plain looking girls, Hannah and Ruth and their chirpy, ten-year-old daughter Sara. Having heard Miklos'singing, in the synagogue, Mr. Pascine offered to take him on, as an apprentice Cantor, in exchange for lodging and board. A completely unexpected and very attractive proposal that Miklos with few options- accepted, without hesitation.

Living with them, rekindled Miklos' religious beliefs and he eagerly embraced the role of apprentice Cantor, in the small, ultra-religious Hasidic Jewish community.

Some years passed, during which, he celebrated several pleasant, memorable Rosh Hashanahs' (New Years) and

Yom Kippurs (day of Atonements), with the community and the Pascine family. During this period, he remained concerned about his parents and would regularly send letters and postcards to their last known address and even to their neighbour and good family friend, Mrs. Kovacs. But got no response. He feared the worst. The uncertainty was eating away at him. He bitterly regretted his decision to leave. Daily, he would visit the Lyon American Express office to check for any mail (as per their arrangement). No luck. However, Returning back to Hungary was not feasible. Desperate, Miklos wondered, whether his uncle, Rubin, in America, may have some information? With nothing to lose, driven by guilt and anxiety, he decided, on the daunting, hazardous option. He had to travel to America.

Chapter 10

Determined to uncover more about his grandparents and his father's past. Dov had almost taken up residence, in the magnificent State Library of Kansas City. He had trawled the enormous, four level, high domed building and scoured the database- with no success. He had spent days at one of the wooden tables on the ground floor, attempting to sort through stacks of books and files, by the light of the desk lamp with its bright green lampshade. One of the many, bright green, dots that sprinkled the ground floor. But had no luck.

Eventually, he had sought the help of the Head Librarian. In her 50s. The slim, grey-haired lady, had black wire spectacles, that made her kind grey eyes appear, like dinner plates. She took pity on the obsessed Hasidic teenager and a personal interest in his endeavour. With her help, he discovered, that Miklos Goldstein was born in Budapest in 1900, he had arrived in America, in 1930 and lived in Queens. A further search of the archives revealed that his parents, Feri and Maria died in Hungary in 1921, leaving Miklos, an orphan (at age 21).

The Head Librarian, eventually, located a Hungarian newspaper article, in the 'Magyar Iras,' dated May 1921. The article, added further details regarding this event. It was reported that the couple had moved back to their previous lodging in Rakoczi Ut, in order that their son, who had recently moved overseas could find them on his return. Unfortunately, so did the Army. It was at this address, they were picked up and then imprisoned, along with thousands of other Jews, as part of the 'White Terror' period in Hungary. They were never seen again. Their friend and neighbour Mrs. Kovacs, reported.

All this new, unexpected, tragic information, traumatised Dov. He felt terrible, distraught and was heartbroken for his father. It felt super weird, how their lives seemed to have had a parallel trajectory. Both orphaned, at a relatively early age (Dov at 17 and Miklos at 21). It made him feel even closer to his dead father and helped to explain his stoic and reserved behaviour.

Dov felt these additional findings, were yet more bizarre pieces of information, to add to his already accumulated over-full Memory file.

Acting like an obsessive Film Director. Dov stage-managed the scene for his revelation, to his father. On a grey, rainy afternoon, they moved into his father's study. The small room was cheerful and cosy from the wood-burning, open fire, which Dov had pre stoked. They sat on the comfortable, well-worn leather couch that looked onto the rain-drenched back garden. Surrounded by two walls of leather-bound books, which exuded a not unpleasant smell of old leather, which balanced the smell of the burning wood.

Dov proudly revealed his findings, with a mix of anxiety and justified satisfaction. However, as each discovery was outlined. He was shocked to note, instead of welcoming the information, each disclosure was like opening, another door to powerful feelings long suppressed and extremely unpleasant. After the final revelation, his father, began to rock to and fro, as he sobbed with grief. The intensity of his father's feelings, astounded and shocked Dov. It made him feel guilty at the pain and grief, his meddling had provoked. The situation left them both - extremely embarrassed.

Dov was disturbed and mystified by his father's reaction. However, he found a clue in his father's repeated lament, as he rocked to and fro, sobbing. "Why did I leave?" And a final emphatic heartbreaking wail. "I should have stayed", Dov a man well acquainted with guilt, realised Miklos felt an unjustifiable guilt, about leaving his parents, moving to France, then to America. Particularly, as his parents prayed, while they desperately waited for his return. They had moved back to their long-standing residents, so Miklos could find them. Unfortunately, it also made it much easier for the Army.

To date, that was by far the most traumatic event in his young life. By comparison, the stress of his upcoming Bar Mitzvah was insignificant. But to witness, his moral compass, his role model, crumble before his eyes, had rocked his world and his sense of security. The impact compounded by, the totally unexpected reaction, to Dov's hard-earned revelations. Witnessing, his hero's public collapse, made Dov determined, to discover, some more details, regarding his family and in particular his father's journey and background.

Chapter 11

After further, extensively searching, the files and archives. He eventually, established, his father arrived in New York, by ship, in the early 1930s. Miklos, much like most Italian and Jewish migrants, one of more than 12 million who entered America via the portal of Ellis Island, between 1892 and 1954. They required no passport, but did undergo a medical examination and a lengthy legal questioning, all of which took several hours. Before they could step on American soil. Mike passed and found his way to Queens. The bustling cosmopolitan nature of the area apparently appealed to the multicultural young immigrants.

Meanwhile, avidly reading his mother's meticulously kept, intimate, disconcertingly honest, Journal, Dov noted her growing disenchantment with country life, in Denton. The teenage Elisabeth Cumming had become more and more frustrated and resentful, about the limitations of life in a rural country town. She was seeking more from life, than was possible in Denton. Her best friend Marge Cornhuckster (Ne Sullivan), tried to discourage her, but Elizabeth was determined to go.

It was only much later, Dov gleaned from his mother's Journal, what happened with his parents: how they happened to meet, their courtship, and all the dramatic events leading up to their wedding.

Dov was startled and eagerly read, how and why his mother decided to convert, despite her long-standing Catholic background. The bitter conflict and loud arguments, as her family tried to dissuade her from her decision. The striking similarity between his mother (Elizabeth's) situation and Jane's was obvious, heartrending, endearing, and had an almost mystical quality.

All this new information, propelled Dov into a foreign, uncomfortable world. He was forced to adjust his long-standing views regarding his parents. His long-standing opinions, had to be re-evaluated. Elizabeth's conversion, had never been mentioned to the teenager. He was stunned and had to readjust his view, regarding his parents. Although Miklos was a devout Cantor. It was with Elizabeth, that he spent countless hours, during his early formative days. In addition. She was the one that kept the strict kosher household that set the 24/7 Jewish tone in the household. She was his major influence. He had never suspected her conversion. Although, in hindsight. At her well-attended funeral. A distant cousin, previously unknown to the family, had surprisingly appeared. He had travelled from Denton and seemed confused and irritated, by all the pronounced Hebrew symbolism and prayers.

Dov avidly read, how the mid–late 20s young Elizabeth Cummings arrived in New York. How she discovered

Queens and in particular 79th Street, Middle Village. How she was awestruck by the bustle, the sights, sounds and smells of this cosmopolitan precinct. How she spent days gaping at the streetscape, so different from Main Street Denton.

One bright day, as she strolled from her nearby boarding house and hungrily inspected the cafes, restaurants, and delicatessens. She was drawn to one, particular delicatessen, which had a huge cheese in the window surrounded by a variety of fresh and pickled vegetables and a huge assortment of freshly baked bread and rolls. Drawn by the delightful exotic aromas' emanating from the shop, she hesitantly entered.

She stood in line behind the counter, awestruck by the variety of foodstuffs on the shelves and in the glass display case. Suddenly, she heard a deep, accented voice ask. "Nu. Can I help you?" She was startled, as she gazed at the source of the question. Standing behind the counter was a tall, 30 something young man with a bushy beard and moustache, wearing a white apron and a white shirt with sleeves rolled up above the elbow, revealing muscular forearms. He was also wearing a small skullcap, which she later learned was a yarmulke. She stared tongue-tied and attracted by this exotic young man, so different from the boys back in Denton.

When she didn't reply, he repeated the question, but she seemed to have lost the ability to speak. Taking pity on her obvious discomfort, he indicated the line of plates on the counter, offering tasting samples. He lowered his voice and kindly said in a thick accent. "Maybe try a few and see what you like?" Still, she couldn't move or speak. He shrugged good-naturedly, picked up a pair of tongs, selected a small piece of cheese and offered it, as he said. "It's okay. Try it", obligingly, as though in slow motion, she did. The flavour, seemed to explode in her mouth and her eyes bulged. Noting her expression, he laughed and said. "Nu, good?" She silently nodded as she hurriedly swallowed the cheese. She was mortified, by her star-struck behaviour, but unable to do anything about it. He laughed, a full-throated belly laugh and she was struck by his vitality and found it attractive. He noticed her obvious interest, leaned over the counter, extended his hand and introduced himself, in a deep husky, accented voice. "Miklos, from Hungary," corrected himself. "But in America, they call me Mike", they shook hands. She hoped, he did not notice her shaking and sweaty palms. She liked the firm handshake and his warm callused hand. She cleared her throat and finally managed. "Elizabeth Cummings, from Denton", he seemed reluctant to let her hand go. Still holding her hand announced. "It would be my great honour, to be your private guide to show you around Queens," startled, she managed to withdraw her hand and silently reviewed his offer. Impatient, he jokingly added. "Nu, what's to consider? A pretty young woman like you shouldn't, walk around this area, by yourself. I promise to show you all the places and promise to behave – no 'funny business,' Elizabeth had to smile at the offer, although she was somewhat disappointed about the funny business proviso.

This is how. Dov's parents met and their relationship began.

As Dov read Elizabeth's, frank, detailed Journal. He felt a mix of embarrassment, at the intimate disclosures and some guilt, at reading something so private. However, their honesty and humanity further endeared them in his heart.

Finally, he read, in full, graphic heart-breaking, detail how they wed. Stories to catalogue and add to his memory File. A File that included: the trauma of -witnessing his father's sudden public death, from a heart attack, at a family wedding, when Dov was 15. Witnessing his mother's valiant, but futile fight with breast cancer, right up to her painful death, when he was17 and approaching 18. Another series of memories to catalogue and add to his already overfull File.

Memories of his life and the lives and deaths of his parents were enmeshed, intertwined. Precious, unforgettable memories, that were all kept and stored in his 'Memory File.'

But the ones that kept intruding and demanded, 'Screen time,' were all related to Jacob. Unwilling to face them- loath to observe his 'Thought Screen.' Dov drove himself without mercy. He strode in a frenzied haze, along the Hudson Embankment.

Chapter 12

The passing landscape was a smudged blur that didn't register, on his psyche. Indefatigable, he walked on and on. He walked past, Manhattan, Albert Embankment with no pause and no recollection.

He was fuelled by what appeared, an inexhaustible, source of Darwinian triggered adrenaline. His automatic, self-preservation, fight-flight response, was in overdrive. Terrified-if he stopped and viewed his 'Thought Screen'-it could result in insanity and maybe even death.

His parents passing had been the key factor, leading to Dov's Odyssey as a near-adult, nigh penniless, orphan. This was the file that now-burst uninvited, on his 'Thought Screen'.

Unwilling. To confront and review their deaths, he drove himself mercilessly. The images now whizzed past at 30 time's normal speed and were just a blur, hardly identifiable. Consequently, not confronting. However, when they slowed to a more identifiable 12 time's normal speed, he recognised the vision. He now 'viewed,' their battered old Chevy car as it laboriously parked in the Deity car park, the relieved family getting out and making their way to the wedding reception.

Dov became terrified about what was soon to be revealed. So, he redoubled his efforts and now the images speeded back up, to 30 time's normal speed and comfortably, unrecognisable and hence not confronting. He continued to desperately stride on and on.

Sometime later. He gradually realised the screen had again slowed down to 12 time's the normal speed. He could now recognise the images. He now viewed his return to Denton for the Centennial celebrations. These were not confronting and he was comfortable to 'view' these images.

Soon it was, "Showtime," he strode onstage for his comeback performance. He felt uncomfortable, but was not threatened, as he watched his near falter, he felt uplifted, as Jane came on stage. With a light- heart, he viewed their duet and was again thrilled and overjoyed, when Jane revealed, she was in remission.

At a near normal speed, he now elatedly viewed the show finale, as the whole Ensemble joined in.

Still, at a near normal speed, he reviewed their move to Buffalo, New York State, despite her parents' objections. He again experienced, exhilaration and delight at Jane's announcement, that she was going to convert, in spite of Clem's strong objections. It confirmed, she cared for him and how much she loved him, she was willing to go against her parents' wishes, her own strict upbringing and undergo two years of rigorous study.

Jubilantly, he viewed, and relived, their wedding at the Saranac synagogue in Saranac Avenue, Buffalo, New York State.

He recalled his first impression of the Saranac synagogue.

Outside. The front of the modest, red brick synagogue, there was a brick –arch, below it, there was a horizontal rectangular pane of stained glass, in a wooden frame, that topped the front, double wooden doors. Five steps, bordered by handrails, led to the elevated entrance.

Inside. The modest, low ceiling building, had parallel rows of dark wooden pews. On the back wall there was a tall bookcase, filled with leather bound prayer books. The bookcase was adjacent, to a high arched, rear, double wooden door.

At the front of the synagogue there was a raised bema, with a wooden lectern. The side walls had a series of vertical, rectangular stained glass windows with wooden frames. These allowed light to flood into the space.

Out back. There was a low ceiling separate, Kiddush area. It had several, large round white clothed tables and a large rectangular clothed, "head" table, with associated black metal and leather chairs.

Chapter 13

The attending Rabbi, for the wedding ceremony, was a rotund, 40 something, American-born, Hasidic Jew. They initially, met him, when they booked the synagogue for their Sunday wedding. He asked them a host of questions regarding their backgrounds and their courtship. When Jane revealed her conversion, in Kansas City. Coincidently, he knew and was friendly with the Rabbi. He was impressed by her attitude and her decision to convert.

During their long conversation, his wife, a forty something, modestly attractive woman, dressed in all black, quietly slipped in. She offered everyone tea? Dov and Jane politely declined and continued their conversation with the Rabbi.

He was sympathetic and intrigued, patently fascinated by their history. Duly, he performed the ceremony with confident grace.

After a long, sometimes, heated argument with Marge, Clem reluctantly, agreed to accompany her, to the ceremony. They arrived in their Sunday best garments and sat, uncomfortable and interested in the front pew.

Alberto was the proud best man and Betty Lou, was the matron of honour. The recently engaged couple appreciated the honour and had a wonderful time. They spent most of the time cuddling and discreetly kissing, in a secluded alcove, they found, outside the venue.

José, made the long journey. Out of breath, he arrived late, resplendent in his new suit, bought for his son's recent engagement. Breathlessly, he took a seat next to the uneasy Clem and engaged him, in casual conversation.

When Dov arrived, looking resplendent, in the suit made by Alberto's tailor, all the guests turned and stared. After an appropriate time, Jane made her entrance, stunning in a splendid white gown, the guests turned and gaped in appreciation.

The nervous couple stood under the chuppa. When Dov, vigorously stomped on the glass and broke it. The guest clapped and loudly shouted." Mazel".

When Jane quizzed, her parents, at the lavish Kiddush, after the ceremony. They admitted, they found the food at the Kiddush, initially strange, but very tasty and the ceremony interesting and somewhat touching, even Clem.

Their big day, had turned out to be as great, as each, could have wished for and much more. It seemed to be an excellent omen, for their future life together.

Dov slowed down and eagerly reviewed their subsequent honeymoon, on his, 'Thought Screen.'

Chapter 14

After the wedding, the fatigued, but exuberant pair were driven by Alberto and Betty Lou, in Alberto's shiny new 1950's Chevy, with a mandatory sign, 'Just Married' and several long strands of string connecting a number of cans trailing, loudly behind it. The car generated considerable interest, as it drove to a nearby Bar, their proposed hotel.

Inside the Bar. They settled in the low lit, dining area, at a vacant table. Alberto ordered champagne, for everyone, when Jane protested, he exclaimed. "We have to to celebrate, this moment in style", Dov and Betty- Lou nodded in agreement, Jane went along with the group decision.

After several drinks, when Alberto became quite boisterous and Betty- Lou sensed that the newlyweds were ready to go, she repeatedly nudged Alberto then, firmly announced. "We'll fix up the bill. You two lovebirds, go and enjoy yourselves," Alberto, somewhat taken back, remained silent, but a prod from Betty- Lou kick-started him, he exclaimed. "Yes! Go and enjoy," he started to push Dov towards the exit, Dov happily complied, grabbed Jane's hand and led her away. At the door, they both turned, faced their friends and gratefully exclaimed. "Thanks for everything. See you later," and quickly departed, with their Carry On cases.

It was only a two minute walk. To the Curtis Hotel in Franhen Street. The main entrance, was through a huge double glass door that opened on to the spacious Lobby. Two Bell boys approached and took the 'Carry Ons', inside. They followed and approached the Receptionist.

After signing in and receiving their room keys, one of the staff escorted them up the stairs, to their first-floor suite. Unbeknown, to them, Alberto, had booked them in to the 'Honeymoon suite.' When they entered, they were surprised and impressed by the size, the luxury and the complimentary champagne, chocolates and strawberries, tastefully laid out, on their lounge table. Their first impression, was reinforced, by a further inspection of their suite. The good sized bedroom, had a king-sized bed, with a prominent bed head, two bedside tables with standard lamps, on each side and a two seat plush couch at the foot of the bed. The marble bathroom, was pure luxury, with a bath tub and a double sink.

By now, it was late afternoon. It felt great to be finally alone. Dov suggested a glass of champagne? Jane was initially ambivalent, then finally agreed. However, Dov sensed she was somewhat nervous. She kept glancing at the big double bed. The 'elephant,' in the room. Dov was sympathetic and tried to put her at ease. He realised, if he hadn't had the affair with Angeline, he would also be extremely apprehensive, about the upcoming, situation. As it was, he was confident and bursting with anticipation.

During their relatively short courtship. They had limited their 'intimacy', to passionate kisses and cuddles, which were tantalising and frustrating. So he could understand, Jane would have some nervousness about, moving into full 'intimacy.' He chose to ignore the 'elephant,' in the room and tried to reassure Jane, with some casual chatter. He decided, to let Jane take the initiative, when she felt comfortable.

After some hours, the sun had set and evening had descended. After finishing her glass of champagne, Jane stood, stretched and softly announced. "I'm bushed. I think I'll freshen up, won't be long," she went into the bathroom and shut the door. Dov heaved a sigh of relief and quickly finished his champagne, got undressed and put on the available, complimentary Dressing Gown. Then, got into the bed. It felt so good. The crisp white sheets, smelt of something wonderful, he wondered, was it lavender? He had dozed off, when the light from the bathroom and Jane's bright. "Hello, dear husband," woke him. He stared at Jane, as she straddled the doorway, in a Dressing Gown. When she saw, he was awake, she swayed to the bed and provocatively, slowly, pirouetted. Then, she suggestively, slid the gown off one shoulder, then the other, until the Gown was only kept up by her cloth belt. She was bare to the waist. Now, she certainly had Dov's attention, he stared appreciatively, at her firm generous breasts with their pronounced pink areolas and nipples.

He sat up in bed and hoarsely announced. "Wow!" You are stunning," patted the bed and added. "Come here, you seductive Jewish minx," Jane played coy, but he could see she was buoyed by his response. She pirouetted again, but remained at the foot of the bed. Intrigued and aroused by her unexpected behaviour, Dov hurriedly got out of bed, in his Dressing Gown and pretended to move towards her. Jane backed away and huskily said. "What's the hurry Darling, we have all night," with that, she undid the cloth belt and let the Dressing Gown drop to the floor, leaving her completely naked. He watched awestruck and aroused as she again, slowly pirouetted around, under his gaze. Dov couldn't get enough of her beauty. He had been besotted and addicted by Angeline's beauty. But the combination of Jane's beauty and his love for her, put Jane in a much higher category.

After some moments. Jane rebuked. "Come on, are you going to keep staring for ever? I was hoping for more, on our honeymoon," Dov realised, it was time to act. He faced Jane and dropped his Dressing Gown, to reveal his profound arousal. Jane stepped back and gasped. "My gosh! Wow! We're wasting time", Dov needed no further encouragement. He stepped towards her and was agreeably met by the advancing Jane. They kissed and embraced, body to body, then fell onto the bed.

Chapter 15

After a torrid, erotic night. The couple slept in and just made it for breakfast, in the Hotels, plush breakfast area. They sat at one of the vacant, white clothed, round tables facing a wall of glass. They had the room to themselves, apart from several waitresses. Obviously, the other guests had already finished.

After a hearty breakfast, they decided to head back to their room. After entering, Dov turned to Jane and asked "should I put on the, 'Do Not Disturb Sign?' She smiled coyly, then announced. "Definitely!" Dov did, then reached out, kissed and embraced the willing Jane.

Still in a post- coital haze, Jane lay contentedly, beside Dov and idly ran her fingers over his bare chest. After a moment, she finally remarked. "Wow. You're full of surprises. For a yeshiva guy. Surprisingly, you are a, hell of a lover. Jane felt as though, he was a maestro pianist and she was the obliging piano on which he "played", an exquisite tormenting, delicious Melody, culminating in a thundering, catasmyslic climax. How come?" Dov was put on the spot. He didn't think, it was appropriate, to confess to her, about Angeline. He attempted to deflect the question. Instead of answering, he enthused. "For a good Catholic virgin, you are a hell of a passionate lover", she accepted and enjoyed the compliment, but realised he had evaded her question. She offered, an enigmatic smile, as she responded. "Thanks, but it takes two to tango. I can't take all the credit", Dov readily accepted the compliment and hoped, she would not pursue her, original query. Dov allowed his hand to drop, to her firm breast and began to caress it, until the nipples distended. Meanwhile, Jane's hand, had also been busy, under the sheets. Soon, they turned to each other and began coupling, again.

Afterwards. After yet another, cataclysmic orgasm. Jane's thoughts again returned to the troublesome issue, she had recently raised with Dov. How could a naive, secluded, Yeshiva guy, be such an accomplished lover? Jane felt as though, he was a maestro pianist and she was the obliging piano on which he "played", an exquisite tormenting, delicious malady, culminating in a thundering, catasmyslic climax. The incongruity of this bothered her. Although, on reflection, if she was completely honest. During, their courting days, even though, they were only modestly 'intimate', she already had some suspicion, regarding this issue.

She loved him dearly, even more so now. So, she wanted to know all about him. She resolved, she would pursue this topic, until she got an acceptable explanation.

Meanwhile. Dov was also reviewing their recent, erotic, passionate encounter. Although, he didn't intend to, he automatically compared it, to his experience with

Angeline. Being a complete naive, virgin, at the time. That, had blown him away. However, if he was honest. His experience with Jane, even though she was inexperienced, was profound and much more emotional, because of his deep love. Yet again, he elatedly concluded. He was a fortunate, blessed man.

Chapter 16

This was the pattern, for their next four days. On the morning of the fifth day, when they returned to their room, after breakfast. They finished their modest packing, grateful they had a complimentary, late checkout. To make the most of their additional time, they decided to make a cup of tea in the room and chill out. After Jane, finished her tea. She tentatively asked. "Did the Honeymoon, meet your expectations?" Dov was surprised, she even had to ask. He readily replied. "No, it was much better. You were – are amazing", he realised that was patently true and fully comprehended, he was an extremely fortunate man. This was a blatant truth. He promised himself to fuse this thought, in to his brain. So, whatever happened in the future, whatever befell them, this would remain his ballast, his beacon. He sincerely thanked G-d for bestowing him with such good fortune.

Dov mulled, all this over and suddenly realised, the persistent, pervasive memory of Angeline, which had physically and emotionally enveloped him, like restrictive over – tight corset – was gone. It had vanished, like a fine mist, when the bright sun, finally climbed above the horizon. He was free from the memory, the burden and the dependency. He felt unrestricted and liberated. He welcomed the dramatic change and the unhindered opportunity, to relax and enjoy, a future life with Jane. He couldn't wait to start their new life.

Jane seemed to be able to read his mind. She kissed him on the cheek and whispered. "You know, I was just thinking. I am such a lucky woman", he was startled and gratified that they were on the same page. He enthusiastically hugged her, when their kiss, became somewhat more heated, he reluctantly pulled free and stated. "Unfortunately, we need to check out, get out of this lovely, sensual cocoon and back to the real world," Jane pouted as she responded. "Must we?" Then, reluctantly added. "I guess we must," she moved away.

They did a final check of their room, to make sure they had everything. Then they picked up their, Carry Ons'. Dov did a final check of his watch, paused, then suddenly announced. "Look. We still have time for one more outing," looked at Jane and suggested. "We never got round to checking out the Rooftop Cocktail Bar. Should we?" Jane put her Carry On, down and enthusiastically responded. "Let's do it!" Dov put his down and indicated the door. "Let's go, our last hurrah, before we leave this sensual nest," they strode out to the lift and took it to the top floor. They got out and hurried to the Vue Rooftop Cocktail Lounge and hastened inside. The lows ceilinged room had a Fire Pit at one end and a wall of glass, facing the street. Along, the opposite wall, there was a long granite topped bar, with tall bar stools, that had high backs.

Parallel to the glass wall, there was a row of large round tables, with matching chairs. There was a couple sitting at a table, near the window, nursing cocktails. A waitress hovered nearby and the uniformed Barman, stood idly behind the bar. They went over and ordered two Margaritas, which the Barman, deftly produced. After tasting them and finding them delicious. They strolled to the glass wall, to check the view. There was a panoramic view of Downtown Buffalo, Lake Eire and the Canadian shoreline. Holding hands, they sat at an adjacent table and leisurely sipped their cocktails. It was a perfect way, to culminate this chapter, of their shared journey. They set contentedly, enjoying, the view, their cocktails, the ambience in the Lounge and each other's company. Reluctantly, they finished their drinks, Dov checked his watch, held his hand out to Jane and grudgingly muttered. "We really must go", she nodded and stood. Holding hands they left, and went back to their room. Got there Carry Ons,' went downstairs and regretfully, checked out.

Chapter 17

At this point, the image on Dov's 'Thought Screen', was becoming threatening, he reflexively speeded up and they now whizzed past 12 time's normal speed. It was 1981 and he was back in New York, again.

Chapter 18

New York 1981

Two weeks, after his traumatic return to New York and two days, before Jacob's funeral. Dov and Alberto anxiously, hovered around the exit of the Port Authority Coach Station. Jane's coach had arrived five minutes earlier. She and the children should be through anytime soon. The pair eagerly scrutinised each group of departing passengers, as they emerged through the door. Finally, they saw Jane pulling a suitcase and holding Sara by her other hand. Alberto towing his suitcase, followed.

Jane looked dishevelled and tired. But brightened, as she heard their shouted greeting. Several emerging passengers later, Betty Lou appeared, accompanied by Lewis aged 13, Maria aged 15, and Oscar aged 11, each pulling their suitcases.

Betty Lou smiled with glee, as she saw the welcoming duo. She bounded over and enthusiastically hugged Dov, offered her condolences, then hugged and kissed Alberto.

Dov and Alberto grabbed the suitcases from their wives and shepherded the families to the exit and the waiting

Limousine. The children were all impressed and in unison yelled. "Wow!" The uniformed driver guided, everyone into the vehicle, packed the cases into the boot. Then they drove off.

An hour, later, they pulled up outside their hotel in Manhattan. After booking in at Reception. They were shown their adjacent, plush, connecting Suits. Once again, the kids were suitably impressed and provided a chorus of loud. "Wows!" Then they scurried through the rooms, to explore their accommodation, all accompanied by a chorus, of loudly expressed delight.

Settled and unpacked, the exhausted families, decided to stay in their rooms for dinner and ordered room service.

The next morning, somewhat refreshed. They met for a late buffet breakfast in the bright breakfast area, over-looking the Empire State Building. This would be their last 'free', day before Jacob's funeral.

Chapter 19

Following breakfast. The two families had a meeting and by mutual consent, agreed to have a 'lazy' day, browsing and sightseeing around Manhattan. They decided to take a, Hop on, Hop off, bus and were blown away by, the range of iconic sites; the Empire State building, Central Park, Lincoln centre, the Statue of Liberty, the Museum of modern Art, Madison Square Garden, Carnegie Hall.

Blessed with seasonally, unusually good weather. They then spent several relaxed, happy hours, checking the shops and theatres in the area. They did a tour of the Theatre district and were blown away by the rich offerings that were available; Blood Brothers, Cats, Mamma Mia, the Lion King, the Phantom of the Opera, Starlight Express, The Woman in Black. The children were desperate to see the Lion King, but with the funeral, the next day realised that was not practical and settled for a tour through Grand Central Station, the massive high roofed, jaw-dropping architecture, had a bustling energy and vitality from the countless travellers, scurrying around like frenzied ants. Exhausted, they decided to have lunch in the first floor, Oyster Bar.

They moved two tables together and gratefully sat down. After a light lunch, they decided to head back to their hotel and rest up for the next day.

It was at this point, Dov's dormant depression and grief, which had been somewhat suppressed by the arrival of his and Alberto's family- resurfaced. The imminent prospect of Jacob's funeral catapulted him back into brutal, confronting reality.

He felt the onset of non-ignorable, mounting anxiety and a sense of crippling, terrifying dread. He felt both dizzy and lightheaded at the same time and had a gaping void in the pit of his stomach. It felt as if it had been ripped out and he'd been left, with a cavernous cavity. His neck and shoulder muscles seemed to knot into an iron fist. He broke out into a cold sweat and had trouble breathing in enough oxygen.

Unwilling, to alarm the others. He offered a lame excuse and made a hasty exit. He rushed back to the hotel.

Chapter 20

After breakfast, the following day. The two families checked out and waited in the Lobby. They sat silently around, on plump red sofas, with their suitcases nearby.

Punctually, at 11 AM their driver bounded in. He was greeted by Dov, then he organised the Bell Hops to take all the suitcases out to the Limousine. Once this was accomplished, he herded everyone into the vehicle. As the car weaved through the New York traffic, he began an accomplished and welcomed commentary on the city and the buildings. It broke the stifling silence in the Limousine. No one had any stomach to make idle chitchat.

An hour later. The Limousine pulled up at the Third Shearith Israel, Jewish cemetery. The group clambered out of the car and looked around curiously. In the distance they could see, two Gravediggers, in open neck, short-sleeved shirts, baggy long trousers, and big black working boots, as they idly leaned on shovels, next to a three-foot high, mound of red clay. Rabbi Abraham Bassous, in full Rabbi gear, stood nearby. The group stood in a tennis court sized area of manicured grass that had no tombstones. Obviously, this was their destination.

The two families slowly made their way between tombstones towards the manicured area and the group. As the group neared, the manicured area, the Rabbi bounded up and warmly greeted Dov and Alberto. He then hurried over and had a brief word with the Gravediggers, who then strode away.

Chapter 21

It was a marshmallow, soft, sunny day. The unseasonal fine weather had again, ironically blessed them. The nearby, great Oak tree, afforded the group some welcome shade.

Dov reviewed the scene and wryly thought. He had made the right choice for Jacob's grave. In different circumstances, it would have been, an ideal setting for a two family picnic. It was beautiful and tranquil, blissfully silent, except for the, buzzing, of the irritating blowflies, the soft-droning of some bees and the twittering of the birds in the adjacent Oak tree.

Chapter 22

Then, shortly. The silence was disrupted by the sound of harsh, loud creaking. It heralded, the Gravediggers, imminent return.

They slowly reappeared, over a gentle rise, laboriously pulling an old roughly made, two-wheeled, creaking, wooden cart carrying a pine coffin. Huffing and puffing, they pulled up next to the open grave. Dov viewed their reappearance, with a sinking feeling. The arrival of his dead son, made everything way too real.

He watched with mounting anxiety, as they casually placed two dark cloth belts, under the coffin. Satisfied, they looked at the Rabbi. He stared at Dov and Alberto and softly asked. "Can you help?"

Startled, with some hesitation, they nodded. The Rabbi indicated the coffin and the Gravediggers, offered Alberto and Dov, the end of one of the cloth belts, while they retained the other end.

Together, the four men slowly lifted the coffin off the cart and placed it on the ground, adjacent to the open grave. The older of the two Gravediggers muttered to Dov and Alberto. "Keep hold of the belts,"

The Rabbi stepped forward and the two families crowded closer together, as he began to sing, a short Hebrew prayer. As the Rabbi sang, Dov, from some deep, unsuspected, recessed memory, began to spontaneously, emotionally sing along. He was astonished that he knew the melody and the words. It was only on later reflection. He realised, this was the same prayer he had emotionally witnessed at both his fathers' and mothers' funeral. Nonetheless, that was over 20 years ago. Obviously, it had been retained and implanted in his traumatised subconscious.

Jane noting his emotions, moved alongside and draped a comforting arm around his shoulders. At the end of the prayer, the Rabbi stepped forward, cleared his throat and earnestly addressed the gathering, in his broken English. "Thank you all, for attending Jacob's funeral," the two families silently shuffled closer, to better hear Jacob's eulogy.

Chapter 23

As Dov listened, he was gratified he and Alberto had spent considerable time briefing, the Rabbi, on Jacob's all too short life. The time had been well spent.

The Rabbi's eulogy was bespoke, regarding Jacob, rather than a generic speech. He listed many of Jacob's successes, achievements and also noted some of his occasional, less than memorable episodes. Each recollection, was readily recognised by the group and was met with a chuckle and/or a sigh of deep regret.

As Dov listened, he shed silent tears, as did Alberto. Their wives were also caught up in the experience and dabbed their eyes with handkerchiefs. The children were sobbing and shuffled closer together for support.

When Dov felt, he couldn't bear to listen to anymore. The Rabbi thankfully finished, with a Jewish blessing.

Chapter 24

After the Rabbi finished, he nodded to the Gravediggers, they, in turn, nodded and then asked, Alberto and Dov to hold on to the cloth belts and help lift the Coffin. The four men did.

Yet again, Dov wondered, was he still involved in a Kafka play? As a struggled to lift his son's coffin. Once aloft, they moved it over the open grave and slowly lowered it to the bottom. Then, the Gravediggers pulled on the belts and hauled them free. Once that was accomplished. The younger of the Gravediggers picked up a shovel, stood beside the mound of clay and vigorously scooped up a full shovel load and deposited it, on top of the coffin, with an accompanying loud Thump that shattered the tranquil scene and caused Dov to jump.

He repeated this, several times, then offered the shovel to the other Gravedigger. He repeated the procedure. Each Thump! Made Dov wince and instinctively flinch. Jane noted his distress, tearful, she again sidled up and this time tenderly grabbed his hand. After several shovel loads, the second Gravedigger, had enough and tentatively offered his shovel to Dov. He hesitated, but then took it. This would be the last thing he could do for his son. He tentatively, tackled the mound of clay and gently deposited a shovel load onto the coffin. He felt it would be disrespectful, to Jacob, to let it Thump, rudely on the top. After several shovel-fulls, he offered his shovel to Alberto. He took it and mimicked Dov's actions. Subsequently, the two boys, each grabbed a shovel from the clay mound and continued to fill the grave.

Dov was mortified how quickly his son had been buried. Now reaches 18, the near 19 memorable years, and been suppressed. However, he knew he would always remember and cherish his memory.

When the Rabbi was satisfied he beckoned the group to come closer and he began to sing another Hebrew prayer. Dov struggled to hold back tears, but joined in.

Then it was over. Dov and Alberto thanked the Rabbi and the Gravediggers, then wandered away to wash their hands at a nearby sink. Then they got back into the Limousine. The rest of the group followed.

In the limousine, on the silent, long drive back. After Dov reviewed, the two grief-stricken families, Alberto, Betty Lou, and their three children. Jane and his two children. He was overwhelmed, by emotion. He felt a burning, overwhelming tidal wave of, joy and love for each and every one of them. He recalled, the jubilant statement he had made to himself on their honeymoon and joyfully, to Jane just prior to that first 3 AM cruel phone call. 'I'm a very lucky man,' he now realised, despite everything, that had subsequently happened, this was still emphatically true.

Yes, he had cruelly lost, his beloved, eldest son. But, he and his family had their health. He was blessed with, a wife he adored an she in turn him. He had two healthy, wonderful children. And a friend, he trusted and loved. Who was married to a woman, both he and Jane adored, as they did their three children, who they considered, as part of their own family. Yes, notwithstanding everything that had happened, he was most definitely, a lucky man.

He managed to desperately hold onto that thought, on the long, silent, drive back to the hotel. Consequently, the terrible reality of what had just taken place, remained repressed and in the background.

However, on their arrival. As he got out of the Limousine, it returned with a knockout impact. He staggered with the weight of his emotions, but remained poker-faced and upright. Realising, he was about to drown in his memories, he offered a brief apology, to the group and hurried away. Out of sight, he instinctively, feverishly, again, began to stride along the Hudson Embankment.

Chapter 25

Dov felt quite 'comfortable,' as he briskly strode along. His recent experience along the Hudson Embankment was reassuring. He felt he could probably, 'manage', his, 'Thought Screen.'

As he started this journey, the first image that appeared on his, 'Thought Screen,' was the culmination of his come-back concert at the Denton Centennial celebrations. He viewed it with fond nostalgia, it was a welcomed memory. The event had launched, his successful comeback, as a major singer-songwriter, after his disastrous, on stage public, meltdown. The concert had relaunched his career. A successful career, he would maintain for the next 20 years.

The successful comeback had given him the courage to propose to Jane. She was still "basking", in her recent diagnosis of remission. She loved him and was keen to get married and have children. She readily agreed, although concerned about her parents' reaction. However, Dov's reclaimed success, had somewhat reduced Clem's objections.

The next image that presented and he was happy to linger on it, was when Jane revealed, she was willing to convert. He felt joyful and lightheaded, as he recalled his happiness and pleasure at her decision and the fact that she had volunteered it. In his mind, her religion had been an unspoken, subconscious obstruction to their future together. Judaism was in his DNA. Even though he desperately loved and wanted to marry Jane. He had difficulty, accepting, that his children would not be considered Jewish (because of the Matrilineal aspect in Judaism). The fact Jane had volunteered to follow his mother's example and convert, added yet another level, to his already high feelings for her. It augmented his love and attachment.

Following Jane's announcement. He felt as if, all his hopes and dreams now seemed to have been, completely fulfilled and answered. It was a glorious, deliriously happy time for both.

Jane's decision meant, they now definitely had to live, initially, at least, in Kansas City. This was necessary for many reasons, as Jane and Dov patiently tried to explain to Clem and Marge; first for Dov's career, second so Jane could attend the two-year conversion course with a Rabbi. Finally, it allowed Jane to attend an appropriate Teachers College. Although, Dov felt that Kansas City was not the ideal location to attempt to launch his career, he was willing to compromise. Particularly, as Jane had already made a huge commitment, regarding conversion. However, he insisted if, after she had finished the two years of conversion and her studies; he had no success, regarding his career, then they would go to New York. She agreed, but was again, apprehensive about passing this information on to her parents.

After the mandatory two years. She successfully converted and was now, also qualified to commence teaching. They were now in a position to get married. Unfortunately, to that point, Dov had no success in relaunching his career. Consequently, they decided to review their New York option. After considerable home-work, they mutually agreed, New York State would be a better choice. It was close enough to New York City (one and a half hours by train, or plane. Although, eight hours by coach). In addition, the house prices were more afford-able (at least a quarter of what it would cost in New York City). It seemed a much preferred environment to raise a young family.

They were fortunate and found an affordable family home (at least a quarter of the price of New York real estate), in South Williamsville, an upmarket area of Buffalo, in New York State and broke the news to Clem and Marge.

As Jane had feared. Their decision was met with surprise and disapproval. They patiently, outlined their reasons, with limited success. However, eventually Clem and Marge, reluctantly bowed to their argument and some months later, together with Alberto and Betty-Lou, they tearfully bade them goodbye.

When they arrived in Buffalo, they made arrangements for their wedding at the Saranac Synagogue in Saranac Avenue, Buffalo. New York State.

The ceremony was attended by their Denton friends and family and their Kansas City friends. Plus the two families' relatives.

Within two years, post marriage. Jane had become profoundly pregnant and duly, after several painful hours of labour. During which Dov had obsessively, paced the hospital corridor – not unlike his current pacing of the Hudson Embankment. However, on the previous occasion, the recently engaged Alberto and Betty Lou had travelled to Buffalo in New York State, for the event and were able to provide Dov and Jane with moral support.

When the images began to display Jacob's early years, Dov felt uneasy and increased his pace, similarly, the images also speeded up, now at 12 time's normal speed and hence, less confronting, as they whizzed past.

Dov was content to continue at that pace and only realised hours had passed, since he started his current journey when the sun, slowly sank below the horizon and the lampposts and street lights lit up.

Mentally, he now felt more settled. He decided to head back to their hotel. He was a bizarre figure, in his traditional Hasidic gear (all back and with a prominent hat). He continued to briskly walk the path, with a fixed 6-mile stare. Other pedestrians gave him strange looks and Gave him a wide berth, as did cyclists. Some passing cars slowed, to get a better look and occasionally, tooted their horn, but drove on.

The image and the thought that he repeatedly, desperately, tried to retrieve were of the two families in the

Limousine on the long drive back from the cemetery. Accompanied by the profound, repeated, revelation, and the clear realisation, of how fortunate, he was. That on the scale of things, despite the recent tragedy, he was a blessed, lucky man.

By the time, he stumbled into the Foyer of his hotel. It had become imprinted, in his mind. Suddenly, he was near-bowled over as Jane rushed up and enthusiastically hugged and kissed him. She was followed by an equally enthusiastic and buoyant Alberto and Betty Lou, who did the same. Lavishly inundated by this overt, effusive affection, love, and warmth, from his closest and dearest. Seemed a direct and immediate confirmation - a QED, of his previous conclusion.

Arm's tight around each other. Jane and Dov bounded up the stairs to their room. Alberto and Betty Lou, a degree less emotional, held hands as they hurried to the lift and up to their room.

Chapter 26

In the privacy of their room. Jane gave him another, but a much, more emotional, passionate kiss and huskily exclaimed. "Thank G-d your back. I love you so much," Dov was pleasantly taken back by her overt emotions and enthusiastically kissed her back. As their breaths and saliva intermingled, he felt her love, almost like an overwhelming, ectoplasmic force, as it infused, warmed and comforted him.

In turn, he sought to release and transfer his abundant love, back to her via their kiss.

As they floated in this almost out – of – body experience. Dov experienced, a transformational clarity. Yes, he had suffered a major tragedy, but in the scheme of things, as events continued to demonstrate, he was a fortunate man.

Consequently, he could either, continue to be consumed and fixated on what he had tragically lost. Alternatively, he could refocus, embrace the future and relish, and appreciate all the positives he still had and be prepared to, delight in those, which potentially, lay in the future.

There and then, he firmly decided. He was now ready to move on with his life and receptive, even eager, to experience the future, with the prospect of its boundless, potential of; new, happy milestones, birthdays, marriages, grandchildren, et cetera. In all respects. He felt a fulfilled, contented man.

As Dov tightly embraced Jane. Unbidden, bubbling up from some deep subconscious, region of his brain, two of his songs, resonated in his mind. Songs that would not be stilled or silenced. Songs that seemed divinely appropriate, to their situation and circumstance.

He felt compelled, to express them, even though it had been over 20 years since he had sung either. They were so exquisitely fitting, applicable, they demanded to be heard. He stared tenderly at Jane and began to emotionally, softly sing.

DOV (OUR LOVE)

From that first glance
You overwhelmed my heart
You ignited something, that's burning deep inside.
Much sweeter than a thousand guitars.

As Jane listened, Dov noticed that silent tears slowly, trickled down her cheeks. Then, she enthusiastically joined in the chorus. Somehow, she too had miraculously, remembered the melody and the words. Together, they jubilantly belted it out.

JANE and DOV

Our love's brighter than Haley's comet.
Sweeter than a Shakespearean sonnet.
More uplifting than Gandhi's marchers.
Stronger than all of the Eiffel's arches.
That's our love
Aaahhh!
That's our love.

At the end of the song. They again embraced and kissed. However, another song demanded, to be also heard. Dov leaned back, ardently faced Jane and began to softly sing.

DOV (TOGETHER)

I have lived the depths of despair.
Even when fame and glory, were there.
Seeking that elusive prize.
Now I know it's right here, by my side.

Dov and Jane reached out and held hands. Holding hands, they jubilantly faced the future. Yet again. Somehow, she had remarkably, also remembered the melody and the words. For Dov, it had again, confirmed, there intimate, almost mystical bond.

They defiantly, sang the chorus and loudly proclaimed their mutual commitment.

Suddenly, there was a loud knock on the door. Then they heard, Alberto anxiously shout. "Dov and Jane are you guys okay?" Betty Lou joined in with a shouted. "Is there anything we can do to help?" Dov and Jane silently stared at each other for a moment, then began to laugh, uproariously. After a few seconds, they loudly resumed the chorus.

JANE and DOV

Your love fills my being and my soul
Beyond happiness, way beyond control.
You're the missing fragment that I need
Now the jigsaw of my being, is complete.
Together we can face anything.
Defy the lions' roar, Break the chains of doubt
Together we're invincible, we soar,
Now fate has brought you back to me once more

The songs and the unexpected laughter, seemed to have been cathartic for both. At the end they held hands, both were crying, but it seemed as if a huge weight had been lifted off both their shoulders. Together, they had stumbled back from the abyss and returned to something approaching normality.

They had their health, their children, their love, their friends, and that was enough-

More than enough.

THE END.